MAIN-TRAVELLED ROADS

HAMLIN GARLAND

2015 by McAllister Editions (MCALLISTEREDITIONS@GMAIL.COM). This book is a classic, and a product of its time. It does not reflect the same views on race, gender, sexuality, ethnicity, and interpersonal relations as it would if it was written today.

CONTENTS

MAIN-TRAVELLED

ROADS

To

My Father And Mother Whose Half-Century Pilgrimage on the Main-Travelled Road of Life Has Brought Them Only Toil and Deprivation, This Book of Stories Is Dedicated By a Son to Whom Every Day Brings a Deepening Sense of His Parents' Silent Heroism

The main-travelled road in the West (as everywhere) is hot and dusty in summer, and desolate and drear with mud in fall and spring, and in winter the winds sweep the snow across it; but it does sometimes cross a rich meadow where the songs of the larks and bobolinks and blackbirds are tangled. Follow it far enough, it may lead past a bend in the river where the water laughs eternally over its shallows.

Mainly it is long and wearyful and has a dull little town at one end, and a home of toil at the other. Like the main-travelled road of life, it is traversed by many classes of people, but the poor and the weary predominate.

PREFACE

In the summer of 1887, after having been three years in Boston and six years absent from my old home in northern Iowa, I found myself with money enough to pay my railway fare to Ordway, South Dakota, where my father and mother were living, and as it cost very little extra to go by way of Dubuque and Charles City, I planned to visit Osage, Iowa, and the farm we had opened on Dry Run prairie in 1871.

Up to this time I had written only a few poems and some articles descriptive of boy life on the prairie, although I was doing a good deal of thinking and lecturing on land reform, and was regarded as a very intense disciple of Herbert Spencer and Henry George a singular combination, as I see it now. On my way westward, that summer day in 1887, rural life presented itself from an entirely new angle. The ugliness, the endless drudgery, and the loneliness of the farmer's lot smote me with stern insistence. I was the militant reformer.

The farther I got from Chicago the more depressing the landscape became. It was bad enough in our former home in Mitchell County, but my pity grew more intense as I passed from northwest Iowa into southern Dakota. The houses, bare as boxes, dropped on the treeless plains, the barbed-wire fences running at right angles, and the towns mere assemblages of flimsy wooden sheds with painted-pine battlement, produced on me the effect of an almost helpless and sterile poverty.

My dark mood was deepened into bitterness by my father's farm, where I found my mother imprisoned in a small cabin on the enormous sunburned, treeless plain, with no expectation of ever living anywhere else. Deserted by her sons and failing in health, she endured the discomforts of her life uncomplainingly-but my resentment of "things as they are" deepened during my talks with her neighbors, who were all housed in the same unshaded cabins in equal poverty and loneliness. The fact that at twenty-seven I was without power to aid my mother in any substantial way added to my despairing mood.

My savings for the two years of my teaching in Boston were not sufficient to enable me to purchase my return ticket, and when my father offered me a stacker's wages in the harvest field I accepted and for two weeks or more proved my worth with the fork, which was still mightier-with me-than the pen.

However, I did not entirely neglect the pen. In spite of the dust and heat of the wheat rieks I dreamed of poems and stories. My mind teemed with subjects for fiction, and one Sunday morning I set to work on a story which had been suggested to me by a talk with my mother, and a few hours later I read to her (seated on the low sill of that treeless cottage) the first two thousand words of "Mrs. Ripley's Trip," the first of the series of sketches which became Main-Travelled Roads.

I did not succeed in finishing it, however, till after my return to Boston in September. During the fall and winter of '87 and the winter and spring of '88, I wrote the most of the stories in Main-Travelled Roads, a novelette for the

Century Magazine, and a play called "Under the Wheel." The actual work of the composition was carried on in the south attic room of Doctor Cross's house at 21 Seaverns Avenue, Jamaica Plain.

The mood of bitterness in which these books were written was renewed and augmented by a second visit to my parents in 1889, for during my stay my mother suffered a stroke of paralysis due to overwork and the dreadful heat of the summer. She grew better before the time came for me to return to my teaching in Boston, but I felt like a sneak as I took my way to the train, leaving my mother and sister on that bleak and sun-baked plain.

"Old Paps Flaxen," "Jason Edwards," "A Spoil of Office," and most of the stories gathered into the second volume of Main-Travelled Roads were written in the shadow of these defeats. If they seem unduly austere, let the reader remember the times in which they were composed. That they were true of the farms of that day no one can know better than I, for I was there-a farmer.

Life on the farms of Iowa and Wisconsin-even on the farms of Dakota-has gained in beauty and security, I will admit, but there are still wide stretches of territory in Kansas and Nebraska where the farmhouse is a lonely shelter. Groves and lawns, better roads, the rural free delivery, the telephone, and the motorcar have done much to bring the farmer into a frame of mind where he is contented with his lot, but much remains to be done before the stream of young life from the country to the city can be checked.

The two volumes of Main-Travelled Roads can now be taken to be what William Dean Howells called them, "historical fiction," for they form a record of the farmer's life as I lived it and studied it. In these two books is a record of the privations and hardships of the men and women who subdued the midland wilderness and prepared the way for the present golden age of agriculture.

H.G.

March 1, 1922

1. A BRANCH ROAD

I

"Keep the main-travelled road till you come to a branch leading off-keep to the right."

IN the windless September dawn a voice went singing, a man's voice, singing a cheap and common air. Yet something in the elan of it all told he was young, jubilant, and a happy lover.

Above the level belt of timber to the east a vast dome of pale undazzling gold was rising, silently and swiftly. Jays called in the thickets where the maples flamed amid the green oaks, with irregular splashes of red and orange. The grass was crisp with frost under the feet, the road smooth and gray-white in color, the air was indescribably sweet, resonant, and stimulating. No wonder the man sang.

He came Into view around the curve in the lane. He had a fork on his shoulder, a graceful and polished tool. His straw hat was tilted on the back of his head, his rough, faded coat was buttoned close to the chin, and he wore thin buckskin gloves on his hands. He looked muscular and intelligent, and was evidently about twenty-two or -three years of age.

As he walked on, and the sunrise came nearer to him, he stopped his song. The broadening heavens had a majesty and sweetness that made him forget the physical joy of happy youth. He grew almost sad with the great vague thoughts and emotions which rolled in his brain as the wonder of the morning grew.

He walked more slowly, mechanically following the road, his eyes on the ever-shifting streaming banners of rose and pale green, which made the east too glorious for any words to tell. The air was so still it seemed to await expectantly the coming of the sun.

Then his mind flew back to Agnes. Would she see it? She was at work, getting breakfast, but he hoped she had time to see it. He was in that mood so common to him now, when he could not fully enjoy any sight or sound unless he could share it with her. Far down the road he heard the sharp clatter of a wagon. The roosters were calling near and far, in many keys and tunes. The dogs were barking, cattle bells jangling in the wooded pastures, and as the youth passed farmhouses, lights in the kitchen windows showed that the women were astir about breakfast, and the sound of voices and curry-combs at the barn told that the men were at their daily chores.

And the east bloomed broader. The dome of gold grew brighter, the faint clouds here and there flamed with a flush of red. The frost began to glisten with a reflected color. The youth dreamed as he walked; his broad face and deep earnest eyes caught and reflected some of the beauty and majesty of the sky.

But as he passed a farm gate and a young man of about his own age joined him, his brow darkened. The other man was equipped for work like himself.

"Hello, Will!"

"Hello, Ed!"

"Going down to help Dingman thrash?"

"Yes," replied Will shortly. It was easy to see he didn't welcome company.

"So'm I. Who's goin' to do your thrashin-Dave McTurg?"

"Yes, I guess so. Haven't spoken to anybody yet."

They walked on side by side. Will didn't feel like being rudely broken in on in this way. The two men were rivals, but Will, being the victor, would have been magnanimous, only he wanted to be alone with his lover's dream.

"When do you go back to the sem'?" Ed asked after a little.

"Term begins next week. I'll make a break about second week."

"Le's see: you graduate next year, don't yeh?"

"I expect to, if I don't slip up on it."

They walked on side by side, both handsome fellows; Ed a little more showy in his face, which had a certain clean-cut precision of line and a peculiar clear pallor that never browned under the sun. He chewed vigorously on a quid of tobacco, one of his most noticeable bad habits.

Teams could be heard clattering along on several roads now, and jovial voices singing. One team coming along behind the two men, the driver sung out in good-natured warning, "Get out o' the way, there." And with a laugh and a chirp spurred his horses to pass them.

Ed, with a swift understanding of the driver's trick, flung out his left hand and caught the end-gate, threw his fork in, and leaped after it. Will walked on, disdaining attempt to catch the wagon. On all sides now the wagons of the plowmen or threshers were getting out into the fields, with a pounding, rumbling sound.

The pale red sun was shooting light through the leaves, and warming the boles of the great oaks that stood in the yard, and melting the frost off the great gaudy threshing machine that stood between the stacks. The interest, picturesqueness of it all got hold of Will Hannan, accustomed to it as he was. The homes stood about in a circle, hitched to the ends of the six sweeps, all shining with frost.

The driver was oiling the great tarry cogwheels underneath. Laughing fellows were wrestling about the yard. Ed Kinney had scaled the highest stack, and stood ready to throw the first sheaf. The sun, lighting him where he stood, made his fork handle gleam like dull gold. Cheery words, jests, and snatches of song everywhere. Dingman bustled about giving his orders and placing his men, and the voice of big Dave McTurg was heard calling to the men as they raised the long stacker into place:

"Heave-ho, there! Up she rises!"

And, best of all, Will caught a glimpse of a smiling girl face at the kitchen window that made the blood beat in his throat.

"Hello, Will!" was the general greeting, given with some constraint by most of the young fellows, for Will had been going to Rock River to school for some years, and there was a little feeling of jealousy on the part of those who pretended to sneer at the "seminary chaps like Will Hannan and Milton Jennings."

Dingrnan came up. "Will, I guess you'd better go on the stack with Ed."

"All ready. Hurrah, there!" said David in his soft but resonant bass voice that always had a laugh in it. "Come, come, every sucker of yeh git hold o' something. All ready!" He waved his hand at the driver, who climbed upon his platform. Everybody scrambled into place.

"Chk, chk! All ready, boys! Stiddy there, Dan! Chk, chk! All ready, boys! Stiddy there, boys! All ready now!" The horses began to strain at the sweeps. The cylinder began to hum.

"Grab a root there! Where's my band cutter? Here, you, climb on here!" And David reached down and pulled Shep Watson up by the shoulder with his gigantic hand.

Bogogoom, Boo-woo-wogoouroourow-owm, yarryarr! The whirling cylinder boomed, roared, and snarled as it rose in speed. At last, when its tone became a rattling yell, David nodded to the pitchers, rasped his hands together, the sheaves began to fall from the stack, the band cutter, knife in hand, slashed the bands in twain, and the feeder with easy majestic motion gathered them under his arm, rolled them out into an even belt of entering wheat, on which the cylinder tore with its frightful, ferocious snarl.

Will was very happy in Its quiet way. He enjoyed the smooth roll of his great muscles, the sense of power he felt in his hands as he lifted, turned, and swung the heavy sheaves two by two down upon the table, where the band cutter madly slashed away. His frame, sturdy rather than tall, was nevertheless lithe, and he made a fine figure to look at, so Agnes thought, as she came out a moment and bowed and smiled to both the young men.

This scene, one of the jolliest and most sociable of the western farm, had a charm quite aside from human companionship. The beautiful yellow straw entering the cylinder; the clear yellow-brown wheat pulsing out at the side; the broken straw, chaff, and dust puffing out on the great stacker; the cheery whistling and calling of the driver; the keen, crisp air, and the bright sun somehow weirdly suggestive of the passage of time.

Will and Agnes had arrived at a tacit understanding of mutual love only the night before, and Will was power-fully moved to glance often toward the house, but feared somehow the jokes of his companions. He worked on, therefore, methodically, eagerly; but his thoughts were on the future-the rustle of the oak tree nearby, the noise of whose sere leaves he could distinguish beneath the booming snarl of the machine; on the sky, where great fleets of clouds were sailing on the rising wind, like merchantmen bound to some land of love and plenty.

When the Dingmans first came in, only a couple of years before, Agnes had been at once surrounded by a swarm of suitors. Her pleasant face and her abounding good nature made her an instant favorite with all. Will, however, had disdained to become one of the crowd, and held himself aloof, as he could easily do, being away at school most of the time.

The second winter, however, Agnes also attended the seminary, and Will saw her daily and grew to love her. He had been just a bit jealous of Ed Kinney all the time, for Ed had a certain rakish grace in dancing and a dashing skill in handling a team which made him a dangerous rival.

But, as Will worked beside him all this Monday, he felt so secure in his knowledge of the caress Agnes had given him at parting the night before that he was perfectly happy-so happy that he didn't care to talk, only to work on and dream as he worked.

Shrewd David McTurg had his joke when the machine stopped for a few minutes. "Well, you fellers do better'n I expected yeh to, after bein' out so late last night. The first feller I find gappin' has got to treat to the apples."

"Keep your eye on me," said Shep.

"You?" laughed one of the others. "Anybody knows if a girl so much as looked crossways at you, you'd fall in a fit."

"Another thing," said David. "I can't have you fellers carryin' grain, going to the house too often for fried cakes or cookies."

"Now you git out," said Bill Young from the straw pile. "You ain't goin' to have all the fun to yerself."

Will's blood began to grow hot in his face. If Bill had said much more, or mentioned her name, he would have silenced him. To have this rough joking come so close upon the holiest and most exquisite evening of his life was horrible. It was not the words they said, but the tones they used, that vulgarized it all. He breathed a sigh of relief when the sound of the machine began again.

This jesting made him more wary, and when the call for dinner sounded and he knew he was going in to see her, he shrank from it. He took no part in the race of the dust-blackened, half-famished men to get at the washing place first. He took no part in the scurry to get seats at the first table.

Threshing time was always a season of great trial to the housewife. To have a dozen men with the appetites of dragons to cook for was no small task for a couple of women, in addition to their other everyday duties. Preparations usually began the night before with a raid on a hen roost, for "biled chickun" formed the piece de resistance of the dinner. The table, enlarged by boards, filled the sitting room. Extra seats were made out of planks placed on chairs, and dishes were borrowed of neighbors who came for such aid, in their turn.

Sometimes the neighboring women came in to help; but Agnes and her mother were determined to manage the job alone this year, and so the girl, with a neat dark dress, her eyes shining, her cheeks flushed with the work, received the men as they came in dusty, coatless, with grime behind their ears, but a jolly good smile on every face.

Most of them were farmers of the neighborhood and schoolmates. The only one she shrank from was Young, with his hard, glittering eyes and red, sordid face. She received their jokes, their noise, with a silent smile which showed her even teeth and dimpled her round cheek. "She was good for sore eyes," as one of the fellows said to Shep. She seemed deliciously sweet and dainty to these roughly dressed fellows.

They ranged along the table with a great deal of noise, boots thumping, squeaking, knives and forks rattling, voices bellowing out.

"Now hold on, Steve! Can't have yeh so near that chickun!"

"Move along, Shep! I want to be next to the kitchen door! I won't get nothin' with you on that side o' me."

"Oh, that's too thin! I see what you're-"

"No, I won't need any sugar, if you just smile into it." This from gallant David, greeted with roars of laughter.

"Now, Dave, s'pose your wife 'ud hear o' that?"

"She'd snatch 'im bald-headed, that's what she'd do."

"Say, somebody drive that ceow down this way," said Bill.

"Don't get off that drive! It's too old," criticised Shep, passing the milk jug.

Potatoes were seized, cut in halves, sopped in gravy, and taken one, two! Corn cakes went into great jaws like coal into a steam engine. Knives in the right hand cut and scooped gravy up. Great, muscular, grimy, but wholesome fellows they were, feeding like ancient Norse, and capable of working like demons. They were deep in the process; half-hidden by steam from the potatoes and stew, in less than sixty seconds from their entrance.

With a shrinking from the comments of the others upon his regard for Agnes, Will assumed a reserved and almost haughty air toward his fellow workmen, and a curious coldness toward her. As he went in, she came forward smiling brightly.

"There's one more place, Will." A tender, involuntary droop in her voice betrayed her, and Will felt a wave of hot blood surge over him as the rest roared.

"Ha, ha! Oh, there'd be a place for him!"

"Don't worry, Will! Always room for you here!"

Will took his seat with a sudden angry flame. "Why can't she keep it from these fools?" was his thought. He didn't even thank her for showing him the chair.

She flushed vividly, but smiled back. She was so proud and happy, she didn't care very much if they did know it. But as Will looked at her with that quick angry glance, and took his seat with scowling brow, she was hurt and puzzled. She redoubled her exertions to please him, and by so doing added to the amusement of the crowd that gnawed chicken bones, rattled cups, knives and forks, and joked as they ate with small grace and no material loss of time.

Will remained silent through it all, eating in marked contrast to the others, using his fork instead of his knife in eating his potato, and drinking his tea from his cup rather than from his saucer—"finickies" which did not escape the notice of the girl nor the sharp eyes of the other workmen.

"See that? That's the way we do down to the sem! See? Fork for pie in yer right hand! Hey? I can't do it. Watch me."

When Agnes leaned over to say, "Won't you have some more tea, Will?" they nudged each other and grinned. "Aha! What did I tell you?"

Agnes saw at last that for some reason Will didn't want her to show her regard for him, that be was ashamed of it in some way, and she was wounded. To cover it up, she resorted to the feminine device of smiling and chatting with the others. She asked Ed if he wouldn't have another piece of pie.

"I will-with a fork, please."

"This is 'bout the only place you can use a fork," said Bill Young, anticipating a laugh by his own broad grin.

"Oh, that's too old," said Shep Watson. "Don't drag that out agin. A man that'll eat seven taters-"

"Shows who does the work."

"Yes, with his jaws," put in Jim Wheelock, the driver. "If you'd put in a little more work with soap 'n' water before comin' in to dinner, it 'ud be a religious idee," said David.

"It ain't healthy to wash."

"Well, you'll live forever, then."

"He ain't washed his face sence I knew 'im."

"Oh, that's a little too tough! He washes once a week," said Ed Kinney.

"Back of his ears?" inquired David, who was munching a doughnut, his black eyes twinkling with fun.

"What's the cause of it?"

"Dade says she won't kiss 'im if he don't." Everybody roared.

"Good fer Dade! I wouldn't if I was in her place."

Wheelock gripped a chicken leg imperturbably, and left it bare as a toothpick with one or two bites at it. His face shone in two clean sections around his nose and mouth. Behind his ears the dirt lay undisturbed. The grease on his hands could not be washed off.

Will began to suffer now because Agnes treated the other fellows too well. With a lover's exacting jealousy, he wanted her in some way to hide their tenderness from the rest, but to show her indifference to men like Young and Kinney. He didn't stop to inquire of himself the justice of such a demand, nor just how it was to be done. He only insisted she ought to do it.

He rose and left the table at the end of his dinner, without having spoken to her, without even a tender, significant glance, and he knew, too, that she was troubled and hurt. But he was suffering. It seemed as if he had lost something sweet, lost it irrecoverably.

He noticed Ed Kinney and Bill Young were the last to come out, just before the machine started up again after dinner, and he saw them pause outside the threshold and laugh back at Agnes standing in the doorway. Why couldn't she keep those fellows at a distance, not go out of her way to bandy jokes with them?

Some way the elation of the morning was gone. He worked on doggedly now, without looking up, without listening to the leaves, without seeing the sunlighted clouds. Of course he didn't think that she meant anything by it, but it irritated him and made him unhappy. She gave herself too freely.

Toward the middle of the afternoon the machine stopped for a time for some repairing; and while Will lay on his stack in the bright yellow sunshine, shelling wheat in his hands and listening to the wind in the oaks, he heard his name and her name mentioned on the other side of the machine, where the measuring box stood. He listened.

"She's pretty sweet on him, ain't she? Did yeh notus how she stood around over him?"

"Yes; an' did yeh see him when she passed the cup o' tea down over his shoulder?"

Will got up, white with wrath as they laughed.

"Some way he didn't seem to enjoy it as I would. I wish she'd reach her arm over my neck that way."

Will walked around the machine, and came on the group lying on the chaff near the straw pile.

"Say, I want you fellers to understand that I won't have any more of this talk. I won't have it."

There was a dead silence. Then Bill Young rose up.

"What yeh goen' to do about it?" he sneered.

"I'm going to stop it."

The wolf rose in Young. He moved forward, his ferocious soul flaming from his eyes.

"W'y, you damned seminary dude, I can break you in two!"

An answering glare came into Will's eyes. He grasped and slightly shook his fork, which he had brought with him unconsciously.

"If you make one motion at me, I'll smash your head like an eggshell!" His voice was low but terrific. There was a tone in it that made his own blood stop in his veins. "If you think I'm going to roll around on this ground with a hyena like you, you've mistaken your man. I'll kill you, but I won't fight with such men as you are."

Bill quailed and slunk away, muttering some epithet like "coward."

"I don't care what you call me, but just remember what I say: you keep your tongue off that girl's affairs."

"That's the talk!" said David. "Stand up for your girl always, but don't use a fork. You can handle him without that:'

"I don't propose to try," said Will, as he turned away. As he did so, he caught a glimpse of Ed Kinney at the well, pumping a pail of water for Agnes, who stood beside him, the sun on her beautiful yellow hair. She was laughing at something Ed was saying as he slowly moved the handle up and down.

Instantly, like a foaming, turbid flood, his rage swept out toward her. "It's all her fault," he thought, grinding his teeth. "She's a fool. If she'd hold herself in like other girls! But no; she must smile and smile at everybody." It was a beautiful picture, but it sent a shiver through him.

He worked on with teeth set, white with rage. He had an impulse that would have made him assault her with words as with a knife. He was possessed with a terrible passion which was hitherto latent in him, and which he now felt to be his worst self. But he was powerless to exorcise it. His set teeth ached with the stress of his muscular tension, and his eyes smarted with the strain.

He had always prided himself on being cool, calm, above these absurd quarrels that his companions had so often indulged in. He didn't suppose he could be so moved. As he worked on, his rage settled down into a sort of stubborn bitterness-stubborn bitterness of conflict between this evil nature and his usual self. It was the instinct of possession, the organic feeling of proprietorship of a woman, which rose to the surface and mastered him. He was not a self-analyst, of course, being young, though he was more introspective than the ordinary farmer.

He had a great deal of time to think it over as he worked on there, pitching the heavy bundles, but still he did not get rid of the miserable desire to punish Agnes; and when she came out, looking very pretty in her straw hat, and came around near his stack, he knew she came to see him, to have an explanation, a smile; and yet he worked away with his hat pulled over his eyes, hardly noticing her.

Ed went over to the edge of the stack and chatted with her; and she-poor girl!-feeling Will's neglect, could only put a good face on the matter, and show that she didn't mind it, by laughing back at Ed.

All this Will saw, though he didn't appear to be looking. And when Jim Wheelock-Dirty Jim-with his whip in his hand, came up and playfully pretended to pour oil on her hair, and she laughingly struck at him with a handful of straw, Will wouldn't have looked at her if she had called him by name.

She looked so bright and charming in her snowy apron and her boy's straw hat tipped jauntily over one pink ear that David and Steve and Bill, and even Shep, found a way to get a word with her, and the poor fellows in the high straw pile looked their disappointment and shook their forks in mock rage at the lucky dogs on the ground. But Will worked on like a fiend, while the dapples of light and shade fell on the bright face of the merry girl.

To save his soul from hell flames he couldn't have gone over there and smiled at her. It was impossible. A wall of bronze seemed to have arisen between them. Yesterday, last night, seemed a dream. The clasp of her hands at his neck, the touch of her lips, were like the caresses of an ideal in some dim reverie.

As night drew on, the men worked with a steadier, more mechanical action. No one spoke now. Each man was intent on his work. No one had any strength or breath to waste. The driver on his power changed his weight on weary feet, and whistled and sang at the tired horses. The feeder, his face gray with dust, rolled the grain into the cylinder so even, so steady, so swift that it ran on with a sullen, booming roar. Far up on the straw pile the stackers worked with the steady, rhythmic action of men rowing a boat, their figures looming vague and dim in the flying dust and chaff, outlined against the glorious yellow and orange-tinted clouds.

"Phe-e-eew-ee," whistled the driver with the sweet, cheery, rising notes of a bird. "Chk, chk, chk! Phe-e-eewee. Go on there, boys! Chk, chk, chk! Step up, there Dan, step up! (Snap!) Phe-e-eew-ee! G'-wan-g'-wan, g'-wan! Chk, clik, chk! Wheest, wheest, wheest! Clik, chk!"

In the house the women were setting the table for supper. The sun had gone down behind the oaks, flinging glorious rose color and orange shadows along the edges of the slate-blue clouds. Agnes stopped her work at the kitchen window to look up at the sky and cry silently. "What was the matter with Will?" She felt a sort of distrust of him now. She thought she knew him so well, but now he was so strange.

"Come, Aggie," said Mrs. Dingman, "they're gettin' most down to the bottom of the stack. They'll be pilin' in here soon."

"Phe-e-eew-ee! G'-wan, Doll! G'-wan, boys! Chk, chk, chk! Phe-e-eew-ee!" called the driver out in the dusk, cheerily swinging the whip over the horses' backs. Boomogogoom! roared the machine, with a muffled, monotonous, solemn tone. "G'-wan, boys! G'-wan, g'-wan!"

Will had worked unceasingly all day. His muscles ached with fatigue. His hands trembled. He clenched his teeth, however, and worked on, determined not to yield. He wanted them to understand that he could do as much pitching as any of them and read Caesar's Commentaries besides. It seemed as if each bundle were the last he could raise. The sinews of his wrist pained him so, they seemed swollen to twice their natural size. But still he worked on grimly, while the dusk fell and the air grew chill.

At last the bottom bundle was pitched up, and he got down on his knees to help scrape the loose wheat into baskets. What a sweet relief it was to kneel down, to release the fork and let the worn and cramping muscles settle into rest! A new note came into the driver's voice, a soothing tone, full of kindness and admiration for the work his team had done.

"Wgo-o, lads! Stiddy-y-y, boys! Wgo-o, there, Dan. Stiddy, stiddy, old man! Ho, there!" The cylinder took on a lower key, with short rising yells, as it ran empty for a moment. The horses had been going so long that they came to a stop reluctantly. At last David called, "Turn out!" The men seized the ends of the sweep, David uncoupled the tumbling rods, and Shep threw a sheaf of grain into the cylinder, choking it into silence.

The stillness and the dusk were very impressive. So long had the bell-metal cogwheel sung its deafening song into Will's ear that, as he walked away into the dusk, he had a weird feeling of being suddenly deaf, and his legs were so numb that he could hardly feel the earth. He stumbled away like a man paralyzed.

He took out his handkerchief, wiped the dust from his face as best he could, shook his coat, dusted his shoulders with a grain sack, and was starting away, when Mr. Dingman, a rather feeble elderly man, came up.

"Come, Will, supper's all ready. Go in and eat."

"I guess I'll go home to supper."

"Oh, no, that won't do. The women'll be expecting yeh to stay."

The men were laughing at the well, the warm yellow light shone from the kitchen, the chill air making it seem very inviting, and she was there, waiting! But the demon rose in him. He knew Agnes would expect him, that she would cry that night with disappointment, but his face hardened. "I guess I'll go home," he said, and his tone was relentless. He turned and walked away, hungry, tired—so tired he stumbled, and so unhappy he could have wept.

II

ON Thursday the county fair was to be held. The fair is one of the gala days of the year in the country districts of the West, and one of the times when the country lover rises above expense to the extravagance of hiring a top buggy in which to take his sweetheart to the neighboring town.

It was customary to prepare for this long beforehand, for the demand for top buggies was so great the livery-men grew dictatorial and took no chances. Slowly but surely the country beaux began to compete with the clerks, and in many cases actually outbid them, as they furnished their own horses and could bid higher, in consequence, on the carriages.

Will had secured his brother's "rig," and early on Thursday morning he was at work, busily washing the mud from the carriage, dusting the cushions, and polishing up the buckles and rosettes on his horses' harnesses. It was a beautiful, crisp, clear dawn-the ideal day for a ride; and Will was singing as he worked. He had regained his real sell, and, having passed through a bitter period of shame, was now joyous with anticipation of forgiveness. He looked forward to the day with its chances of doing a thousand little things to show his regret and his love.

He had not seen Agnes since Monday, because Tuesday he did not go back to help thresh, and Wednesday he had been obliged to go to town to see about board for the coming term; but he felt sure of her. It had all been arranged the Sunday before; she'd expect him, and he was to call at eight o'clock.

He polished up the colts with merry tick-tack of the brush and comb, and after the last stroke on their shining limbs, threw his tools in the box and went to the house.

"Pretty sharp last night," said his brother John, who was scrubbing his face at the cistern.

"Should say so by that rim of ice," Will replied, dipping his hands into the icy water.

"I ought'o stay home today an' dig tates," continued the older man thoughtfully as they went into the wood-shed and wiped consecutively on the long roller towel. "Some o' them Early Rose lay right on top o' the ground. They'll get nipped sure."

"Oh, I guess not. You'd better go, Jack; you don't get away very often. And then it would disappoint Nettie and the children so. Their little hearts are overflowing," he ended as the door opened and two sturdy little boys rushed out.

"B'ekfuss, Poppa; all yeady!"

The kitchen table was set near the stove; the room was full of sun, and the smell of sizzling sausages and the aroma of coffee filled the room. The kettle was doing its duty cheerily, and the wife with flushed face and smiling eyes was hurrying to and fro, her heart full of anticipation of the day's outing.

There was a hilarity almost like some strange intoxication on the part of the two children. They danced, and chattered, and clapped their chubby brown hands, and ran to the windows ceaselessly.

"Is yuncle Will goin' yide flour buggy?"

"Yus; the buggy and the colts."

"Is he goin' to take his girl?"

Will blushed a little, and John roared.

"Yes, I'm goin'-"

"Is Aggie your girl?"

"H'yer! h'yer! young man," called John, "you're gettin' personal."

"Well, set up," said Nettie, and with a good deal of clatter they drew around the cheerful table.

Will had already begun to see the pathos, the pitiful significance of this great joy over a day's outing, and he took himself a little to task at his own selfish freedom. He resolved to stay at home some time and let Nettie go in his place. A few hours in the middle of the day on Sunday, three or four holidays in summer; the rest for this cheerful little wife and her patient husband was work-work that some way accomplished so little and left no trace on their souls that was beautiful.

While they were eating breakfast, teams began to clatter by, huge lumber wagons with three seats across, and a boy or two jouncing up and down with the dinner baskets near the end-gate. The children rushed to the window each time to announce who it was, and how many there were in.

But as Johnny said "fifteen" each time, and Ned wavered between "seven" and "sixteen," it was doubtful if they could be relied upon. They had very little appetite, so keen was their anticipation of the ride and the wonderful sights before them. Their little hearts shuddered with joy at every fresh token of preparation-a joy that made Will say, "Poor little men!"

They vibrated between the house and the barn while the chores were being finished, and their happy cries started the young roosters into a renewed season of crowing. And when at last the wagon was brought out and the horses hitched to it, they danced like mad sprites.

After they had driven away, Will brought out the colts, hitched them in, and drove them to the hitching post. Then he leisurely dressed himself in his best suit, blacked his boots with considerable exertion, and at about 7:30 o'clock climbed into his carriage and gathered up the reins.

He was quite happy again. The crisp, bracing air, the strong pull of the spirited young team put all thought of sorrow behind him. He had planned it all out. He would first put his arm around her and kiss her-there would not need to be any words to tell her how sorry and ashamed he was. She would know!

Now, when he was alone and going toward her on a beautiful morning, the anger and bitterness of Monday fled away, became unreal, and the sweet dream of the Sunday parting grew the reality. She was waiting for him now. She had on her pretty blue dress and the wide hat that always made her look so arch. He had said about eight o'clock.

The swift team was carrying him along the crossroad, which was little travelled, and he was alone with his thoughts. He fell again upon his plans. Another year at school for them both, and then he'd go into a law office. Judge Brown had told him he'd give him-"Whoa! Ho!"

There was a swift lurch that sent him flying over the dasher. A confused vision of a roadside ditch full of weeds and bushes, and then he felt the reins in his hands and heard the snorting horses trample on the hard road.

He rose dizzy, bruised, and covered with dust. The team he held securely and soon quieted. He saw the cause of it all: the right forewheel had come off, letting the front of the buggy drop. He unhitched the excited team from the carriage, drove them to the fence and tied them securely, then went back to find the wheel and the "nut" whose failure to hold its place had done all the mischief. He soon had the wheel on, but to find the burr was a harder task. Back and forth he ranged, looking, scraping in the dust, searching the weeds.

He knew that sometimes a wheel will run without the burr for many rods before coming off, and so each time he extended his search. He traversed the entire half-mile several times, each time his rage and disappointment getting more bitter. He ground his teeth in a fever of vexation and dismay.

He had a vision of Agnes waiting, wondering why he did not come. It was this vision that kept him from seeing the burr in the wheel-track, partly covered by a clod.

Once he passed it looking wildly at his watch, which was showing nine o'clock. Another time he passed it with eyes dimmed with a mist that was almost tears of anger.

There is no contrivance that will replace an axle burr, and farmyards have no unused axle burrs, and so Will searched. Each moment he said: "I'll give it up, get onto one of the horses, and go down and tell her." But searching for a lost axle burr is like fishing: the searcher expects each moment to find it. And so he groped, and ran breathlessly, furiously, back and forth, and at last kicked away the clod that covered it, and hurried, hot and dusty, cursing his stupidity, back to the team.

It was ten o'clock as he climbed again into the buggy and started his team on a swift trot down the road. What would she think? He saw her now with tearful eyes and pouting lips. She was sitting at the window, with hat and gloves on; the rest had gone, and she was waiting for him.

But she'd know something had happened, because he had promised to be there at eight. He had told her what team he'd have. (He had forgotten at this moment the doubt and distrust he had given her on Monday.) She'd know he'd surely come.

But there was no smiling or tearful face watching at the window as he came down the lane at a tearing pace and turned into the yard. The house was silent and the curtains down. The silence sent a chill to his heart. Something rose up in his throat to choke him.

"Agnes!" he called. "Hello! I'm here at last!"

There was no reply. As he sat there, the part he had played on Monday came back to him. She may be sick! he thought with a cold thrill of fear.

An old man came around the corner of the house with a potato fork in his hands, his teeth displayed in a grin.

"She ain't here. She's gone."

"Gone!"

"Yes-more'n an hour ago."

"Who'd she go with?"

"Ed Kinney," said the old fellow with a malicious grin. "I guess your goose is cooked."

Will lashed the horses into a run and swung round the yard and out of the gate. His face was white as a dead man's, and his teeth were set like a vise. He glared straight ahead. The team ran wildly, steadily homeward, while their driver guided them unconsciously. He did not see them. His mind was filled with a tempest of rages, despairs, and shames.

That ride he will never forget. In it he threw away all his plans. He gave up his year's schooling. He gave up his law aspirations. He deserted his brother and his friends. In the dizzying whirl of passions he had only one clear idea-to get away, to go West, to get away from the sneers and laughter of his neighbors, and to make her suffer by it all.

He drove into the yard, did not stop to unharness the team, but rushed into the house and began packing his trunk. His plan was formed, which was to drive to Cedarville and hire someone to bring the team back. He had no thought of anything but the shame, the insult she had put upon him. Her action on Monday took on the same levity it wore then, and excited him in the same way. He saw her laughing with Ed over his dismay. He sat down and wrote a letter to her at last-a letter that came from the ferocity of the medieval savage in him:

"It you want to go to hell with Ed Kinney, you can. I won't say a word. That's where he'll take you. You won't see me again."

This he signed and sealed, and then he bowed his head and wept like a girl. But his tears did not soften the effect of the letter. It went as straight to its mark as he meant it should. It tore a seared and ragged path to an innocent, happy heart, and be took a savage pleasure in the thought of it as he rode away on the cars toward the South.

III

The seven years lying between 1880 and 1887 made a great change in Rock River and in The adjacent farming land. Signs changed and firms went out of business with characteristic Western ease of shift. The trees grew rapidly, dwarfing The houses beneath them, and contrasts of newness and decay thickened.

Will found The country changed, as he walked along The dusty road from Rock River toward "The Corners." The landscape was at its fairest and liberalest, with its seas of corn deep green and moving with a mournful rustle, in sharp contrast to its flashing blades; its gleaming fields of barley, and its wheat already mottled with soft gold in The midst of its pea-green.

The changes were in The hedges, grown higher, In The greater predominance of cornfields and cattle pastures, but especially in The destruction of homes. As he passed on Will saw The grass growing and cattle feeding on a dozen places where homes had once stood. They had given place to The large farm and The stock raiser. Still the whole scene was bountiful and very beautiful to the eye.

It was especially grateful to Will, for he had spent nearly all his years of absence among The rocks, treeless swells, and bleak cliffs of The Southwest. The crickets rising before his dusty feet appeared to him something sweet and suggestive and The cattle feeding in The clover moved him to deep thought-they were so peaceful and slow-motioned.

As he reached a little popple tree by the roadside, he stopped, removed his broad-brimmed hat, put his elbows on The fence, and looked hungrily upon The scene. The sky was deeply blue, with only here and there a huge, heavy, slow-moving, massive, sharply outlined cloud sailing like a berg of ice in a shoreless sea of azure.

In the fields the men were harvesting the ripened oats and barley, and the sound of their machines clattering, now low, now loud, came to his ears. Flies buzzed near him, and a king bird clattered overhead. He noticed again, as he had many a time when a boy, that The softened sound of The far-off reaper was at times exactly like the hum of a bluebottle fly buzzing heedlessly about his ears.

A slender and very handsome young man was shocking grain near the fence, working so desperately he did not see Will until greeted by him. He looked up, replied to the greeting, but kept on till he had finished his last stook, then he came to the shade of the tree and took off his hat.

"Nice day to sit under a tree and fish."

Will smiled. "I ought to know you, I suppose; I used to live here years ago."

"Guess not; we came in three years ago."

The young man was quick-spoken and very pleasant to look at. Will felt freer with him.

"Are The Kinneys still living over there?" He nodded at a group of large buildings.

"Tom lives there. Old man lives with Ed. Tom ousted The old man some way, nobody seems to know how, and so he lives with Ed."

Will wanted to ask after Agnes, but hardly felt able. "I s'pose John Hannan is on his old farm?"

"Yes. Got a good crop this year."

Will looked again at The fields of rustling wheat over which The clouds rippled, and said with an air of conviction: "This lays over Arizona, dead sure."

"You're from Arizona, then?"

"Yes-a good ways from it'" Will replied in a way that stopped further question. "Good luck!" he added as he walked on down The road toward The creek, musing. "And the spring-I wonder if that's there yet. I'd like a drink." The sun seemed hotter than at noon, and he walked slowly. At the bridge that spanned the meadow brook, just where it widened over a sandy ford, he paused again. He hung over the rail and looked at the minnows swimming there.

"I wonder if they're the same identical chaps that used to boil and glitter there when I was a boy-looks so. Men change from one generation to another, but the fish remain the same. The same eternal procession of types. I suppose Darwin 'ud say their environment remains The same."

He hung for a long time over the railing, thinking of a vast number of things, mostly vague, flitting things, looking into the clear depths of the brook, and listening to the delicious liquid note of a blackbird swinging on the willow. Red lilies starred the grass with fire, and goldenrod and chicory grew everywhere; purple and orange and yellow-green the prevailing tints.

Suddenly a water snake wriggled across the dark pool above the ford, and the minnows disappeared under the shadow of the bridge. Then Will sighed, lifted his head, and walked on. There seemed to be something prophetic in it, and he drew a long breath. That's the way his plans broke and faded away.

Human life does not move with the regularity of a clock. In living there are gaps and silences when the soul stands still in its flight through abysses-and then there come times of trial and times of struggle when we grow old without knowing it. Body and soul change appallingly.

Seven years of hard, busy life had made changes in Will.

His face had grown bold, resolute, and rugged, some of its delicacy and all of its boyish quality gone. His figure was stouter, erect as of old, but less graceful. He bore himself like a man accustomed to look out for himself in all kinds of places. It was only at times that there came into his deep eyes a preoccupied, almost sad look that showed kinship with his old self.

This look was on his face as he walked toward the clump of trees on the right of the road.

He reached the grove of popple trees and made his way at once to the spring. When he saw it, it gave him a shock. They had let it fill up with leaves and dirt.

Overcome by the memories of the past, he flung him-sell down on the cool and shadowy bank, and gave him-sell up to the bittersweet reveries of a man returning to his boyhood's home. He was filled somehow with a strange and powerful feeling of the passage of time; with a vague feeling of the mystery and elusiveness of human life. The leaves whispered it overhead, the birds sang it in chorus with the insects, and far above, in the measureless spaces of sky, the hawk told it in the silence and majesty of his flight from cloud to cloud.

It was a feeling hardly to be expressed in words—one of those emotions whose springs lie far back in the brain. He lay so still, the chipmunks came curiously up to his very feet, only to scurry away when he stirred like a sleeper in pain.

He had cut himself off entirely from the life at The Corners. He had sent money home to John, but had concealed his own address carefully. The enormity of this folly now came back to him, racking him till he groaned.

He heard the patter of feet and the half-mumbled monologue of a running child. He roused up and faced a small boy, who started back in terror like a wild fawn. He was deeply surprised to find a man there where only boys and squirrels now came. He stuck his fist in his eye, and was backing away when Will spoke.

"Hold on, sonny! Nobody's hit you. Come, I ain't goin' to eat yeh." He took a bit of money from his pocket. "Come here and tell me your name. I want to talk with you."

The boy crept upon the dime.

Will smiled. "You ought to be a Kinney. What is your name?"

"Tomath Dickinthon Kinney. I'm thix and a half. I've got a colt," lisped the youngster breathlessly as he crept toward the money.

"Oh, you are, eh? Well, now, are you Tom's boy or Ed's?"

"Tomth's boy. Uncle Ed hith gal-"

"Ed got a boy?"

"Yeth, thir- lii baby. Aunt Agg letth me hold 'im"

"Agg! Is that her name?"

"That's what Uncle Ed callth her."

The man's head fell, and it was a long time before he asked his next question.

"How is she, anyhow?"

"Purty well," piped the boy with a prolongation of the last words into a kind of chirp. "She'th been thick, though," he added.

"Been sick? How long?"

"Oh, a long time. But she ain't thick abed; she'th awuul poor, though. Gran'pa thayth she'th poor ath a rake."

"Oh, he does, eh?"

"Yeth, thir. Uncle Ed he jawth her, then she crieth."

Will's anger and remorse broke out in a groaning curse. "O my God! I see it all. That great lunkin' houn' has made life a hell fer her." Then that letter came back to his mind; he had never been able to put it out of his mind-he never would till he saw her and asked her pardon.

"Here, my boy, I want you to tell me some more. Where does your Aunt Agnes live?"

"At gran'pa'th. You know where my gran'pa livth?"

"Well, you do. Now I want you to take this letter to her. Give it to her." He wrote a little note and folded it. "Now dust out o' here."

The boy slipped away through the trees like a rabbit; his little brown feet hardly rustled. He was like some little wood animal. Left alone, the man went back into a reverie that lasted till the shadows fell on the thick little grove around the spring. He rose ~ last and, taking his stick in hand, walked out to the wood again and stood there, gazing at the sky. He seemed loath to go farther. The sky was full of flame-colored clouds floating in a yellow-green sea, where bars of faint pink streamed broadly away.

As he stood there, feeling the wind lift his hair, listening to the crickets' ever-present crying, and facing the majesty of space, a strange sadness and despair came into his eyes.

Drawing a quick breath, he leaped the fence and was about going on up the road, when he heard, at a little distance, the sound of a drove of cattle approaching, and he stood aside to allow them to pass. They snuffed and shied at the silent figure by the fence, and hurried by with snappug heels-a peculiar sound that made the man smile with pleasure.

An old man was driving the cows, crying out:

"St, boy, there! Go on, there. Whay, boss!"

Will knew that hard-featured, wiry old man, now entering his second childhood and beginning to limp painfully. He had his hands full of hard clods which he threw impatiently at the lumbering animals.

"Good evening, uncle!"

"I ain't y'r uncle, young man."

His dim eyes did not recognize the boy he had chased out of his plum patch years before.

"I don't know yeh, neither."

"Oh, you will, later on. I'm from the East. I'm a sort of a relative to John Hannan."

"I wanto know if y' be!" the old man exclaimed, peering closer.

"Yes. I'm just up from Rock River. John's harvesting, I s'pose?"

"Where's the youngest one-Will?"

"William? Oh! he's a bad aig-he lit out fr the West somewhere. He was a hard boy. He stole a hatful o' my plums once. He left home kind o' sudden. He! he! I s'pose he was purty well cut up jest about them days."

"How's that?"

The old man chuckled.

"Well, y' see, they was both courtin' Agnes then, an' my son cut William out. Then William he lit out fr the West, Arizony 'r California 'r somewhere out West. Never been back sence."

"Ain't, heh?"

"No. But they say he's makin' a terrible lot o' money," the old man said in a hushed voice. "But the way he makes it is awful scaly. I tell my wife if I had a son like that an' he'd send me home a bushel basket o' money, earnt like that, I wouldn't touch finger to it-no, sir!"

"You wouldn't? Why?"

"'Cause it ain't right. It ain't made right no way, you-"

"But how is it made? What's the feller's trade?"

"He's a gambler-that's his trade! He plays cards, and every cent is bloody. I wouldn't touch such money no how you could fix it~"

"Wouldn't, hay?" The young man straightened up. "Well, look-a-here, old man: did you ever hear of a man foreclosing a mortgage on a widow and two boys, getting a farm fr one quarter what it was really worth? You damned old hypocrite! I know all about you and your whole tribe-you old bloodsucker!"

The old man's jaw fell; he began to back away.

"Your neighbors tell some good stories about you. Now skip along after those cows or I'll tickle your old legs for you!"

The old man, appalled and dazed at this sudden change of manner, backed away, and at last turned and racked off up the road, looking back with a wild face at which the young man laughed remorselessly.

"The doggoned old skeesucks!" Will soliloquized as he walked up the road. "So that's the kind of a character he's been givin' me!"

"Hullo! A whippoorwrn. Takes a man back into childhood-No, don't 'whip poor Will'; he's got all he can bear now."

He came at last to the little farm Dingman had owned, and he stopped in sorrowful surprise. The barn had been moved away, the garden plowed up, and the house, turned into a granary, stood with boards nailed across its dusty cobwebbed windows. The tears started into the man's eyes; he stood staring at it silently.

In the face of this house the seven years that he had last lived stretched away into a wild waste of time. It stood as a symbol of his wasted, ruined life. It was personal, intimately personal, this decay of her home.

All that last scene came back to him: the booming roar of the threshing machine, the cheery whistle of the driver, the loud, merry shouts of the men. He remembered how warmly the lamplight streamed out of that door as he turned away tired, hungry, sullen with rage and jealousy. Oh, if he had only had the courage of a man!

Then he thought of the boy's words. She was sick. Ed abused her. She had met her punishment. A hundred times he had been over the whole scene. A thousand times he had seen her at the pump smiling at Ed Kinney, the sun lighting her bare head; and he never thought of it without hardening.

At this very gate he had driven up that last forenoon, to find that she had gone with Ed. He had lived that sickening, depressing moment over many times, but not times enough to keep down the bitter passion he had felt then, and felt now as he went over it in detail.

He was so happy and confident that morning, so perfectly certain that all would be made right by a kiss and a cheery jest. And now! Here he stood sick with despair and doubt of all the world. He turned away from the desolate homestead and walked on.

"But I'll see her-just once more. And then-" And again the mighty significance, responsibility of life fell upon him. He felt as young people seldom do the irrevocableness of living, the determinate, unalterable character of living. He determined to begin to live in some new way-just how he could not say.

IV

OLD man Kinney and his wife were getting their Sunday school lessons with much bickering, when Will drove up the next day to the dilapidated gate and hitched his team to a leaning post under the oaks. Will saw the old man's head at the open window, but no one else, though he looked eagerly for Agnes as he walked up the familiar path. There stood the great oak under whose shade he had grown to be a man. How close the great tree seemed to stand to his heart, some way! As the wind stirred in the leaves, it was like a rustle of greeting.

In that low old house they had all lived, and his mother had toiled for thirty years. A sort of prison after all. There they were all born, and there his father and his little sister had died. And then it had passed into old Kinney's hands.

Walking along up the path he felt a serious weakness in his limbs, and he made a pretense of stopping to look at a flowerbed containing nothing but weeds. After seven years of separation he was about to face once more the woman whose life came so near being a part of his- Agnes, now a wife and a mother.

How would she look? Would her face have that old-time peachy bloom, her mouth that peculiar beautiful curve? She was large and fair, he recalled, hair yellow and shining, eyes blue-He roused himself. This was nonsense! He was trembling. He composed himself by looking around again.

"The old scoundrel has let the weeds choke out the flowers and surround the beehives. Old man Kinney neverbelieved in anything but a petty utility."

Will set his teeth, and marched up to the door and struck it like a man delivering a challenge. Kinney opened the door, and started back in fear when he saw who it was.

"How de do? How de do?" said Will, walking in' his eyes fixed on a woman seated beyond, a child in her lap.

Agnes rose, without a word; a fawnlike, startled widening of the eyes, her breath coming quick, and her face flushing. They couldn't speak; they only looked at each other an instant, then Will shivered, passed his hand over his eyes, and sat down.

There was no one there but the old people, who were looking at him in bewilderment. They did not notice any confusion in Agnes's face. She recovered first.

"I'm glad to see you back, Will," she said, rising and putting the sleeping child down in a neighboring room. As she gave him her hand, he said:

"I'm glad to get back, Agnes. I hadn't ought to have gone." Then he turned to the old people: "I'm Will Hannan. You needn't be scared, daddy; I was jokin' last night."

"Dew tell! I wanto know!" exclaimed granny. "Wal I never! An, you're my little Willy boy who ust 'o he in my class. Well! well! W'y, Pa, ain't he growed tall! Growed handsome tew. I ust 'o think he was a drelful humly boy; but my sakes, that mustache-"

"Wal, he give me a tumble scare last night. My land! scared me out of a year's growth," cackled the old man.

This gave them all a chance to laugh and the air was cleared. It gave Agnes time to recover herself and to be able to meet Will's eyes. Will himself was powerfully moved; his throat swelled and tears came to his eyes every time he looked at her.

$he was worn and wasted incredibly. The blue of her eyes seemed dimmed and faded by weeping, and the oldtime scariet of her lips had been washed away. The sinews of her neck showed painfully when she turned her head, and her trembling hands were worn, discolored, and lumpy at the joints.

Poor girl! She felt that she was under scrutiny, and her eyes felt hot and restless. She wished to run away and cry, but she dared not. She stayed, while Will began to tell her of his life and to ask questions about old friends.

The old people took it up and relieved her of any share in it; and Will, seeing that she was suffering, told some funny stories which made the old people cackle in spite of themselves.

But it was forced merriment on Will's part. Once in a while Agnes smiled with just a little flash of the old-time sunny temper. But there was no dimple in the cheek now, and the smile had more suggestion of an invalid~r even a skeleton. He was almost ready to take her in his arms and weep, her face appealed so pitifully to him.

"It's most time f'r Ed to be gittin' back, ain't it' Pa?"

"Sh'd say 'twas! He jist went over to Hobkirk's to trade horses. It's dretful tryin' to me to have him go off tradin' horses on Sunday. Seems if he might wait till a rainy day, 'r do it evenin's. I never did believe in horse tradin' anyhow."

"Have y' come back to stay, Willie?" asked the old lady.

"Well-it's hard-tellin'," answered Will, looking at Agnes.

"Well, Agnes, ain't you goin' to get no dinner? I'm 'bout ready f'r dinner. We must git to church eariy today. Elder Wheat is goin' to preach an' they'll be a crowd. He's goin' to hold communion."

"You'll stay to dinner, Will?" asked Agnes.

"Yes-if you wish it."

"I do wish it."

"Thank you; I want to have a good visit with you. I don't know when I'll see you again."

As she moved about, getting dinner on the table, Will sat with gloomy face, listening to the "clack" of the old man. The room was a poor little sitting room, with furniture worn and shapeless; hardly a touch of pleasant color, save here and there a little bit of Agnes's handiwork. The lounge, covered with calico, was rickety; the rocking chair matched it, and the carpet of rags was patched and darned with twine in twenty places. Everywhere was the influence of the Kinneys. The furniture looked like them, in fact.

Agnes was outwardly calm, but her real distraction did not escape Mrs. Kinney's hawklike eyes.

"Well, I declare if you hain't put the butter on in one o' my blue chainy saucers! Now you know I don't allow that saucer to be took down by nobody. I don't see what's got into yeh. Anybody'd s'pose you never see any comp'ny b'fore-wouldn't they, Pa?"

"Sh'd say th' would," said Pa, stopping short in a long story about Ed. "Seems if we couldn't keep anything in this' house sep'rit from the rest. Ed he uses my currycomb-"

He launched out a long list of grievances, which Will shut his ears to as completely as possible, and was thinking how to stop him, when there was a sudden crash. Agnes had dropped a plate.

"Good land o' Goshen!" screamed Granny. "If you ain't the worst I ever see. I'll bet that's my grapevine plate. If it is-well, of all the mercies, it ain't! But it might 'a' ben. I never see your beat-never! That's the third plate since I came to live here."

"Oh, look-a-here, Granny," said Will desperately. "Don't make so much fuss about the plate. What's it worth, anyway? Here's a dollar."

Agnes cried quickly:

"Oh, don't do that, Will! It ain't her pate. It's my plate, and I can break every plate in the house if I want'o," she cried defiantly.

"'Course you can," Will agreed.

"Well, she can't! Not while I'm around," put in Daddy. "I've helped to pay f'r them plates, if she does call 'em hern-"

"What the devul is all this row about? Agg, can't you get along without stirring up the old folks everytime I'm out o' the house?"

The speaker was Ed, now a tail and slouchily dressed man of thirty-two or - three; his face still handsome in a certain dark, cleanly cut style, but he wore a surly loo'k and lounged along in a sort of hangdog style, in greasy overalls and vest unbuttoned.

"Hello, Will! I heard you'd got home. John told me as I came along."

They shook bands, and Ed slouched down on the lounge. Will could have kicked him for laying the blame of the dispute upon Agnes; it showed him in a flash just how he treated her. He disdained to quarrel; he simply silenced and dominated her.

Will asked a few questions about crops, with such grace as he could show, and Ed, with keen eyes in his face, talked easily and stridently.

"Dinner ready?" he asked of Agnes. "Where's Pete?"

"He's asleep."

"All right. Let 'im sleep. Well, let's go out an' set 'up. Come, Dad, sling away that Bible and come to grub. Mother, what the devul are you sniffling at? Say, now, look here. If I hear any more about this row, I'll simply let you walk down to meeting. Come, Will, set up."

He led the way out into the little kitchen where the dinner was set.

"What was the row about? Hain't been breakin' some dish, Agg?"

"Yes, she has."

"One o' the blue ones?" winked Ed.

"No, thank goodness, it was a white one."

"Well, now, I'll git into that dod-gasted cubberd some day an' break the whole eternal outfit. I ain't goin' to have this damned jawin' goin' on," he ended, brutally unconscious of his own "jawin'."

After this the dinner proceeded in comparative silence, Agnes sobbing under breath. The room was small and very hot; the table was warped so badly that the dishes had a tendency to slide to the center; the walls were bare plaster grayed with time; the food was poor and scant, and the flies absolutely swarmed upon everything, like bees. Otherwise the room was clean and orderly.

"They say you've made a pile o' money out West, Bill. I'm glad of it. We fellers back here don't make anything. It's a dam tight squeeze. Agg, it seems to me the flies are devilish thick today. Can't you drive 'em out?"

Agnes felt that she must vindicate herself a little. "I do drive 'em out, but they come right in again. The screen door is broken, and they come right in."

"I told Dad to fix that door."

"But he won't do it for me."

Ed rested his elbows on the table and fixed his bright black eyes on his father.

"Say, what d'you mean by actin' like a mule? I swear I'll trade you off f'r a yaller dog. What do I keep you round here. for anyway-to look purty?"

"I guess I've as good a right here as you have, Ed Kinney."

"Oh, go soak y'r head, old man. If you don't tend out here a little better, down goes your meat house! I won't drive you down to meetin' till you promise to fix that door. Hear me!"

Daddy began to snivel. Agnes could not look up for shame. Will felt sick. Ed laughed.

"I kin bring the old man to terms that way; he can't walk very well late years, an' he can't drive my colt. You know what a cuss I used to be about fast nags? Well, I'm just the same. Hobkirk's got a colt I want. Say, that re-minds me: your team's out there by the fence. I forgot. I'll go and put 'em up."

"No, never mind; I can't stay but a few minutes."

"Goin' to be round the country long?"

"A week-maybe."

Agnes looked up a moment and then let her eyes fall.

"Goin' back West, I s'pose?"

"No. May go East, to Europe mebbe."

"The devul y' say! You must 'a' made a ten-strike out West."

"They say it didn't come lawful," piped Daddy over his blackberries and milk.

"Oh, you shet up. Who wants your put-in? Don't work in any o' your Bible on us."

Daddy rose to go into the other room.

"Hold on, old man. You goin' to fix that door?"

"'Course I be," quavered he.

"Well see't y' do, that's all. Now git on y'r duds, an'

I'll go an' hitch up." He rose from the table. "Don't keep me waiting."

He went out unceremoniously, and Agnes was alone with Will.

"Do you go to church? "he asked. She shook her head. "No, I don't go anywhere now. I have too much to do; I haven't strength left. And I'm not fit anyway."

"Agnes, I want to say something to you; not now-after they're gone."

He went into the other room, leaving her to wash the dinner things. She worked on in a curious, almost dazed way, a dream of something sweet and irrevocable in her eyes. He represented so much to her. His voice brought up times and places that thrilled her like song. He was associated with all that was sweetest and most carefree and most girlish in her life.

Ever since the boy had handed her that note she had been reliving those days. In the midst of her drudgery she stopped to dream-to let some picture come back into her mind. She was a student again at the seminary, and stood in the recitation room with suffocating beat of the heart. Will was waiting outside-waiting in a tremor like her own, to walk home with her under the maples.

Then she remembered the painfully sweet mixture of pride and fear with which she walked up the aisle of the little church behind him. Her pretty new gown rustled, the dim light of the church had something like romance in it, and he was so strong and handsome. Her heart went out in a great silent cry to God- "Oh, let me be a girl again!"

She did not look forward to happiness. She hadn't power to look forward at all.

As she worked, she heard the high, shrill voices of the old people as they bustled about and nagged at each other.

"Ma, where's my specticles?"

"I ain't seen y'r specticles."

"You have, too."

"I ain't neither."

"You had 'em this forenoon."

"Didn't no such thing. Them was my own brass-bowed ones. You had yourn jest 'fore goin' to dinner. If you'd put 'em into a proper place you'd find 'em again."

"I want'o know if I would," the old man snorted'.

"Wal, you'd orter know."

"Oh, you're awful smart, ain't yeh? You never have no trouble, and use mine-do yeh?-an' lose 'em so't I can't

"And if this is the thing that goes on when I'm here, it must be hell when visitors are gone," thought Will.

"Willy, ain't you goin' to meetin'?"

"No, not today. I want to visit a little with Agnes, then I've got to drive back to John's."

"Wal, we must be goin'. Don't you leave them dishes f't me to wash," she screamed at Agnes as she went out the door. "An' if we don't get home by five, them caaves orter be fed."

As Agnes stood at the door to watch them drive away, Will studied her, a smothering ache in his heart as he saw how thin and bent and weary she was. In his soul he felt that she was a dying woman unless she had rest and tender care.

As she turned, she saw something in his face-a pity and an agony of self-accusation-that made her weak and white. She sank into a chair, putting her hand on her chest, as if she felt a failing of breath. Then the blood came back to her face, and her eyes filled with tears.

"Don't-don't look at me like that," she said in a whisper. His pity hurt her.

At sight of her sitting there pathetic, abashed, bewildered, like some gentle animal, Will's throat contracted so that he could not speak. His voice came at last in one terrible cry-"Oh, Agnes! for God's sake forgive me!" He knelt by her side and put his arm about her shoulders and kissed her bowed head. A curious numbness involved his whole body; his voice was husky, the tears burned in his eyes. His whole soul and body ached with his pity and remorseful, self-accusing wrath.

"It was all my fault. Lay it all to me. .. I am the one to bear it. . . . Oh, I've dreamed a thousand times of sayin' this to you, Aggie! I thought if I could only see you again and ask your forgiveness, I'd-" He ground his teeth together in his assault upon himself. "I threw my life away an' killed you-that's what I did!"

He rose and raged up and down the room till he had mastered himself.

"What did you think I meant that day of the thrashing?" he said, turning suddenly. He spoke of it as if it were but a month or two past.

She lifted her head and looked at him in a slow way. She seemed to be remembering. The tears lay on her hollow cheeks.

"I thought you was ashamed of me. I didn't know-why-"

He uttered a snarl of sell-disgust.

"You couldn't know. Nobody could tell what I meant. But why didn't you write? I was ready to come back. I only wanted an excuse-only a line."

"How could I, Will-after your letter?"

He groaned and turned away.

"And Will, I-I got mad too. I couldn't write."

"Oh, that letter-I can see every line of it! F'r God's sake, don't think of it again! But I didn't think, even when I wrote that letter, that I'd find you where you are. I didn't think, I hoped anyhow, Ed Kinney wouldn't-"

She stopped him with a startled look in her great eyes. "Don't talk about him-it ain't right. I mean it don't do any good. What could I do, after Father died? Mother and I. Besides, I waited three years to hear from you, Will."

He gave a strange, choking cry. It burst from his throat—that terrible thing, a man's sob of agony. She went on, curiously calm now.

"Ed was good to me; and he offered a home, anyway, for Mother—"

"And all the time I was waiting for some line to break down my cussed pride, so I could write to you and explain. But you did go with Ed to the fair," he ended suddenly, seeking a morsel of justification for himself.

"Yes. But I waited an' waited; and I thought you was mad at me, and so when they came I-no, I didn't really go with Ed. There was a wagonload of them."

"But I started," he explained, "but the wheel came off. I didn't send word because I thought you'd feel sure I'd come. If you'd only trusted me a little more-No! it was all my fault. I acted like a crazy fool. I didn't stop to reason about anything."

They sat in silence alter these explanations. The sound of the snapping wings of the grasshoppers came through the~windows, and a locust high in a poplar sent down his ringing whir.

"It can't be helped now, Will," Agnes said at last, her voice full of the woman's resignation. "We've got to bear it."

Will straightened up. "Bear it?" He paused. "Yes, I s'pose so. If you hadn't married Ed Kinney! Anybody but him. How did you do it?"

"Oh' I don't know," she answered, wearily brushing her hair back from her eyes. "It seemed best when I did it-and it can't be helped now." There was infinite, dull despair and resignation in her voice.

Will went over to the window. He thought how bright and handsome Ed used to be, and he felt after all that it was no wonder that she married him. Life pushes us into such things. Suddenly he turned, something resolute and imperious in his eyes and voice.

"It can be helped, Aggie," he said. "Now just listen to me. We've made an awful mistake. We've lost seven years o' life, but that's no reason why we should waste the rest of it. Now hold on; don't interrupt me just yet. I come back thinking just as much of you as ever. I ain't going to say a word more about Ed; let the past stay past. I'm going to talk about the future."

She looked at him in a daze of wonder as he went on. "Now I've got some money, I've got a third interest in a ranch, and I've got a standing offer to go back on the Sante Fee road as conductor. There is a team standing out there. I'd like to make another trip to Cedarville-with you-"

"Oh, Will, don't!" she cried; "for pity's sake don't talk-"

"Wait!" he said imperiously. "Now look at it Here you are in hell! Caged up with two old crows picking the life out of you. They'll kill you-I can see it; you're being killed by inches. You can't go anywhere, you can't have anything. Life is just torture for you-"

She gave a little moan of anguish and despair and turned her face to her chairback. Her shoulders shook with weeping, but she listened. He went to her and stood with his hand on the chairback.

His voice trembled and broke. "There's just one way to get out of this, Agnes. Come with me. He don't care for you; his whole idea of women is that they are created for his pleasure and to keep house. Your whole life is agony. Come! Don't cry. There's a chance for life yet."

She didn't speak, but her sobs were less violent; his voice growing stronger reassured her.

"I'm going East, maybe to Europe; and the woman who goes with me will have nothing to do but get strong and well again. I've made you suffer so, I ought to spend the rest of my life making you happy. Come! My wife will sit with me on the deck of the steamer and see the moon rise, and walk with me by the sea, till she gets strong and happy again-till the dimples get back into her cheeks. I never will rest till I see her eyes laugh again.

She rose flushed, wide-eyed, breathing hard with the emotion his vibrant voice called up, but she could not speak. He put his hand gently upon her shoulder, and she sank down again. And he went on with hi~s appeal. There was something hypnotic, dominating in his voice and eyes.

On his part there was no passion of an ignoble sort, only a passion of pity and remorse, and a sweet, tender, reminiscent love. He did not love the woman before him so much as the girl whose ghost she was-the woman whose promise she was. He held himself responsible for it all, and he throbbed with desire to repair the ravage he had indirectly caused. There was nothing equivocal in his position-nothing to disown. How others might look at it he did not consider and did not care. His impetuous soul was carried to a point where nothing came in to mar or divert.

"And then after you're well, after our trip, we'll come back to Houston, and I'll build my wife a house that'll make her eyes shine. My cattle and my salary will give us a good living, and she can have a piano and books, and go to the theater and concerts. Come, what do you think of that?"

Then she heard his words beneath his voice Somehow, and they produced pictures that dazzled her. Luminous shadows moved before her eyes, drifting across the gray background of her poor, starved, work-weary life.

As his voice ceased the rosy clouds faded, and she realized again the faded, musty little room, the calico~ covered furniture, and looking down at her own cheap and ill-fitting dress, she saw her ugly hands lying there. Then she cried out with a gush of tears:

"Oh, Will, I'm so old and homely now, I ain't fit to go with you now! Oh, why couldn't we have married then?"

She was seeing herself as she was then, and so was he; but it deepened his resolution. How beautiful she used to be! He seemed to see her there as if she stood in perpetual sunlight, with a warm sheen in her hair and dimples in her cheeks.

She saw her thin red wrists, her gaunt and knotted hands. There was a pitiful droop in the thin pale lips, and the tears fell slowly from her drooping lashes. He went on:

"Well, it's no use to cry over what was. We must think of what we're going to do. Don't worry about your looks; you'll be the prettiest woman in the country when we get back. Don't wait, Aggie; make up your mind."

She hesitated, and was lost.

"What will people say?"

"I don't care what they say," he flamed out. "They'd say, stay here and be killed by inches. I say you've had your share of suffering. They'd say-the liberal ones-stay and get a divorce; but how do we know we can get one after you've been dragged through the mud of a trial? We can get one just as well in some other state. Why should you be worn out at thirty? What right or justice is there in making you bear all your life the consequences of our-my schoolboy folly?"

As he went on, his argument rose to the level of Browning's philosophy.

"We can make this experience count for us yet. But we mustn't let a mistake ruin us-it should teach us. What right has anyone to keep you in a hole? God don't expect a toad to stay in a stump and starve if it can get out. He don't ask the snakes to suffer as you do."

She had lost the threads of right and wrong out of her hands. She was lost in a maze. She was not moved by passion. Flesh had ceased to stir her; but there was vast power in the new and thrilling words her deliverer spoke. He seemed to open a door for her, and through it turrets shone and great ships crossed on dim blue seas.

"You can't live here, Aggie. You'll die in less than five years. It would kill me to see you die here. Come! It's suicide."

She did not move, save the convulsive motion of her breath and the nervous action of her fingers. She stared down at a spot in the carpet; she couldn't face him.

He grew insistent, a sterner note creeping into his voice.

"If I leave this time, of course you know I never come back."

Her hoarse breathing, growing quicker each moment, was her only reply.

"I'm done," he said with a note of angry disappointment. He did not give her up, however. "I've told you what I'd do for you. Now if you think-"

"Oh, give me time to think, Will!" she cried out, lifting her face.

He shook his head. "No. You might as well decide now. It won't be any easier tomorrow. Come, one minute more and I go out o' that door-unless-" He crossed the room slowly, doubtful himself of his desperate last measure. "My hand is on the knob. Shall I open it?"

She stopped breathing; her fingers closed convulsively on the chair. As he opened the door she sprang up.

"Don't go, Will! Don't go, please don't! I need you here-I-"

"That ain't the question. Are you going with me, Agnes?"

"Yes, yes! I tried to speak before. I trust you, Will; you'r-"

He flung the door open wide. "See the sunlight out there shining on that field o' wheat? That's where I'll take you-out into the sunshine. You shall see it shining on the Bay of Naples. Come, get on your hat; don't take anything more'n you actually need. Leave the past behind you."

The woman turned wildly and darted into the little bedroom. The man listened. He whistled in surprise almost comical. He had forgotten the baby. He could hear the mother talking, cooing.

"Mommie's 'ittle pet. She wasn't goin' to leave her 'ittle man-no, she wasn't! There, there, don't 'e cry. Mommie ain't goin' away and leave him-wicked Mommie ain't-'ittle treasure!"

She was confused again; and when she reappeared at the door, with the child in her arms, there was a wandering look on her face pititul to see. She tried to speak, tried to say, "Please go, Will,"

He designedly failed to understand her whisper. He stepped forward. "The baby! Sure enough. Why, certainly! to the mother belongs the child. Blue eyes, thank heaven!"

He put his arm about them both. She obeyed silently. There was something irresistible in his frank, clear eyes, his sunny smile, his strong brown hand. He slammed the door behind them.

"That closes the door on your sufferings," he said' smiling down at her. "Goodbye to it all."

The baby laughed and stretched out its hands toward the light.

"Boo, boo!" he cried.

"What's he talking about?"

She smiled in perfect trust and fearlessness, seeing her child's face beside his own. "He says it's beautiful."

"Oh, he does? I can't follow his French accent."

She smiled again, in spite of herself. Will shuddered with a thrill of fear, she was so weak and worn. But the sun shone on the dazzling, rustling wheat, the fathomless sky blue, as a sea, bent above them-and the world lay before them.

2. UP THE COULEE. A STORY OF WISCONSIN

"Keep the main-travelled road up the coulee-it's the second house after crossin' the crick."

I

THE ride from Milwaukee to the Mississippi is a fine ride at any time, superb in summer. To lean back in a reclining chair and whirl away in a breezy July day, past lakes, groves of oak, past fields of barley being reaped, past hayfields, where the heavy grass is toppling before the swift sickle, is a panorama of delight, a road full of delicious surprises, where down a sudden vista lakes open, or a distant wooded hill looms darkly blue, or swift streams, foaming deep down the solid rock, send whiffs of cool breezes in at the window.

It has majesty, breadth. The farming has nothing apparently petty about it. All seems vigorous, youthful, and prosperous. Mr. Howard McLane in his chair let his newspaper fall on his lap and gazed out upon it with dreaming eyes. It had a certain mysterious glamour to him; the lakes were cooler and brighter to his eye, the greens fresher, and the grain more golden than to anyone else, for he was coming back to it all after an absence of ten years. It was, besides, his West. He still took pride in being a Western man.

His mind all day flew ahead of the train to the little town far on toward the Mississippi, where he had spent his boyhood and youth. As the train passed the Wisconsin River, with its curiously carved cliffs, its cold, dark, swift-swirling water eating slowly under cedar-clothed banks, Howard began to feel curious little movements of the heart, like a lover as he nears his sweetheart.

The hills changed in character, growing more intimately recognizable. They rose higher as the train left the ridge and passed down into the Black River valley, and specifically into the La Crosse valley. They ceased to have any hint of upheavals of rock, and became simply parts of the ancient level left standing after the water had practically given up its postglacial, scooping action.

It was about six o'clock as he caught sight of the dear broken line of hills on which his baby eyes had looked thirty-five years ago. A few minutes later and the train drew up at the grimy little station set in at the hillside, and, giving him just time to leap off, plunged on again toward the West. Howard felt a ridiculous weakness in his legs as he stepped out upon the broiling hot splintery planks of the station and faced the few idlers lounging about. He simply stood and gazed with the same intensity and absorption one of the idlers might show standing before the Brooklyn Bridge.

The town caught and held his eyes first. How poor and dull and sleepy and squalid it seemed! The one main street ended at the hillside at his left and stretched away to the north, between two rows of the usual village stores, unrelieved by a tree or a touch of beauty. An unpaved street, drab-colored, miserable, rotting wooden buildings, with the inevitable battlements-the same, only worse, was the town.

The same, only more beautiful still, was the majestic amphitheater of green wooded hills that circled the horizon, and toward which he lifted his eyes. He thrilled at the sight.

"Glorious!" he cried involuntarily.

Accustomed to the White Mountains, to the Allghenies, he had wondered if these hills would retain their old-time charm. They did. He took off his hat to them as he stood there. Richly wooded, with gently sloping green sides, rising to massive square or rounded tops with dim vistas, they glowed down upon the squalid town, gracious, lofty in their greeting, immortal in their vivid and delicate beauty.

He was a goodly figure of a man as he stood there beside his valise. Portly, erect, handsomely dressed, and with something unusually winning in his brown mustache and blue eyes, something scholarly suggested by the pinch-nose glasses, something strong in the repose of the head. He smiled as he saw how unchanged was the grouping of the old loafers on the salt barrels and nail kegs. He recognized most of them-a little dirtier, a little more bent, and a little grayer.

They sat in the same attitudes, spat tobacco with the same calm delight, and joked each other, breaking into short and sudden fits of laughter, and pounded each other on the back, just as when he was a student at the La Crosse Seminary and going to and fro daily on the train.

They ruminated on him as he passed, speculating in a perfectly audible way upon his business.

"Looks like a drummer."

"No, he ain't no drummer. See them Boston glasses?"

"That's so. Guess he's a teacher."

"Looks like a moneyed cuss."

"Bos'n, I guess."

He knew the one who spoke last-Freeme Cole, a man who was the fighting wonder of Howard's boyhood, now degenerated into a stoop-shouldered, faded, garrulous, and quarrelsome old man. Yet there was something epic in the old man's stories, something enthralling in the dramatic power of recital.

Over by the blacksmith shop the usual game of quaits" was in progress, and the drug clerk on the corner was chasing a crony with the squirt pump, with which he was about to wash the windows. A few teams stood ankle-deep in the mud, tied to the fantastically gnawed pine pillars of the wooden awnings. A man on a load of hay was "jawing" with the attendant of the platform scales, who stood below, pad and pencil in hand.

"Hit 'im! hit 'im! Jump off and knock 'im!" suggested a bystander, jovially.

Howard knew the voice.

"Talk's cheap. Takes money t' buy whiskey," he said when the man on the load repeated his threat of getting off and whipping the scalesman.

"You're William McTurg," Howard said, coming up to him.

"I am, sir," replied the soft-voiced giant turning and looking down on the stranger with an amused twinkle in his deep brown eyes. He stood as erect as an Indian, though his hair and beard were white.

"I'm Howard McLane."

"Ye begin t' look it," said McTurg, removing his right hand from his pocket. "How are yeh?"

"I'm first-rate. How's Mother and Grant?"

"Saw 'im plowing corn as I came down. Guess he's all right. Want a boost?"

"Well, yes. Are you down with a team?"

"Yep. 'Bout goin' home. Climb right in. That's my rig, right there," nodding at a sleek bay colt hitched in a covered buggy. "Heave y'r grip under the seat."

They climbed into the seat after William had lowered the buggy top and unhitched the horse from the post. The loafers were mildly curious. Guessed Bill had got hooked onto by a lightnin'-rod peddler, or somethin' o' that kind.

"Want to go by river, or 'round by the hills?"

"Hills, I guess."

The whole matter began to seem trivial, as if he had only been away for a month or two.

William McTurg was a man little given to talk. Even the coming back of a nephew did not cause any flow of questions or reminiscences. They rode in silence. He sat a little bent forward, the lines held carelessly in his hands, his great leonine head swaying to and fro with the movement of the buggy.

As they passed familiar spots, the younger man broke the silence with a question.

"That's old man McElvaine's place, ain't it?"

"Old man living?"

"I guess he is. Husk more corn 'n any man he c'n hire."

On the edge of the village they passed an open lot on the left, marked with circus rings of different eras.

"There's the old ball ground. Do they have circuses on it just the same as ever?"

"Just the same."

"What fun that field calls up! The games of ball we used to have! Do you play yet?"

"Sometimes. Can't stoop so well as I used to." He smiled a little. "Too much fat."

It all swept back upon Howard in a flood of names and faces and sights and sounds; something sweet and stirring somehow, though it had little of esthetic charm at the time. They were passing along lanes now, between superb fields of corn, wherein plowmen were at work. Kingbirds flew from post to post ahead of them; the insects called from the grass. The valley slowly outspread below them. The workmen in the fields were "turning out" for the night; they all had a word of chaff with McTurg.

Over the western wall of the circling amphitheater the sun was setting. A few scattering clouds were drifting on the west wind, their shadows sliding down the green and purple slopes. The dazzling sunlight flamed along the luscious velvety grass, and shot amid the rounded, distant purple peaks, and streamed in bars of gold and crimson across the blue mist of the narrower upper coulee.

The heart of the young man swelled' with pleasure almost like pain, and the eyes of the silent older man took on a far-off, dreaming look, as he gazed at the scene which had repeated itself a thousand times in his life, but of whose beauty he never spoke.

Far down to the left was the break in the wall through which the river ran on its way to join the Mississippi. As they climbed slowly among the hills, the valley they had left grew still more beautiful, as the squalor of the little town was hid by the dusk of distance. Both men were silent for a long time. Howard knew the peculiarities of his companion too well to make any remarks or ask any questions, and besides it was a genuine pleasure to ride with one who could feel that silence was the only speech amid such splendors.

Once they passed a little brook singing in a mourn-fully sweet way its eternal song over its pebbles. It called back to Howard the days when he and Grant, his younger brother, had fished in this little brook for trout, with trousers rolled above the knee and wrecks of hats upon their heads.

"Any trout left?" he asked.

"Not many. Little fellers." Finding the silence broken, William asked the first question since he met Howard. "Le's see: you're a show feller now? B'long to a troupe?"

"Yes, yes; I'm an actor."

"Pay much?"

"Pretty well."

That seemed to end William's curiosity about the matter.

"Ah, there's our old house, ain't it?" Howard broke out, pointing to one of the houses farther up the coulee. "It'll be a surprise to them, won't it?"

"Yep; only they don't live there."

"What! They don't!"

"Who does?"

"Dutchman."

Howard was silent for some moments. "Who lives on the Dunlap place?"

"'Nother Dutchman."

"Where's Grant living, anyhow?"

"Farther up the conlee."

"Well, then I'd better get out here, hadn't I?"

"Oh, I'll drive yeh up."

"No, I'd rather walk."

The sun had set, and the coulee was getting dusk when Howard got out of McTurg's carriage and set off up the winding lane toward his brother's house. He walked slowly to absorb the coolness and fragrance and color of the hour. The katydids sang a rhythmic song of welcome to him. Fireflies were in the grass. A whippoorwill in the deep of the wood was calling weirdly, and an occasional night hawk, flying high, gave his grating shriek, or hollow boom, suggestive and resounding.

He had been wonderfully successful, and yet had carried into his success as a dramatic author as well as actor a certain puritanism that made him a paradox to his fellows. He was one of those actors who are always in luck, and the best of it was he kept and made use of his luck. Jovial as he appeared, he was inflexible as granite against drink and tobacco. He retained through it all a certain freshness of enjoyment that made him one of the best companions in the profession; and now as he walked on, the hour and the place appealed to him with great power. It seemed to sweep away the life that came between.

How close it all was to him, after all! In his restless life, surrounded by the giare of electric lights, painted canvas, hot colors, creak of machinery, mock trees, stones, and brooks, he had not lost but gained appreciation for the coolness, quiet and low tones, the shyness of the wood and field.

In the farmhouse ahead of him a light was shining as he peered ahead, and his heart gave another painful movement. His brother was awaiting him there, and his mother, whom he had not seen for ten years and who had grown unable to write. And when Grant wrote, which had been more and more seldom of late, his letters had been cold and curt.

He began to feel that in the pleasure and excitement of his life he had grown away from his mother and brother. Each summer he had said, "Well, now I'll go home this year sure." But a new play to be produced, or a yachting trip, or a tour of Europe, had put the homecoming off; and now it was with a distinct consciousness of neglect of duty that he walked up to the fence and looked into the yard, where William had told him his brother lived.

It was humble enough-a small white house, story-and-a-half structure, with a wing, set in the midst of a few locust trees; a small drab-colored barn, with a sagging ridge pole; a barnyard full of mud, in which a few cows were standing, fighting the flies and waiting to be milked. An old man was pumping water at the well; the pigs were squealing from a pen nearby; a child was crying.

Instantly the beautiful, peaceful valley was forgotten. A sickening chill struck into Howard's soul as he looked at it all. In the dim light he could see a figure milking a cow. Leaving his valise at the gate, he entered and walked up to the old man, who had finished pumping and was about to go to feed the hogs.

"Good evening," Howard began. "Does Mr. Grant McLane live here?"

"Yes, sir, he does. He's right over there milkin'."

"I'll go over there an-"

"Don't b'lieve I would. It's darn muddy over there. It's been turrible rainy. He'll be done in a minute, any-way."

"Very well; I'll wait."

As he waited, he could hear a woman's fretful voice, and the impatient jerk and jar of kitchen things, indicative of ill temper or worry. The longer he stood absorbing this farm scene, with all its sordidness, dullness, triviality, and its endless drudgeries, the lower his heart sank. All the joy of the homecoming was gone, when the figure arose from the cow and approached the gate, and put the pail of milk down on the platform by the pump.

"Good evening," said Howard out of the dusk.

Grant stared a moment. "Good. evening."

Howard knew the voice, though it was older and deeper and more sullen. "Don't you know me, Grant? I am Howard.

The man approached him, gazing intently at his face. "You are?" after a pause. "Well, I'm glad to see yeh, but I can't shake hands. That damned cow had laid down in the mud."

They stood and looked at each other. Howard's cuffs, collar, and shirt, alien in their elegance, showed through the dusk, and a glint of light shot out from the jewel of his necktie, as the light from the house caught it at the right angle. As they gazed in silence at each other, Howard divined something of the hard, bitter feeling which came into Grant's heart as he stood there, ragged, ankle-deep in muck, his sleeves rolled up, a shapeless old straw hat on his head.

The gleam of Howard's white hands angered him. When he spoke, it was in a hard, gruff tone, full of rebellion.

"Well, go in the house and set down. I'll be in soon's I strain the milk and wash the dirt off my hands."

"But Mother-"

"She's 'round somewhere. Just knock on the door under the porch 'round there."

Howard went slowly around the corner of the house, past a vilely smelling rain barrel, toward the west. A gray-haired woman was sitting in a rocking chair on the porch, her hands in her lap, her eyes fixed on the faintly yellow sky, against which the hills stood dim purple silhouettes and the locust trees were etched as fine as lace. There was sorrow, resignation, and a sort of dumb despair in her attitude.

Howard stood, his throat swelling till it seemed as if he would suffocate. This was his mother-the woman who bore him, the being who had taken her life in her hand for him; and he, in his excited and pleasurable life, had neglected her!

He stepped into the faint light before her. She turned and looked at him without fear. "Mother!" he said. She uttered one little, breathing, gasping cry, called his name, rose, and stood still. He bounded up the steps and took her in his arms.

"Mother! Dear old Mother!"

In the silence, almost painful, which followed, an angry woman's voice could be heard inside: "I don't care. I am't goin' to wear myself out fer him. He c'n eat out here with us, or else-"

Mrs. McLane began speaking. "Oh, I've longed to see yeh, Howard. I was afraid you wouldn't come till-too late."

"What do you mean, Mother? Ain't you well?"

"I don't seem to be able to do much now 'cept sit around and knit a little. I tried to pick some berries the other day, and I got so dizzy I had to give it up."

"You mustn't work. You needn't work. Why didn't you write to me how you were?" Howard asked in an agony of remorse.

"Well, we felt as if you probably had all you could do to take care of yourself."

"Are you married, Howard?"

"No, Mother; and there ain't any excuse for me-not a bit," he said, dropping back into her colloquialisms. "I'm ashamed when I think of how long it's been since I saw you. I could have come."

"It don't matter now," she interrupted gently. "It's the way things go. Our boys grow up and leave us."

"Well, come in to supper," said Grant's ungracious voice from the doorway. "Come, Mother."

Mrs. McLane moved with difficulty. Howard sprang to her aid, and leaning on his arm she went through the little sitting room, which was unlighted, out into the kitchen, where the supper table stood near the cookstove.

"How, this is my wife," said Grant in a cold, peculiar tone.

Howard bowed toward a remarkably handsome young woman, on whose forehead was a scowl, which did not change as she looked at him and the old lady.

"Set down, anywhere," was the young woman's cordial invitation.

Howard sat down next to his mother, and facing the wife, who had a small, fretful child in her arms. At Howard's left was the old man, Lewis. The supper was spread upon a gay-colored oilcloth, and consisted of a pan of milk, set in the midst, with bowls at each plate. Beside the pan was a dipper and a large plate of bread, and at one end of the table was a dish of fine honey.

A boy of about fourteen leaned upon the table, his bent shoulders making him look like an old man. His hickory shirt, like that of Grant, was still wet with sweat, and discolored here and there with grease, or green from grass. His hair, freshly wet and combed, was smoothed away from his face, and shone in the light of the kerosene lamp. As he ate, he stared at Howard, as if he would make an inventory of each thread of the visitor's clothing.

"Did I look like that at his age?" thought Howard.

"You see we live jest about the same's ever," said Grant as they began eating, speaking with a grim, almost challenging inflection.

The two brothers studied each other curiously, as they talked of neighborhood scenes. Howard seemed incredibly elegant and handsome to them all, with his rich, soft clothing, his spotless linen, and his exquisite enunciation and ease of speech. He had always been "smooth-spoken," and he had become "elegantly persuasive," as his friends said of him, and it was a large factor in his success.

Every detail of the kitchen, the heat, the flies buzzing aloft, the poor furniture, the dress of the people-all smote him like the lash of a wire whip. His brother was a man of great character. He could see that now. His deep-set, gray eyes and rugged face showed at thirty a man of great natural ability. He had more of the Scotch in his face than Howard, and he looked much older.

He was dressed, like the old man and the boy, in a checked shirt without vest. His suspenders, once gay-colored, had given most of their color to his shirt, and had marked irregular broad bands of pink and brown and green over his shoulders. His hair was uncombed, merely pushed away from his face. He wore a mustache only, though his face was covered with a week's growth of beard. His face was rather gaunt and was brown as leather.

Howard could not eat much. He was disturbed by his mother's strange silence and oppression, and sickened by the long-drawn gasps with. which the old man ate his bread and milk, and by the way the boy ate. He had his knife gripped tightly in his fist, knuckles up, and was scooping honey upon his bread.

The baby, having ceased to be afraid, was curious, gazing silently at the stranger.

"Hello, little one! Come and see your uncle. Eh? 'Course 'e will," cooed Howard in the attempt to escape the depressing atmosphere. The little one listened to his inflections as a kitten does, and at last lifted its arms in sign of surrender.

The mother's face cleared up a little. "I declare, she wants to go to you."

"'Course she does. Dogs and kittens always come to me when I call 'em. Why shouldn't my own niece come?"

He took the little one and began walking up and down the kitchen with her, while she pulled at his beard and nose. "I ought to have you, my lady, in my new comedy. You'd bring down the house."

"You don't mean to say you put babies on the stage, Howard," said his mother in surprise.

"Oh, yes. Domestic comedy must have a baby these days."

"Well, that's another way of makin' a livin', sure," said Grant. The baby had cleared the atmosphere a little. "I s'pose you fellers make a pile of money."

"Sometimes we make a thousand a week; oftener we don't."

"A thousand dollars!" They all stared.

"A thousand dollars sometimes, and then lose it all the next week in another town. The dramatic business is a good deal like gambling-you take your chances."

"I wish you weren't in it, Howard. I don't like to have my son-"

"I wish I was in somethin' that paid better'n farmin'. Anything under God's heavens is better'n farmin'," said Grant.

"No, I ain't laid up much," Howard went on, as if explaining why he hadn't helped them. "Costs me a good deal to live, and I need about ten thousand dollars lee-way to work on. I've made a good living, but I-I ain't made any money."

Grant looked at him, darkly meditative.

Howard went on:

"How'd ye come to sell the old farm? I was in hopes-"

"How'd we come to sell it?" said Grant with terrible bitterness. "We had something on it that didn't leave anything to sell. You probably don't remember anything about it, but there was a mortgage on it that eat us up in just four years by the almanac. 'Most killed Mother to leave it. We wrote to you for money, but I don't s'pose you remember that."

"No, you didn't."

"Yes, I did."

"When was it? I don't-why, it's-I never received it. It must have been that summer I went with Rob Manning to Europe." Howard put the baby down and faced his brother. "Why, Grant, you didn't think I refused to help?"

"Well, it locked that way. We never heard a word from yeh all summer, and when y' did write, it was all about yerself 'n plays 'n things we didn't know anything about. I swore to God I'd never write to you again, and I won't."

"But, good heavens! I never got it."

"Suppose you didn't. You might of known we were poor as Job's off-ox. Everybody is that earns a living. We fellers on the farm have to earn a livin' for ourselves and you fellers that don't work. I don't blame yeh. I'd do it if I could."

"Grant, don't talk so! Howard didn't realize-"

"I tell yeh I don't blame 'im. Only I don't want him to come the brotherly business over me, after livin' as he has-that's all." There was a bitter accusation in the man's voice.

Howard leaped to his feet, his face twitching. "By God, I'll go back tomorrow morning!" he threatened.

"Go, an' be damned! I don't care what yeh do," Grant growled, rising and going out.

"Boys," called the mother, piteously, "it's terrible to see you quarrel."

"But I'm not to blame, Mother," cried Howard in a sickness that made him white as chalk. "The man is a savage. I came home to help you all, not to quarrel."

"Grant's got one o' his fits on," said the young wife, speaking for the first time. "Don't pay any attention to him. He'll be all right in the morning."

"If it wasn't for you, Mother, I'd leave now and never see that savage again."

He lashed himself up and down in the room, in horrible disgust and hate of his brother and of this home in his heart. He remembered his tender anticipations of the homecoming with a kind of self-pity and disgust. This was his greeting!

He went to bed, to toss about on the hard, straw-filled mattress in the stuffy little best room. Tossing, writhing under the bludgeoning of his brother's accusing inflections, a dozen times he said, with a half-articulate snarl:

"He can go to hell! I'll not try to do anything more for him. I don't care if he is my brother; he has no right to jump on me like that. On the night of my return, too. My God! he is a brute, a savage!"

He thought of the presents in his trunk and valise which he couldn't show to him that night, after what had been said. He had intended to have such a happy evening of it, such a tender reunion! It was to be so bright and cheery!

In the midst of his cursings, his hot indignation, would come visions of himself in his own modest rooms. He seemed to be yawning and stretching in his beautiful bed, the sun shining in, his books, foils, pictures around him, to say good morning and tempt him to rise, while the squat little clock on the mantel struck eleven warningly.

He could see the olive walls, the unique copper-and-crimson arabesque frieze (his own selection), and the delicate draperies; an open grate full of glowing coals, to temper the sea winds; and in the midst of it, between a landscape by Enneking and an Indian in a canoe in a canyon, by Brush, he saw a somber landscape by a master greater than Millet, a melancholy subject, treated with pitiless fidelity.

A farm in the valley! Over the mountains swept jagged, gray, angry, sprawling clouds, sending a freezing, thin drizzle of rain, as they passed, upon a man following a plow. The horses had a sullen and weary look, and their manes and tails streamed sidewise in the blast. The plowman clad in a ragged gray coat, with uncouth, muddy boots upon his feet, walked with his head inclined t~ ward the sleet, to shield his face from the cold and sting of it. The soil rolled away, black and sticky and with a dull sheen upon it. Nearby, a boy with tears on his cheeks was watching cattle, a dog seated near, his back to the gale.

As he looked at this picture, his heart softened. He looked down at the sleeve of his soft and fleecy nightshirt, at his white, rounded arm, muscular yet fine as a woman's, and when he looked for the picture it was gone. Then came again the assertive odor of stagnant air, laden with camphor; he felt the springless bed under him, and caught dimly a few soap-advertising lithographs on the walls. He thought of his brother, in his still more in-hospitable bedroom, disturbed by the child, condemned to rise at five o'clock and begin another day's pitiless labor. His heart shrank and quivered, and the tears started to his eyes.

"I forgive him, poor fellow! He's not to blame."

II

HE woke, however, with a dull, languid pulse and an oppressive melancholy on his heart. He looked around the little room, clean enough, but oh, how poor! how barren! Cold plaster walls, a cheap washstand, a wash set of three pieces, with a blue band around each; the windows, rectangular, and fitted with fantastic green shades.

Outside he could hear the bees humming. Chickens were merrily moving about. Cowbells far up the road were sounding irregularly. A jay came by and yelled an insolent reveille, and Howard sat up. He could hear nothing in the house but the rattle of pans on the back side of the kitchen. He looked at his watch and saw it was half-past seven. His brother was in the field by this time, after milking, currying the horses, and eating breakfast—had been at work two hours and a half.

He dressed himself hurriedly in a neglige shirt with a windsor scad, light-colored, serviceable trousers with a belt, russet shoes, and a tennis hat-a knockabout costume, he considered. His mother, good soul, thought it a special suit put on for her benefit and admired it through her glasses.

He kissed her with a bright smile, nodded at Laura the young wife, and tossed the baby, all in a breath, and with the manner, as he himself saw, of the returned captain in the war dramas of the day.

"Been to breakfast?" He frowned reproachfully. "Why didn't you call me? I wanted to get up, just as I used to, at sunrise."

"We thought you was tired, and so we didn't-"

"Tired! Just wait till you see me help Grant pitch hay or something. Hasn't finished his haying, has he?"

'No, I guess not. He will today if it don't rain again."

"Well, breakfast is all ready-Howard," said Laura, hesitating a little on his name.

"Good! I am ready for it. Bacon and eggs, as I'm a jay! Just what I was wanting. I was saying to myself. 'Now if they'll only get bacon and eggs and hot biscuits and honey-' Oh, say, mother, I heard the bees humming this morning; same noise they used to make when I was a boy, exactly, must be the same bees. Hey, you young rascal! come here and have some breakfast with your uncle."

"I never saw her take to anyone so quick," Laura smiled. Howard noticed her in particular for the first time. She had on a clean calico dress and a gingham apron, and she looked strong and fresh and handsome. Her head was intellectual, her eyes full of power. She seemed anxious to remove the impression of her unpleasant looks and words the night before. Indeed, it would have been hard to resist Howard's sunny good nature.

The baby laughed and crowed. The old mother could not take her dim eyes off the face of her son, but sat smiling at him as he ate and rattled on. When he rose from the table at last, after eating heartily and praising it all, he said with a smile:

"Well, now I'll just telephone down to the express and have my trunk brought up. I've got a few little things in there you'll enjoy seeing. But this fellow," indicating the baby, "I didn't take into account. But never mind; Uncle Howard make that all right."

"You ain't goin' to lay it up agin Grant, be you, my son?" Mrs. McLane faltered as they went out into the best room.

"Of course not! He didn't mean it. Now, can't you send word down and have my trunk brought up? Or shall I have to walk down?"

"I guess I'll see somebody goin' down," said Laura.

"All right. Now for the hayfield," he smiled and went out into the glorious morning.

The circling hills the same, yet not the same as at night. A cooler, tenderer, more subdued cloak of color upon them. Far down the valley a cool, deep, impalpable, blue mist lay, under which one divined the river Ian, under its elms and basswoods and wild grapevines. On the shaven slopes of the hills cattle and sheep were feeding, their cries and bells coming to the ear with a sweet suggestiveness. There was something immemorial in the sunny slopes dotted with red and brown and gray cattle.

Walking toward the haymakers, Howard felt a twinge of pain and distrust. Would he ignore it all and smile—

He stopped short. He had not seen Grant smile in so long-he couldn't quite see him smiling. He had been cold and bitter for years. When he came up to them, Grant was pitching on; the old man was loading, and the boy was raking after.

"Good morning," Howard cried cheerily. The old man nodded, the boy stared. Grant growled something, with-out looking up. These "finical" things of saying good morning and good night are not much practiced in such homes as Grant McLane's.

"Need some help? I'm ready to take a hand. Got on my regimentals this morning."

Grant looked at him a moment.

"You look like it."

"Gimme a hold on that fork, and I'll show you. I'm not so soft as I look, now you bet."

He laid hold upon the fork in Grant's hands, who released it sullenly and stood back sneering. Howard struck the fork into the pile in the old way, threw his left hand to the end of the polished handle, brought it down into the hollow of his thigh, and laid out his strength till the handle bent like a bow. "Oop she rises!" he called laughingly, as the whole pile began slowly to rise, and finally rolled upon the high load.

"Oh, I ain't forgot how to do it," he laughed as he looked around at the boy, who was studying the jacket and hat with a devouring gaze.

Grant was studying him too, but not in admiration.

"I shouldn't say you had," said the old man, tugging at the forkful.

'Mighty funny to come out here and do a little of this. But if you had to come here and do it all the while, you wouldn't look so white and soft in the hands," Grant said as they moved on to another pile. "Give me that fork. You'll be spoiling your fine clothes."

"Oh, these don't matter. They're made for this kind of thing."

"Oh, are they? I guess I'll dress in that kind of a rig. What did that shirt cost? I need one."

"Six dollars a pair; but then it's old."

"And them pants," he pursued; "they cost six dollars, too, didn't they?"

Howard's face darkened. He saw his brother's purpose. He resented it. "They cost fifteen dollars, if you want to know, and the shoes cost six-fifty. This ring on my cravat cost sixty dollars, and the suit I had on last night cost eighty-five. My suits are made by Breckstein, on Fifth Avenue and Twentieth Street, if you want to patronize him," he ended brutally, spurred on by the sneer in his brother's eyes. "I'll introduce you."

"Good idea," said Grant with a forced, mocking smile. "I need just such a get up for haying and corn plowing. Singular I never thought of it. Now my pants cost eighty-five cents, s'penders fifteen, hat twenty, shoes one-fifty; stockin's I don't bother about."

He had his brother at a disadvantage, and he grew fluent and caustic as he went on, almost changing places with Howard, who took the rake out of the boy's hands and followed, raking up the scatterings.

"Singular we fellers here are discontented and mulish, am't it? Singular we don't believe your letters when you write, sayin', 'I just about make a live of it'? Singular we think the country's goin' to hell, we fellers, in a two dollar suit, wadin' around in the mud or sweatin' around in the hayfield, while you fellers lay around New York and smoke and wear good clothes and toady to millionaires?"

Howard threw down the rake and folded his arms. 'My God! you're enough to make a man forget the same mother bore us!"

"I guess it wouldn't take much to make you forget that. You ain't put much thought on me nor her for ten years."

The old man cackled, the boy grinned, and Howard, sick and weak with anger and sorrow, turned away and walked down toward the brook. He had tried once more to get near his brother and had failed. O God! how miserably, pitiably! The hot blood gushed all over him as he thought of the shame and disgrace of it.

He, a man associating with poets, artists, sought after by brilliant women, accustomed to deference even from such people, to be sneered at, outfaced, shamed, shoved aside, by a man in a stained hickory shirt and patched overalls, and that man his brother! He lay down on the bright grass, with the sheep all around him, and writhed and groaned with the agony and despair of it.

And worst of all, underneath it was a consciousness that Grant was right in distrusting him. He had neglected him; he had said, "I guess they're getting along all right." He had put them behind him when the invitation to spend summer on the Mediterranean or in the Adirondacks came.

"What can I do? What can I do?" he groaned.

The sheep nibbled the grass near him, the jays called pertly, "Shame, shame," a quail piped somewhere on the hillside, and the brook sung a soft, soothing melody that took away at last the sharp edge of his pain, and he sat up and gazed down the valley, bright with the sun and apparently filled with happy and prosperous people.

Suddenly a thought seized him. He stood up so suddenly the sheep fled in affright. He leaped the brook, crossed the flat, and began searching in the bushes on the hillside. "Hurrah!" he said with a smile.

He had found an old road which he used to travel when a boy-a road that skirted the edge of the valley, now grown up to brush, but still passable for footmen. As he ran lightly along down the beautiful path, under oaks and hickories, past masses of poison ivy, under hanging grapevines, through clumps of splendid hazelnut bushes loaded with great sticky, rough, green burrs, his heart threw off part of its load.

How it all came back to him! How many days, when the autumn sun burned the frost off the bushes, had he gathered hazelnuts here with his boy and girl friends-Hugh and Shelley McTurg, Rome Sawyer, Orrin McIlvaine, and the rest! What had become of them all? How he had forgotten them!

This thought stopped him again, and he fell into a deep muse, leaning against an oak tree and gazing into the vast fleckless space above. The thrilling, inscrutable mystery of life fell upon him like a blinding light. Why was he living in the crush and thunder and mental unrest of a great city, while his companions, seemingly his equal, in powers, were milking cows, making butter, and growing corn and wheat in the silence and drear monotony of the farm?

His boyish sweethearts! Their names came back to his ear now with a dull, sweet sound as of faint bells. He saw their faces, their pink sunbonnets tipped back upon their necks, their brown ankles flying with the swift action of the scurrying partridge. His eyes softened; he took off his hat. The sound of the wind and the leaves moved him almost to tears.

A woodpecker gave a shrill, high-keyed, sustained cry, "Ki, ki, ki!" and he started from his reverie, the dapples of sun and shade falling upon his lithe figure as he hurried on down the path.

He came at last to a field of corn that tan to the very wall of a large weather-beaten house, the sight of which made his breathing quicker. It was the place where he was born. The mystery of his life began there. In the branches of those poplar and hickory trees he had swung and sung in the rushing breeze, fearless as a squirrel Here was the brook where, like a larger Kildee, he with Grant had waded after crawfish, or had stolen upon some wary trout, rough-cut pole in hand.

Seeing someone in the garden, he went down along the corn row through the rustling ranks of green leaves. An old woman was picking berries, a squat and shapeless figure.

"Good morning," he called cheerily.

"Morgen," she said, looking up at him with a startled and very red face. She was German in every line of her body.

"Ich bin Herr McLane," he said after a pause.

"So?" she replied with a questioning inflection.

"Yah; ich bin Herr Grant's bruder."

"Ach, So!" she said with a downward inflection. "Ich no spick Inglish. No spick Inglis."

"Ich bin durstig," he said. Leaving her pans, she went with him to the house, which was what he wanted to see.

"Ich bin hier geboren."

"Ach, so!" She recognized the little bit of sentiment, and said some sentences in German whose general meaning was sympathy. She took him to the cool cellar where the spring had been trained to run into' a tank containing pans of cream and milk, she gave him a cool draught from a large tin cup, and then at his request they went upstairs. The house was the same, but somehow seemed cold and empty. It was clean and sweet, but it had so little evidence of being lived in. The old part, which was built of logs, was used as best room, and modeled after the best rooms of the neighboring Yankee homes, only it was emptier, without the cabinet organ and the rag carpet and the chromoes.

The old fireplace was bricked up and plastered-the fireplace beside which in the far-off days he had lain on winter nights, to hear his uncles tell tales of hunting, or to hear them play the violin, great dreaming giants that they were.

The old woman went out and left him sitting there, the center of a swarm of memories coming and going like so many ghostly birds and butterflies.

A curious heartache and listlessness, a nerveless mood came on him. What was it worth, anyhow-success? Struggle, strife, trampling on someone else. His play crowding out some other poor fellow's hope. The hawk eats the partridge, the partridge eats the flies and bugs, the bugs eat each other, and the hawk, when he in his turn is shot by man. So, in the world of business, the life of one man seemed to him to be drawn from the life of another man, each success to spring from other failures.

He was like a man from whom all motives had been withdrawn. He was sick, sick to the heart. Oh, to be a boy again! An ignorant baby, pleased with a block and string, with no knowledge and no care of the great un-known! To lay his head again on his mother's bosom and rest! To watch the flames on the hearth!

Why not? Was not that the very thing to do? To buy back the old farm? It would cripple him a little for the next season, but he could do it. Think of it! To see his mother back in the old home, with the fireplace restored, the old furniture in the sitting room around her, and fine new things in the parlor!

His spirits rose again. Grant couldn't stand out when he brought to him a deed of the farm. Surely his debt would be canceled when he had seen them all back in the wide old kitchen. He began to plan and to dream. He went to the windows and looked out on the yard to see how much it had changed.

He'd build a new barn and buy them a new carriage. His heart glowed again, and his lips softened into their usual feminine grace-lips a little full and falling easily into curves.

The old German woman came in at length, bringing some cakes and a bowl of milk, smiling broadly and hospitably as she waddled forward.

"Ach! Goot!" he said, smacking his lips over the pleasant draught.

"Wo ist ihre goot mann?" he inquired, ready for business.

III

WHEN Grant came in at noon, Mrs. McLane met him at the door with a tender smile on her face.

"Where's Howard, Grant?"

"I don't know," he replied in a tone that implied "I don't care."

The dim eyes clouded with quick tears.

"Ain't you seen him?"

"Not since nine o'clock."

"Where d'you think he is?"

"I tell yeh I don't know. He'll take care of himself; don't worry."

He flung off his hat and plunged into the wash basin. His shirt was wet with sweat and covered with dust of the hay and fragments of leaves. He splashed his burning face with the water, paying no further attention to his mother. She spoke again, very gently, in reproof:

"Grant, why do you stand out against Howard so?"

"I don't stand out against him," he replied harshly, pausing with the towel in his hands. His eyes were hard and piercing. "But if he expects me to gush over his coming back, he's fooled, that's all. He's left us to paddle our own canoe all this while, and, so far as I'm concerned, he can leave us alone hereafter. He looked out for his precious hide mighty well, and now he comes back here to play big gun and pat us on the head. I don't propose to let him come that over me."

Mrs. McLane knew too well the temper of her son to say any more, but she inquired about Howard of the old hired man.

"He went off down the valley. He 'n' Grant had s'm words, and he pulled out down toward the old farm. That's the last I see of 'im."

Laura took Howard's part at the table. "Pity you can't be decent," she said, brutally direct as usuaL "You treat Howard as if he was a-a-I do' know what."

"wrn you let me alone?"

"No, I won't. If you think I'm going to set by an' agree to your bullyraggin' him, you're mistaken. It's a shame! You're mad 'cause he's succeeded and you ain't. He ain't to blame for his brains. If you and I'd had any, we'd 'a' succeeded, too. It ain't our fault and it ain't his; so what's the use?"

There was a look came into Grant's face that the wife knew. It meant bitter and terrible silence. He ate his dinner without another word.

It was beginning to cloud up. A thin, whitish, 'all-pervasive vapor which meant rain was dimming the sky, and be forced his hands to their utmost during the afternoon in order to get most of the down hay in before the rain came. He was pitching hay up into the barn when Howard came by just before one o'clock.

It was windless there. The sun fell through the white mist with undiminished fury, and the fragrant hay sent up a breath that was hot as an oven draught. Grant was a powerful man, and there was something majestic in his action as he rolled the huge flakes of hay through the door. The sweat poured from his face like rain, and he was forced to draw his dripping sleeve across his face to clear away the blinding sweat that poured into his eyes.

Howard stood and looked at him in silence, remembering how often he had worked there in that furnace heat, his muscles quivering, cold chills running over his flesh, red shadows dancing before his eyes.

His mother met him at the door anxiously, but smiled as she saw his pleasant face and cheerful eyes.

"You're a little late, m' son."

Howard spent most of the afternoon sitting with his mother on the porch, or under the trees, lying sprawled out like a boy, resting at times with sweet forgetfulness of the whole world, but feeling a dull pain whenever he remembered the stern, silent man pitching hay in the hot sun on the torrid side of the barn.

His mother did not say anything about the quarrel; she feared to reopen it. She talked mainly of old times in a gentle monotone of reminiscence, while he listened, looking up into her patient face.

The heat slowly lessened as the sun sank down toward the dun clouds rising like a more distant and majestic line of mountains beyond the western hills. The sound of cowbells came irregularly to the ear, and the voices and sounds of the haying fields had a jocund, thrilling effect on the ear of the city dweller.

He was very tender. Everything conspired to make him simple, direct, and honest.

"Mother, if you'll only forgive me for staying away so long, I'll surely come to see you every summer."

She had nothing to forgive. She was so glad to have him there at her feet-her great, handsome, successful boy! She could only love him and enjoy him every moment of the precious days. If Grant would only reconcile himself to Howard! That was the great thorn in her flesh.

Howard told her how he had succeeded.

"It was luck, Mother. First I met Cooke, and he introduced me to Jake Saulsman of Chicago. Jake asked me to go to New York with him, and-I don't know why-took a fancy to me some way. He introduced me to a lot of the fellows in New York, and they all helped me along. I did nothing to merit it. Everybody helps me. Anybody can succeed in that way."

The doting mother thought it not at all strange that they all helped him.

At the supper table Grant was gloomily silent, ignoring Howard completely. Mrs. McLane sat and grieved silently, not daring to say a word in protest. Laura and the baby tried to amuse Howard, and under cover of their talk the meal was eaten.

The boy fascinated Howard. He "sawed wood" with a rapidity and uninterruptedness which gave alarm. He had the air of coaling up for a long voyage.

"At that age," Howard thought, "I must have gripped my knife in my right hand so, and poured my tea into my saucer so. I must have buttered and bit into a huge slice of bread just so, and chewed at it with a smacking sound in just that way. I must have gone to the length of scooping up honey with my knife blade."

It was magically, mystically beautiful over all this squalor and toil and bitterness, from five till seven-a moving hour. Again the falling sun streamed in broad banners across the valleys; again the blue mist lay far down the coulee over the river; the cattle called from the hills in the moistening, sonorous air; the bells came in a pleasant tangle of sound; the air pulsed with the deepening chorus of katydids and other nocturnal singers.

Sweet and deep as the very springs of his life was all this to the soul of the elder brother; but in the midst of it, the younger man, in ill-smelling clothes and great boots that chafed his feet, went out to milk the. cows-on whose legs the flies and mosquitoes swarmed, bloated with blood-to sit by the hot side of the cow and be lashed with her tall as she tried frantically to keep the savage insects from eating her raw.

"The poet who writes of milking the cows does it from the hammock, looking on," Howard soliloquized as he watched the old man Lewis racing around the filthy yard after one of the young heifers that had kicked over the pail in her agony with the flies and was unwilling to stand still and be eaten alive.

"So, so! you beast!" roared the old man as he finally cornered the shrinking, nearly frantic creature.

"Don't you want to look at the garden?" asked Mrs. McLane of Howard; and they went out among the vegetables and berries.

The bees were coming home heavily laden and crawling slowly into the hives. The level, red light streamed through the trees, blazed along the grass, and lighted a few old-fashioned flowers into red ai~d gold flame. It was beautiful, and Howard looked at it through his half-shut eyes as the painters do, and turned away with a sigh at the sound of blows where the wet and grimy men were assailing the frantic cows.

"There's Wesley with your trunk," Mrs. McLane said, recalling him to himself.

Wesley helped him carry the trunk in and waved off thanks.

"Oh, that's all right," he said; and Howard knew the Western man too well to press the matter of pay.

As he went in an hour later and stood by the trunk, the dull ache came back into his heart. How he had failed! It seemed like a bitter mockery now to show his gifts.

Grant had come in from his work, and with his feet released from his chafing boots, in his wet shirt and milk-splashed overalls, sat at the kitchen table reading a newspaper which he held close to a small kerosene lamp. He paid no attention to anyone. His attitude, Curiously like his father's, was perfectly definite to Howard. It meant that from that time forward there were to be no words of any sort between them. It meant that they were no longer brothers, not even acquaintances. "How inexorable that face!" thought Howard.

He turned sick with disgust and despair, and would have closed his trunk without showing any of the presents, only for the childish expectancy of his mother and Laura.

"Here's something for you, Mother," he said, assuming a cheerful voice as he took a fold of fine silk from the trunk and held it up. "All the way from Paris."

He laid it on his mother's lap and stooped and kissed her, and then turned hastily away to hide the tears that came to his own eyes as he saw her keen pleasure.

"And here's a parasol for Laura. I don't know how I came to have that in here. And here's General Grant's autobiography for his namesake," he said with an effort at carelessness, and waited to hear Grant rise.

"Grant, won't you come in?" asked his mother quiveringly.

Grant did not reply nor move. Laura took the handsome volumes out and laid them beside him on the table. He simply pushed them to one side and went on with his reading.

Again that horrible anger swept hot as flame over Howard. He could have cursed him. His hands shook as he handed out other presents to his mother and Laura and the baby. He tried to joke.

"I didn't know how old the baby was, so she'll have to grow to some of these things."

But the pleasure was all gone for him and for the rest. His heart swelled almost to a feeling of pain as he looked at his mother. There she sat with the presents in her lap. The shining silk came too late for her. It threw into appalling relief her age, her poverty, her work-weary frame. "My God!" he almost cried aloud, "how little it would have taken to lighten her life!"

Upon this moment, when it seemed as if he could endure no more, came the smooth voice of William McTurg:

"Hello, folkses!"

"Hello, Uncle Bill! Come in."

"That's what we came for," laughed a woman's voice.

"Is that you, Rose?" asked Laura.

"It's me-Rose," replied the laughing girl as she bounced into the room and greeted everybody in a breathless sort of way.

"You don't mean little Rosy?"

"Big Rosy now," said William.

Howard looked at the handsome girl and smiled, saying in a nasal sort of tone, "Wal, wal! Rosy, how you've growed since I saw yeh!"

"Oh, look at all this purple and fine linen! Am I left out?"

Rose was a large girl of twenty-five or thereabouts, and was called an old maid. She radiated good nature from every line of her buxom self. Her black eyes were full of drollery, and she was on the best of terms with Howard at once. She had been a teacher, but that did not prevent her from assuming a peculiar directness of speech. Of course they talked about old friends.

"Where's Rachel?" Howard inquired. Her smile faded away.

"Shellie married Orrin McIlvaine. They're way out in Dakota. Shellie's havin' a hard row of stumps."

There was a little silence.

"And Tommy?"

"Gone West. Most all the boys have gone West. That's the reason there's so many old maids."

"You don't mean to say-"

"I don't need to say-I'm an old maid. Lots of the girls are."

"It don't pay to marry these days."

"Are you married?"

"Not yet." His eyes lighted up again in a humorous way.

"Not yet! That's good! That's the way old maids all talk."

"You don't mean to tell me that no young fellow comes prowling around-"

"Oh, a young Dutchman or Norwegian once in a while. Nobody that counts. Fact is, we're getting like Boston-four women to one man; and when you consider that we're getting more particular each year, the outlook is-well, it's dreadful!"

"It certainly is."

"Marriage is a failure these days for most of us. We can't live on the farm, and can't get a living in the city, and there we are." She laid her hand on his arm. "I declare, Howard, you're the same boy you used to be. I ain't a bit afraid of you, for all your success."

"And you're the same girl? No, I can't say that. It seems to me you've grown more than I have-I don't mean physically, I mean mentally," he explained as he saw her smile in the defensive way a fleshy girl has, alert to ward off a joke.

They were in the midst of talk, Howard telling one of his funny stories, when a wagon clattered up to the door and merry voices called loudly:

"Whoa, there, Sampson!"

"Hullo, the house!"

Rose looked at her father with a smile in her black eyes exactly like his. They went to the door.

"Hullo! What's wanted?"

"Grant McLane live here?"

"Yup. Right here."

A moment later there came a laughing, chatting squad of women to the door. Mrs. McLane and Laura stared at each other in amazement. Grant went outdoors.

Rose stood at the door as if she were hostess.

"Come in, Nettie. Glad to see yeh-glad to see yeh! Mrs. McIlvaine, come right in! Take a seat. Make yerself to home, do! And Mrs. Peavey! Wal, I never! This must be a surprise party. Well, I swan! How many more o' ye air they?"

All was confusion, merriment, handshakings as Rose introduced them in her roguish way.

"Folks, this is Mr. Howard McLane of New York. He's an actor, but it hain't spoiled him a bit as I can see. How, this is Nettie McIlvaine-Wilson that was."

Howard shook hands with Nettie, a tall, plain girl with prominent teeth.

"This is Ma McIlvaine."

"She looks just the same," said. Howard, shaking her hand and feeling how hard and work-worn it was.

And so amid bustle, chatter, and invitations "to lay off y'r things an' stay awhile," the women got disposed about the room at last Those that had rocking chairs rocked vigorously to and fro to hide their embarrassment. They all talked in loud voices.

Howard felt nervous under this furtive scrutiny. He wished his clothes didn't look so confoundedly dressy. Why didn't he have sense enough to go and buy a fifteen-dollar suit of diagonals for everyday wear.

Rose was the life of the party. Her tongue rattled on in the most delightful way.

"It's all Rose an' Bill's doin's," Mrs. McIlvaine explained. "They told us to come over an' pick up anybody we see on the road. So we did."

Howard winced a little at her familiarity of tone. He couldn't help it for the life of him.

"Well, I wanted to come tonight because I'm going away next week, and I wanted to see how he'd act at a surprise party again," Rose explained.

"Married, I s'pose," said Mrs. McIlvaine abruptly.

"No, not yet."

"Good land! Why, y' Inns' be thirty-five, How. Must a dis'p'inted y'r mam not to have a young 'un to call 'er granny."

The men came clumping in, talking about haying and horses. Some of the older ones Howard knew and greeted, but the younger ones were mainly too much changed. They were all very ill at ease. Most of them were in compromise dress-something lying between working "rig" and Sunday dress. Most of them had on clean shirts and paper collars, and wore their Sunday coats (thick woolen garments) over rough trousers. All of them crossed their legs at once, and most of them sought the wall and leaned back perilously upon the hind legs of their chairs, eyeing Howard slowly.

For the first few minutes the presents were the subjects of conversation. The women especially spent a good deal of talk upon them.

Howard found himself forced to taking the initiative, so he inquired about the crops and about the farms.

"I see you don't plow the hills as we used to. And reap'. What a job it ust to be. It makes the hills more beautiful to have them covered with smooth grass and cattle."

There was only dead silence to this touching upon the idea of beauty.

"I s'pose it pays reasonably."

"Not enough to kill," said one of the younger men. "You c'n see that by the houses we live in-that is, most of us. A few that came in early an' got land cheap, like McIlvaine, here-he got a lift that the rest of us can't get."

"I'm a free trader, myself," said one young fellow, blushing and looking away as Howard turned and said cheerily:

"So'm I."

The rest semed to feel that this was a tabooed subject—a subject to be talked out of doors, where one could prance about and yell and do justice to it.

Grant sat silently in the kitchen doorway, not saying a word, not looking at his. brother.

"Well, I don't never use hot vinegar for mine," Mrs. McIlvaine was heard to say. "I jest use hot water, an' I rinse 'em out good, and set 'em bottourside up in the sun. I do' know but what hot vinegar would be more cleansin'."

Rose had the younger folks in a giggle with a droll telling of a joke on herself.

"How'd y' stop 'em from laffin'?"

"I let 'em laugh. Oh, my school is a disgrace-so one director says. But I like to see children laugh. It broadens their cheeks."

"Yes, that's all handwork." Laura was showing the baby's Sunday clothes.

"Goodness Peter! How do you find time to do so much?"

"I take time."

Howard, being the lion of the evening, tried his best to be agreeable. He kept near his mother, because it afforded her so much pride and satisfaction, and because he was obliged to keep away from Grant, who had begun to talk to the men. Howard talked mainly about their affairs, but still was forced more and more into talking of life in the city. As he told of the theater and the concerts, a sudden change fell upon them; they grew sober, and he felt deep down in the hearts of these people a melancholy which was expressed only elusively with little tones or sighs. Their gaiety was fitful.

They were hungry for the world, for art-these young people. Discontented and yet hardly daring to acknowledge it; indeed, few of them could have made definite statement of their dissatisfaction. The older people felt it less. They practically said, with a sigh of pathetic resignation:

"Well, I don't expect ever to see these things now.."

A casual observer would have said, "What a pleasant bucolic-this little surprise party of welcome!" But Howard with his native ear and eye had no such pleasing illusion. He knew too well these suggestions of despair and bitterness. He knew that, like the smile of the slave, this cheerfulness was self-defense; deep down was another self.

Seeing Grant talking with a group of men over by the kitchen door, he crossed over slowly and stood listening. Wesley Cosgrove-a tall, rawboned young fellow with a grave, almost tragic face-was saying:

"Of course I ain't. Who is? A man that's satisfied to live as we do is a fool."

"The worst of it is," said Grant without seeing Howard, a man can't get out of it during his lifetime, and l don't know that he'll have any chance in the next-the speculator'll be there ahead of us."

The rest laughed, but Grant went on grily:

"Ten years ago Wes, here, could have got land in Dakota pretty easy, but now it's about all a feller's life's worth to try it. I tell you things seem shuttin' down on us fellers."

"Plenty o' land to rent?" suggested someone.

"Yes, in terms that skin a man alive. More than that, farmin' ain't so free a life as it used to be. This cattle-raisin' and butter-makin' makes a nigger of a man. Binds him right down to the grindstone, and he gets nothin' out of it-that's what rubs it in. He simply wallers around in the manure for somebody else. I'd like to know what a man's life is worth who lives as we do? How much higher is it than the lives the niggers used to live?"

These brutally bald words made Howard thrill with emotion like some great tragic poem. A silence fell on the group.

"That's the God's truth, Grant," said young Cosgrove after a pause.

"A man like me is helpless," Grant was saying. "Just like a fly in a pan of molasses. There ain't any escape for him. The more he tears around, the more liable he is to rip his legs off."

"What can he do?"

The men listened in silence.

"Oh, come, don't talk politics all night!" cried Rose, breaking in. "Come, let's have a dance. Where's that fiddle?"

"Fiddle!" cried Howard, glad of a chance to laugh. "Well, now! Bring out that fiddle. Is it William's?"

"Yes, Pap's old fiddle."

"Oh, gosh! he don't want to hear me play," protested William. "He's heard s' many fiddlers."

"Fiddlers! I've heard a thousand violinists, but not fiddlers. Come, give us 'Honest John.'"

William took the fiddle in his work-calloused and crooked hands and began tuning it. The group at the kitchen door turned to listen, their faces lighting up a little. Rose tried to get a set on the floor.

"Oh, good land!" said some. "We're all tuckered out. What makes you so anxious?"

"She wants a chance to dance with the New Yorker."

"That's it exactly," Rose admitted.

"Wal, if you'd churned and mopped and cooked for hayin' hands as I have today, you wouldn't be so full o' nonsense."

"Oh, bother! Life's short. Come quick, get Bettie out. Come, Wes, never mind your hobbyhorse."

By incredible exertion she got a set on the floor, and William got the fiddle in tune. Howard looked across at Wesley, and thought the change in him splendidly dramatic. His face had lighted up into a kind of deprecating, boyish smile. Rose could do anything with him.

William played some of the old tunes that had a thou-sand associated memories in Howard's brain, memories of harvest moons, of melon feasts, and of clear, cold winter nights. As he danced, his eyes filled with a tender, luminous light. He came closer to them all than he had been able to do before. Grant had gone out into the kitchen.

After two or three sets had been danced, the company took seats and could not be stirred again. So Laura and Rose disappeared for a few moments, and returning, served strawberries and cream, which she "just happened to have in the house."

And then William played again. His fingers, now grown more supple, brought out clearer, firmer tones. As he played, silence fell on these people. The magic of music sobered every face; the women looked older and more careworn, the men slouched sullenly in their chairs or leaned back against the wall.

It seemed to Howard as if the spirit of tragedy had entered this house. Music had always been William's unconscious expression of his unsatisfied desires. He was never melancholy except when he played. Then his eyes grew somber, his drooping face full of shadows.

He played on slowly, softly, wailing Scotch tunes and mournful Irish songs. He seemed to find in the songs of these people, and especially in a wild, sweet, low-keyed Negro song, some expression for his indefinable inner melancholy.

He played on, forgetful of everybody, his long beard sweeping the violin, his toilworn hands marvelously obedient to his will.

At last he stopped, looked up with a faint, deprecating smile, and said with a sigh:

"Well, folkses, time to go home."

The going was quiet. Not much laughing. Howard stood at the door and said good night to them all, his heart very tender.

"Come and see us," they said.

"I will," he replied cordially. "I'll try and get around to see everybody, and talk over old times, before I go back."

After the wagons had driven out of the yard, Howard turned and put his arm about his mother's neck.

"Tired?"

"A little."

"Well, now, good night. I'm going for a little stroll." His brain was too active to sleep. He kissed his mother good night and went out into the road, his hat in his hand, the cool, moist wind on his hair.

It was very dark, the stars being partly hidden by a thin vapor. On each side the hills rose, every line familiar as the face of an old friend. A whippoorwill called occasionally from the hillside, and the spasmodic jangle of a bell now and then told of some cow's battle with the mosquitoes.

As he walked, he pondered upon the tragedy he had rediscovered in these people's lives. Out here under the inexorable spaces of the sky, a deep distaste of his own life took possession of him. He felt like giving it all up. He thought of the infinite tragedy of these lives which the world loves to call "peaceful and pastoral." HIS mind went out in the aim to help them. What could he do to make life better worth living? Nothing. They must live and die practically as he saw them tonight.

And yet he knew this was a mood, and that in a few hours the love and the habit of life would come back upon him and upon them; that he would go back to the city in a few days; that these people would live on and make the best of it.

"I'll make the best of it," he said at last, and his thought came back to his mother and Grant.

IV

The next day was a rainy day; not a shower, but a steady rain-an unusual thing in midsummer in the West. A cold, dismal day in the fireless, colorless farmhouses. It came to Howard in that peculiar reaction which surely comes during a visit of this character, when thought is a weariness, when the visitor longs for his own familiar walls and pictures and books, and longs to meet his friends, feeling at the same time the tragedy of life which makes friends nearer and more congenial than blood relations.

Howard ate his breakfast alone, save Baby and Laura, its mother, going about the room. Baby and mother alike insisted on feeding him to death. Already dyspeptic pangs were setting in.

"Now ain't there something more I can-"

"Good heavens! No!" he cried in dismay. "I'm likely to die of dyspepsia now. This honey and milk, and these delicious hot biscuits-"

"I'm afraid it ain't much like the breakfasts you have in the city."

"Well, no, it ain't," he confessed. "But this is the kind a man needs when he lives in the open air."

She sat down opposite him, with her elbows on the table, her chin in her palm, her eyes full of shadows.

"I'd like to go to a city once. I never saw a town bigger'n Lumberville. I've never seen a play, but I've read of 'em in the magazines. It must be wonderful; they say they have wharves and real ships coming up to the wharf, and people getting off and on. How do they do it?"

"Oh, that's too long a story to tell. It's a lot of machinery and paint and canvas. If I told you how it was done, you wouldn't enjoy it so well when you come on and see it."

"Do you ever expect to see me in New York?"

"Why, yes. Why not? I expect Grant to come On and bring you all some day, especially Tonikins here. Tonikins, you hear, sir? I expect you to come on you' for birfday, sure." He tried thus to stop the woman's gloomy confidence.

'I hate farm life," she went on with a bitter inflection. "It's nothing but fret, fret and work the whole time, never going any place, never seeing anybody but a lot of neighbors just as big fools as you are. I spend my time fighting flies and washing dishes and churning. I'm sick of it all."

Howard was silent. What could he say to such an indictment? The ceiling swarmed with flies which the cold rain had driven to seek the warmth of the kitchen. The gray rain was falling with a dreary sound outside, and down the kitchen stovepipe an occasional drop fell on the stove with a hissing, angry sound.

The young wife went on with a deeper note:

"I lived in Lumberville two years, going to school, and I know a little something of what city life is. If I was a man, I bet I wouldn't wear my life out on a farm, as Grant does. I'd get away and I'd do something. I wouldn't care what, but I'd get away."

There was a certain volcanic energy back of all the woman said that made Howard feel she'd make the attempt. She didn't know that the struggle for a. place to stand on this planet was eating the heart and soul out of men and women in the city, just as in the country. But he could say nothing. If be had said in conventional phrase, sitting there in his soft clothing, "We must make the best of it all," the woman could justly have thrown the dishcloth in his face. He could say nothing.

"I was a fool for ever marrying," she went on, while the baby pushed a chair across the room. "I made a decent living teaching, I was free to come and go, my money was my own. Now I'm fled right down to a churn or a dishpan, I never have a cent of my own. He's growlin' round half the time, and there's no chance of his ever being different."

She stopped with a bitter sob in her throat. She forgot she was talking to her husband's brother. She was conscious only of his sympathy.

As if a great black cloud had settled down upon him, Howard felt it all-the horror, hopelessness, immanent tragedy of it all. The glory of nature, the bounty and splendor of the sky, only made it the more benumbing. He thought of a sentence Millet once wrote:

I see very well the aureole of the dandelions, and the sun also, far down there behind the hills, flinging his glory upon the clouds. But not alone that-I see in the plains the smoke of the tired horses at the plough, or, on a stony-hearted spot of ground, a back-broken man trying to raise himself upright for a moment to breathe.

The tragedy is surrounded by glories-that is no invention of mine.

Howard arose abruptly and went back to his little bedroom, where he walked up and down the floor till he was calm enough to write, and then he sat down and poured it all out to "Dearest Margaret," and his first sentence was this:

"If it were not for you (just to let you know the mood I'm in)-if it were not for you, and I had the world in my hands, I'd crush it like a puffball; evil so predominates, suffering is so universal and persistent, happiness so fleeting and so infrequent."

He wrote on for two hours, and by the time he had sealed and directed several letters he felt calmer, but still terribly depressed. The rain was still falling, sweeping down from the half-seen hills, wreathing the wooded peaks with a gray garment of mist and filling the valley with a whitish cloud.

It fell around the house drearily. It ran down into the tubs placed to catch it, dripped from the mossy pump, and drummed on the upturned milk pails, and upon the brown and yellow beehives under the maple trees. The chickens seemed depressed, but the irrepressible bluejay screamed amid it all, with the same insolent spirit, his plumage untarnished by the wet. The barnyard showed a horrible mixture of mud and mire, through which Howard caught glimpses of the men, slumping to and fro without more additional protection than a ragged coat and a shapeless felt hat.

In the sitting room where his mother sat sewing there was not an ornament, save the etching he had brought. The clock stood on a small shell, its dial so much defaced that one could not tell the time of day; and when it struck, it was with noticeably disproportionate deliberation, as if it wished to correct any mistake into which the family might have fallen by reason of its illegible dial.

The paper on the walls showed the first concession of the Puritans to the Spirit of Beauty, and was made up of a heterogeneous mixture of flowers of unheard-of shapes and colors, arranged in four different ways along the wall. There were no books, no music, and only a few newspapers in sight—a bare, blank, cold, drab-colored shelter from the rain, not a home. Nothing cozy, nothing heartwarming; a grim and horrible shed.

"What are they doing? It can't be they're at work such a day as this," Howard said, standing at the window.

"They find plenty to do, even on rainy days," answered his mother. "Grant always has some job to set the men at. It's the only way to live."

"I'll go out and see them." He turned suddenly. "Mother, why should Grant treat me so? Have I deserved it?"

Mrs. McLane sighed in pathetic hopelessness. "I don't know, Howard. I'm worried about Grant. He gets more an' more downhearted an' gloomy every day. Seem's if he'd go crazy. He don't care how he looks any more, won't dress up on Sunday. Days an' days he'll go aroun' not sayin' a word. I was in hopes you could help him, Howard."

"My coming seems to have had an opposite effect. He hasn't spoken a word to me, except when he had to, since I came. Mother, what do you say to going home with me to New York?"

"Oh, I couldn't do that!" she cried in terror. "I couldn't live in a big city-never!"

"There speaks the truly rural mind," smiled Howard at his mother, who was looking up at him through her glasses with a pathetic forlornness which sobered him again. "Why, Mother, you could live in Orange, New Jersey, or out in Connecticut, and be just as lonesome as you are here. You wouldn't need to live in the city. I could see you then every day or two."

"Well, I couldn't leave Grant an' the baby, anyway," she replied, not realizing how one could live in New Jersey and do business daily in New York.

"Well, then, how would you like to go back into the old house?" he said, facing her.

The patient hands fell to the lap, the dim eyes fixed in searching glance on his face. There was a wistful cry in the voice.

"Oh, Howard! Do you mean-"

He came and sat down by her, and put his arm about her and hugged her hard. "I mean, you dear, good, patient, work-wear~ old Mother, I'm going to buy back the old farm and put you in it."

There was no refuge for her now except in tears, and she put up her thin, trembling old hands about his neck and cried in that easy, placid, restful way age has.

Howard could not speak. His throat ached with remorse and pity. He saw his forgetfulness of them all once more without relief-the black thing it was!

"There, there, Mother, don't cry!" he said, torn with anguish by her tears. Measured by man's tearlessness, her weeping seemed terrible to him. "I didn't realize how things were going here. It was all my fault-or, at least, most of it. Grant's letter didn't reach me. I thought you were still on the old farm. But no matter; it's all over now. Come, don't cry any more, Mother dear. I'm going to take care of you now."

It had been years since the poor, lonely woman had felt such warmth of love. Her sons had been like her husband, chary of expressing their affection; and like most Puritan families, there was little of caressing among them. Sitting there with the rain on the roof and driving through the trees, they planned getting back into the old house. Howard's plan seemed to her full of splendor and audacity. She began to understand his power and wealth now, as he put it into concrete form before her.

"I wish I could eat Thanksgiving dinner there with you," he said at last, "but it can't be thought of. However, I'll have you all in there before I go home. I'm going out now and tell Grant. Now don't worry any more; I'm going to fix it all up with him, sure." He gave her a parting hug.

Laura advised him not to attempt to get to the barn; but as he persisted in going, she hunted up an old rubber coat for him. "You'll mire down and spoil your shoes," she said, glancing at his neat calf gaiters.

"Darn the difference!" he laughed in his old way. "Besides, I've got rubbers."

"Better go round by the fence," she advised as he stepped out into the pouring rain.

How wretchedly familiar it all was! The miry cow yard, with the hollow trampled out around the horse trough, the disconsolate hens standing under the wagons and sheds, a pig wallowing across its sty, and for atmosphere the desolate, falling rain. It was so familiar he felt a pang of the old rebellious despair which seized him on such days in his boyhood.

Catching up courage, he stepped out on the grass, opened the gate, and entered the barnyard. A narrow ribbon of turf ran around the fence, on which he could walk by clinging with one hand to the rough boards. In this way he slowly made his way around the periphery, and came at last to the open barn door without much harm.

It was a desolate interior. In the open floorway Grant, seated upon a half-bushel, was mending a harness. The old man was holding the trace in his hard brown hands; the boy was lying on a wisp of hay. It was a small barn, and poor at that. There was a bad smell, as of dead rats, about it, and the rain fell through the shingles here and there. To the right, and below, the horses stood, looking up with their calm and beautiful eyes, in which the whole scene was idealized.

Grant looked up an instant and then went on with his work.

"Did yeh wade through?" grinned Lewis, exposing his broken teeth.

"No, I kinder circumambiated the pond." He sat down on the little toolbox near Grant. "Your barn is good deal like that in 'The Arkansas Traveller.' Needs a new roof, Grant." His voice had a pleasant sound, full of the tenderness of the scene through which he had just been. "In fact, you need a new barn."

"I need a good many things more'n I'll ever get," Grant replied shortly.

"How long did you say you'd been on this farm?"

"Three years this fall."

"I don't s'pose you've been able to think of buying-Now hold on, Grant," he cried, as Grant threw his head back. "For God's sake, don't get mad again! Wait till you see what I'm driving at."

"I don't see what you're drivin' at, and I don't care.

All I want you to do is to let us alone. That ought to be easy enough for you."

"I tell you, I didn't get your letter. I didn't know you'd lost the old farm." Howard was determined not to quarrel. "I didn't suppose-"

"You might 'a' come to see."

"Well, I'll admit that. All I can say in excuse is that since I got to managing plays I've kept looking ahead to making a big hit and getting a barrel of money-just as the old miners used to hope and watch. Besides, you don't understand how much pressure there is on me. A hundred different people pulling and hauling to have me go here or go there, or do this or do that. When it isn't yachting, it's canoeing, or

He stopped. His heart gave a painful throb, and a shiver ran through him. Again he saw his life, so rich, so bright, so free, set over against the routine life in the little low kitchen, the barren sitting room, and this still more horrible barn. Why should his brother sit there in wet and grimy clothing mending a broken trace, while he enjoyed all the light and civilization of the age?

He looked at Grant's fine figure, his great strong face; recalled his deep, stern, masterful voice. "Am I so much superior to him? Have not circumstances made me and destroyed him?"

"Grant, for God's sake, don't sit there like that! I'll admit I've been negligent and careless. I can't understand it all myself. But let me do something for you now. I've sent to New York for five thousand dollars. I've got terms on the old farm. Let me see you all back there once more before I return."

"I don't want any of your charity."

"It ain't charity. It's only justice to you." He rose. "Come now, let's get at an understanding, Grant. I can't go on this way. I can't go back to New York and leave you here like this."

Grant rose, too. "I tell you, I don't ask your help. You can't fix this thing up with money. If you've got more brains 'n I have, why it's all right. I ain't got any right to take anything that I don't earn."

"But you don't get what you do earn. It ain't your fault. I begin te see it now. Being the oldest, I had the best chance. I was going to town to school while you were plowing and husking corn. Of course I thought you'd be going soon, yourself. I had three years the start of you. If you'd been in my place, you might have met a man like Cooke, you might have gone to New York and have been where I am'.

"Well, it can't be helped now. So drop it."

"But it must be!" Howard said, pacing about, his hands in his coat pockets. Grant had stopped work, and was gloomily looking out of the door at a pig nosing in the mud for stray grains of wheat at the granary door:

"Good God! I see it all now," Howard burst out in an impassioned tone. "I went ahead with my education, got my start in life, then Father died, and you took up his burdens. Circumstances made me and crushed you. That's all there is about that. Luck made me and cheated you. It ain't right."

His voice faltered. Both men were now oblivious of their companions and of the scene. Both were thinking of the days when they both planned great things in the way of an education, two ambitious, dreamful boys.

"I used to think of you, Grant, when I pulled out Monday morning in my best suit-cost fifteen dollars in those days." He smiled a little at the recollection. "While you in overalls and an old 'wammus' was going out into the field to plow, or husk corn in the mud. It made me feel uneasy, but, as I said, I kept saying to myself, 'His turn'll come in a year or two.' But it didn't."

His voice choked. He walked to the door, stood a moment, came back. His eyes were full of tears.

"I tell you, old man, many a time in my boardinghouse down to the city, when I thought of the jolly times I was having, my heart hurt me. But I said: 'It's no use to cry. Better go on and do the best you can, and then help them afterward. There'll only be one more miserable member of the family if you stay at home.' Besides, it seemed right to me to have first chance. But I never thought you'd be shut off, Grant. If I had, I never would have gone on. Come, old man, I want you to believe that." His voice was very tender now and almost humble.

"I don't know as I blame yeh for that, How," said Grant slowly. It was the first time he had called Howard by his boyish nickname. His voice was softer, too, and higher in key. But he looked steadily away.

"I went to New York. People liked my work. I was very successful, Grant; more successful than you realize. I could have helped you at any time. There's no use lying about it. And I ought to have done it; but some way-it's no excuse, I don't mean it for an excuse, only an explanation-some way I got in with the boys. I don't mean I was a drinker and all that. But I bought pictures and kept a horse and a yacht, and of course I had to pay my share of all expeditions, and, oh, what's the use!"

He broke off, turned, and threw his open palms out toward his brother, as if throwing aside the last attempt at an excuse.

"I did neglect you, and it's a damned shame! and I ask your forgiveness. Come, old man!"

He held out his hand, and Grant slowly approached and took it. There was a little silence. Then Howard went on, his voice trembling, the tears on his face.

"I want you to let me help you, old man. That's the way to forgive me. Will you?"

"Yes, if you can help me."

Howard squeezed his hand. "That's right, old man. Now you make me a boy again. Course I can help you. I've got ten-"

"I don't mean that, How." Grant's voice was very grave. "Money can't give me a chance now."

"What do you mean?"

"I mean life ain't worth very much to me. I'm too old to take a new start. I'm a dead failure. I've come to the conclusion that life's a failure for ninety-nine per cent of us. You can't help me now. It's too late."

The two men stood there, face to face, hands clasped, the one fair-skinned, full-lipped, handsome in his neat sult; the other tragic, somber in his softened mood, his large, long, rugged Scotch face bronzed with sun and scarred with wrinkles that had histories, like saber cuts on a veteran, the record of his battles.

3. AMONG THE CORN ROWS

I

"But the road sometimes passes a rich meadow, where the songs o' larks and bobolinks and blackbirds are tangled."

ROB held up his hands, from which the dough depended in ragged strings.

"Biscuits," he said with an elaborate working of his jaws, intended to convey the idea that they were going to be specially delicious.

Seagraves laughed, but did not enter the shanty door. "How do you like baching it?"

"Oh, don't mention it!" entreated Rob, mauling the dough again. "Come in an' sit down. Why in thunder y' standin' out there for?"

"Oh, I'd rather be where I can see the prairie. Great weather!"

"Im-mense!"

"How goes breaking?"

"Tip-top! A leette dry now; but the bulls pull the plow through two acres a day. How's things in Boomtown?"

"Oh, same old grind."

"Judge still lyin'?"

"Still at it."

"Major Mullens still swearin' to it?"

"You hit it like a mallet. Railroad schemes are thicker'n prairie chickens. You've got grit, Rob. I don't have anything but crackers and sardines over to my shanty, and here you are making soda biscuit."

"I have t' do it. Couldn't break if I didn't. You editors c'n take things easy, lay around on the prairie, and watch the plovers and medderlarks; but we settlers have got to work."

Leaving Rob to sputter over his cooking, Seagraves took his slow way off down toward the oxen grazing in a little hollow. The scene was characteristically, wonderfully beautiful. It was about five o'clock in a day in late June, and the level plain was green and yellow, and infinite in reach as a sea; the lowering sun was casting over its distant swells a faint impalpable mist, through which the breaking teams on the neighboring claims plowed noiselessly, as figures in a dream. The whistle of gophers, the faint, wailing, fluttering cry of the falling plover, the whir of the swift-winged prairie pigeon, or the quack of a lonely duck, came through the shimmering air. The lark's infrequent whistle, piercingly sweet, broke from the longer grass in the swales nearby. No other climate, sky, plain, could produce the same unnamable weird charm. No tree to wave, no grass to rustle; scarcely a sound of domestic life; only the faint melancholy soughing of the wind in the short grass, and the voices of the wild things of the prairie.

Seagraves, an impressionable young man (junior editor of the Boomtown Spike), threw himself down on the sod, pulled his hat rim down over his eyes, and looked away over the plain. It was the second year of Boourtown's existence, and Seagraves had not yet grown restless under its monotony. Around him the gophers played saucily. Teams were moving here and there across the sod, with a peculiar noiseless, effortless motion that made them seem as calm, lazy, and unsubstantial as the mist through which they made their way; even the sound of passing wagons was a sort of low, well-fed, self-satisfied chuckle.

Seagraves, "holding down a claim" near Rob, had come to see his neighboring "bach" because of feeling the need of company; but now that he was near enough to hear him prancing about getting supper, he was content to lie alone on a slope of the green sod.

The silence of the prairie at night was well-nigh terrible. Many a night, as Seagraves lay in his bunk against the side of his cabin, he would strain his ear to hear the slightest sound, and he listening thus sometimes for minutes before the squeak of a mouse or the step of a passing fox came as a relief to the aching sense. In the daytime, however, and especially on a morning, the prairie was another thing. The pigeons, the larks; the cranes, the multitudinous voices of the ground birds and snipes and insects, made the air pulsate with sound-a chorus that died away into an infinite murmur of music.

"Hello, Seagraves!" yelled Rob from the door. "The biscuit are 'most done."

Seagraves did not speak, only nodded his head and slowly rose. The faint clouds in the west were getting a superb flame color above and a misty purple below, and the sun had shot them with lances of yellow light. As the air grew denser with moisture, the sounds of neighboring life began to reach the ear. Children screamed and laughed, and afar off a woman was singing a lullaby. The rattle of wagons and voices of men speaking to their teams multiplied. Ducks in a neighboring lowland were quacking. The whole scene took hold upon Seagraves with irresistible power.

"It is American," he exclaimed. 'No other land or time can match this mellow air, this wealth of color, much less the strange social conditions of life on this sunlit Dakota prairie."

Rob, though visibly affected by the scene also, couldn't let his biscuit spoil or go without proper attention.

"Say, ain't y' comin' t' grub?" he asked impatiently.

"Th a minute," replied his friend, taking a last wistful look at the scene. "I want one more look at the landscape."

"Landscape be blessed! If you'd been breakin' all day-Come, take that stool an' draw up."

"No; I'll take the candle box."

"Not much. I know what manners are, if I am a bull driver."

Seagraves took the three-legged and rather precarious-looking stool and drew up to the table, which was a flat broad box nailed up against the side of the wall, with two strips of board nailed at the outer corners for legs.

"How's that f'r a layout?" Rob inquired proudly.

"Well, you have spread yourself! Biscuit and canned peaches and sardines and cheese. why, this is-is- prodigal."

"It ain't nothin' else."

Rob was from one of the finest counties of Wisconsin, over toward Milwaukee. He was of German parentage, a middle-sized, cheery, wide-awake, good-looking young fellow-a typical claimholder. He was always confident, jovial, and full of plans for the future. He had dug his own well, built his own shanty, washed and mended his own clothing. He could do anything, and do it well. He had a fine field of wheat, and was finishing the plowing of his entire quarter section.

"This is what I call settin' under a feller's own vine an' fig tree"-after Seagraves's compliments-"an' I like it. I'm my own boss. No man can say 'come here' 'n' 'go there' to me. I get up when I'm a min' to, an' go t' bed when I'm a min' t'."

"Some drawbacks, I s'pose?"

"Yes. Mice, f'r instance, give me a devilish lot o' trouble. They get into my flour barrel, eat up my cheese, an' fall into my well. But it ain't no use t' swear."

"The rats and the mice they made such a strife

He had to go to London to buy him a wife,"

quoted Seagraves. "Don't blush. I've probed your secret thought."

"Well, to tell the honest truth," said Rob a little sheepishly, leaning across the table, "I ain't satisfied with my style o' cookin'. It's good, but a little too plain, y' know. I'd like a change. It ain't much fun to break all day and then go to work an' cook y'r own supper."

"No, I should say not."

"This fall I'm going back to Wisconsin. Girls are thick as huckleberries back there, and I'm goin' t' bring one back, now you hear me."

"Good! That's the plan," laughed Seagraves, amused at a certain timid and apprehensive look in his companion's eye. "Just think what a woman 'd do to put this shanty in shape; and think how nice it would be to take her arm and saunter out after supper, and look at the farm, and plan and lay out gardens and paths, and tend the chickens!"

Rob's manly and self-reliant nature had the settler's typical buoyancy and hopefulness, as well as a certain power of analysis, which enabled him now to say: "The fact is, we fellers holdin' down claims out here ain't fools clear to the rine. We know a couple o' things. Now I didn't leave Waupac County f'r fun. Did y' ever see Wanpac? Well, it's one o' the handsomest counties the sun ever shone on, full o' lakes and rivers and groves of timber. I miss 'em all out here, and I miss 'em all out here, and I miss 'em all out here, and I miss 'em all out here, and I miss 'em all out here, and I miss 'em all out here, and I miss 'em all out here, and I miss 'em all out here, and I miss 'em all out here, and I miss 'em all out here, and I miss 'em all out here, and I miss 'em all out here, and I miss 'em all out here, and I miss 'em all out here, and I miss 'em all out here, and I miss 'em all out here, and I miss 'em all out here, and I miss 'em all out here. Land that was good was so blamed high you couldn't touch it with a ten-foot pole from a balloon. Rent was high, if you wanted t' rent, an' so a feller like me had t' get out, an' now I'm out here, I'm goin' f make the most of it. An other thing," he went on, after a pause-"we fellers work-in' out back there got more 'n' more like hands, an' less like human beings. Y'know, Waupac is a kind of a summer resort, and the people that use' t' come in summers looked down on us cusses in the fields an' shops. I couldn't stand it. By God!" he said with a sudden impulse of rage quite unlike him, "I'd rather live on an ice-berg and claw crabs f'r a livin' than have some feller passin' me on the road an' callin' me fellah!'"

Seagraves knew what he meant and listened in astonishment at this outburst.

"I consider myself a sight better 'n any man who lives on somebody else's hard work. I've never had a cent I didn't earn with them hands." He held them up and broke into a grin. "Beauties, ain't they? But they never wore gloves that some other poor cuss earned."

Seagraves thought them grand hands, worthy to grasp the hand of any man or woman living.

"Well, so I come West, just like a thousand other fellers, to get a start where the cussed European aristocracy hadn't got a holt on the people. I like it here-course I'd like the lakes an' meadows of Waupac better-but I'm my own boss, as I say, an' I'm goin' to stay my own boss if I haf to live on crackers an' wheat coffee to do it; that's the kind of a hairpin I am."

In the pause which followed, Seagraves, plunged deep into thought by Rob's words, leaned his head on his hand. This working farmer had voiced the modern idea. It was an absolute overturn of all the ideas of nobility and special privilege born of the feudal past. Rob had spoken upon impulse, but that impulse appeared to Sea-graves to be right.

"I'd like to use your idea for an editorial, Rob," he said.

"My ideas!" exclaimed the astounded host, pausing in the act of filling his pipe. "My ideas! why, I didn't know I had any."

"Well, you've given me some, anyhow."

Seagraves felt that it was a wild, grand upstirring of the modern democrat against the aristocratic, against the idea of caste and the privilege of living on the labor of others. This atom of humanity (how infinitesimal this drop in the ocean of humanity!) was feeling the name-less longing of expanding personality, and had already pierced the conventions of society and declared as nil the laws of the land-laws that were survivals of hate and prejudice. He had exposed also the native spring of the emigrant by uttering the feeling that it is better to be an equal among peasants than a servant before nobles.

"So I have good reasons f'r liking the country," Rob resumed in a quiet way. "The soil is rich, the climate good so far, an' if I have a couple o' decent crops you'll see a neat upright goin' up here, with a porch and a bay winder."

"And you'll still be livin' here alone, frying leathery slapjacks an' choppin' taters and bacon."

"I think I see myself," drawled Rob, "goin' around all summer wearin' the same shirt without washin', an' wipin' on the same towel four straight weeks, an' wearin' holes in my socks, an' eatin' musty gingersnaps, moldy bacon, an' canned Boston beans f'r the rest o' my endurin' days! Oh, yes; I guess not! Well, see y' later. Must go water my bulls."

As he went off down the slope, Seagraves smiled to hear him sing:

"I wish that some kindhearted girl Would pity on me take, And extricate me from the mess I'm in. The angel-how I'd bless her, li this her home she'd make, In my little old sod shanty on the plain!"

The boys nearly fell off their chairs in the Western House dining room, a few days later, at seeing Rob come into supper with a collar and necktie as the finishing touch of a remarkable outfit.

"Hit him, somebody!"

"It's a clean collar!"

"He's started f'r Congress!"

"He's going to get married," put in Seagraves in a tone that brought conviction.

"What!" screamed Jack Adams, O'Neill, and Wilson in one breath. "That man?"

"That man," replied Seagraves, amazed at Rob, who coolly took his seat, squared his elbows, pressed his collar down at the back, and called for the bacon and eggs.

The crowd stared at him in a dead silence.

"Where's he going to do it?" asked Jack Adams. "where's he going to find a girl?"

"Ask him," said Seagraves.

"I ain't tellin'," put in Rob, with his mouth full of potato.

"You're afraid of our competition."

"That's right; our competition, Jack; not your competition. Come, now, Rob, tell us where you found her."

"I ain't found her."

"What! And yet you're goin' away t' get married!"

"I'm goin' t' bring a wife back with me ten days fr'm date."

"I see his scheme," put in Jim Rivers. "He's goin' back East somewhere, an' he's goin' to propose to every girl he meets."

"Hold on!" interrupted Rob, holding up his fork. "Ain't quite right. Every good-lookin' girl I meet."

"Well, I'll be blanked!" exclaimed Jack impatiently; "that simply lets me out. Any man with such a cheek ought to-"

"Succeed," interrupted Seagraves.

"That's what I say," bawled Hank whiting, the proprietor of the house. "You fellers ain't got any enterprise to yeh. Why don't you go to work an' help settle the country like men? 'Cause y' ain't got no sand. Girls are thicker'n huckleberries back East. I say it's a dum shame!"

"Easy, Henry," said the elegant bank clerk, Wilson, looking gravely about through his spectacles. "I commend the courage and the resolution of Mr. Rodemaker. I pray the lady may not

"Mislike him for his complexion, The shadowed livery of the burning sun."

"Shakespeare," said Adams at a venture.

"Brother in adversity, when do you embark? Another season on an untried sea~"

"Hay!" said Rob, winking at Seagraves. "Oh, I go tonight-night train."

"And return?"

"Ten days from date."

"I'll wager a wedding supper he brings a blonde," said Wilson in his clean-cut, languid speech.

"Oh, come now, Wilson; that's too thin! We all know that rule about dark marryin' light."

"I'll wager she'll be tall," continued Wilson. "I'll wager you, friend Rodemaker, she'll be blonde and tall."

The rest roared at Rob's astonishment and contusion. The absurdity of it grew, and they went into spasms of laughter. But Wilson remained impassive, not the twitching of a muscle betraying that he saw anything to laugh at in the proposition.

Mrs. Whiting and the kitchen girls came in, wondering at the merriment. Rob began to get uneasy.

"What is it? What is it?" said Mrs. Whiting, a jolly little matron.

Rivers put the case. "Rob's on his way back to Wisconsin t' get married, and Wilson has offered to bet him that his wife will be a blonde and tall, and Rob dassent bet!" And they roared again.

"Why, the idea! The man's crazy!" said Mrs. Whiting. The crowd looked at each other. This was hint enough; they sobered, nodding at each other.

"Aha! I see; I understand."

"It's the heat."

"And the Boston beans."

"Let up on him, Wilson. Don't badger a poor irresponsible fellow. I thought something was wrong when I saw the collar."

"Oh, keep it up!" said Rob, a little nettled by their evident intention to "have fun" with him.

"Soothe him-sogo-go-the him!" said Wilson. "Don't be harsh."

Rob rose from the table. "Go to thunder! You make me tired."

"The fit is on him again!"

He rose disgustedly and went out. They followed him in single file. The rest of the town "caught on." Frank Graham heaved an apple at him and joined the procession. Rob went into the store to buy some tobacco. They followed and perched like crows on the counters till he went out; then they followed him, as before. They watched him check his trunk; they witnessed the purchase of the ticket. The town had turned out by this time.

"Waupac!" announced the one nearest the victim.

"Waupac!" said the next man, and the word was passed along the street up town.

"Make a note of it," said Wilson: "Waupa-a county where a man's proposal for marriage is honored upon presentation. Sight drafts."

Rivers struck up a song, while Rob stood around, patiently bearing the jokes of the crowd:

"We're lookin' rather seedy now, While holdin' down our claims, And our vittles are not always of the best, And the mice play slyly round us As we lay down to sleep In our little old tarred shanties on the claim.

"Yet we rather like the novelty Of livin' in this way, Though the bill of fare is often rather tame; An' we're happy as a clam On the land of Uncle Sam In our little old tarred shanty on the claim."

The train drew up at length, to the immense relief of Rob, whose stoical resignation was beginning to weaken.

"Don't y' wish y' had sand?" he yelled to the crowd as he plunged into the car, thinking he was rid of them.

But no; their last stroke was to follow him into the car, nodding, pointing to their heads, and whispering, managing in the half-minute the train stood at the platform to set every person in the car staring at the crazy man. Rob groaned and pulled his hat down over his eyes-an action which confirmed his tormentors' words and made several ladies click their tongues in sympathy-"Tick! tick! poor fellow!"

"All abgo-ga-rd!' said the conductor, grinning his appreciation at the crowd, and the train was off.

"Oh, won't we make him groan when he gets back!" said Barney, the young lawyer who sang the shouting tenor.

"We'll meet him with the timbrel and the harp. Anybody want to wager? I've got two to one on a short brunette," said Wilson.

II

"Follow it far enough and it may pass the bend in the river where the water laughs eternally over its shallows."

A CORNFIELD in July is a hot place. The soil is hot and dry; the wind comes across the lazily murmuring leaves laden with a warm sickening smell drawn from the rapidly growing, broad-flung banners of the corn. The sun, nearly vertical, drops a flood of dazzing light and heat upon the field over which the cool shadows run, only to make the heat seem the more intense.

Julia Peterson, faint with fatigue, was tolling back and forth between the corn rows, holding the handles of the double-shovel corn plow while her little brother Otto rode the steaming horse. Her heart was full of bitterness, and her face flushed with heat, and her muscles aching with fatigue. The heat grew terrible. The corn came to her shoulders, and not a breath seemed to reach her, while the sun, nearing the noon mark, lay pitilessly upon her shoulders, protected only by a calico dress. The dust rose under her feet, and as she was wet with perspiration it soiled her till, with a woman's instinctive cleanliness, she shuddered. Her head throbbed dangerously. what matter to her that the king bird pitched jovially from the maples to catch a wandering bluebottle fly, that the robin was feeding its young, that the bobolink was singing? All these things, if she saw them, only threw her bondage to labor into greater relief.

Across the field, in another patch of corn, she could see her father-a big, gruff-voiced, wide-bearded Norwegian-at work also with a plow. The corn must be plowed, and so she toiled on, the tears dropping from the shadow of the ugly sunbonnet she wore. Her shoes, coarse and square-toed, chafed her feet; her hands, large and strong, were browned, or more properly burned, on the backs by the sun. The horse's harness "creak-cracked" as he swung steadily and patiently forward, the moisture pouring from his sides, his nostrils distended.

The field ran down to a road, and on the other side of the road ran a river-a broad, clear, shallow expanse at that point, and the eyes of the boy gazed longingly at the pond and the cool shadow each time that he turned at the fence.

"Say, Jule, I'm goin' in! Come, can't I? Come-say!" he pleaded as they stopped at the fence to let the horse breathe.

"I've let you go wade twice."

"But that don't do any good. My legs is all smarty, 'cause ol' Jack sweats so." The boy turned around on the horse's back and slid back to his rump. "I can't stand it!" he burst out, sliding off and darting under the fence. "Father can't see."

The girl put her elbows on the fence and watched her little brother as be sped away to the pool, throwing off his clothes as he ran, whooping with uncontrollable delight. Soon she could hear him splashing about in the water a short distance up the stream, and caught glimpses of his little shiny body and happy face. How cool that water looked! And the shadows there by the big basswood! How that water would cool her blistered feet! An impulse seized her, and she squeezed between the rails of the fence and stood in the road looking up and down to see that the way was clear. It was not a main-travelled road; no one was likely to come; why not?

She hurriedly took off her shoes and stockings-how delicious the cool, soft velvet of the grass!-and sitting down on the bank under the great basswood, whose roots formed an abrupt bank, she slid her poor blistered, chafed feet into the water, her bare head leaned against the huge tree trunk.

And now as she rested, the beauty of the scene came to her. Over her the wind moved the leaves. A jay screamed far off, as if answering the cries of the boy. A kingfisher crossed and recrossed the stream with dipping sweep of his wings. The river sang with its lips to the pebbles. The vast clouds went by majestically, far above the treetops, and the snap and buzzing and ringing whir of July insects made a ceaseless, slumberous undertone of song solvent of all else. The tired girl forgot her work. She began to dream. This would not last always. Some one would come to release her from such drudgery. This was her constant, tenderest, and most secret dream. He would be a Yankee, not a Norwegian; the Yankees didn't ask their wives to work in the field. He would have a home. Perhaps he'd live in town-perhaps a merchant! And then she thought of the drug clerk in Rock River who had looked at her- A voice broke in on her dream, a fresh, manly voice.

"Well, by jinks! if it ain't Julia! Just the one I wanted to see!"

The girl turned, saw a pleasant-faced young fellow in a derby hat and a fifteen-dollar suit of diagonals.

"Rod Rodemaker! How come-"

She remembered her situation, and flushed, looked down at the water, and remained perfectly still.

"Ain't ye goin' to shake hands? Y' don't seem very glad t' see me."

She began to grow angry. "If you had any eyes you'd see!"

Rob looked over the edge of the bank, whistled, turned away. "Oh, I see! Excuse me! Don't blame yeh a bit, though. Good weather f'r corn," he went on' looking up at the trees. 'Corn seems to be pretty well for-ward," he continued in a louder voice as he walked away, still gazing into the air. "Crops is looking first-class in Boomtown. Hello! This Otto? H'yare y' little scamp! Get onto that horse agin. Quick, 'r I'll take y'r skin off an, hang it on the fence. what y' been doing?"

"Ben in swimmm'. Jimminy, ain't it fun! when 'd y' get back?" said the boy, grinning.

"Never you mind," replied Rob, leaping the fence by laying his left hand on the top rail. "Get onto that horse." He tossed the boy up on the horse, hung his coat on the fence. "I s'pose the ol' man makes her plow same as usual?"

"Yup," said Otto.

"Dod ding a man that'll do that! I don't mind if it's necessary, but it ain't necessary in his case." He continued to mutter in this way as he went across to the other side of the field. As they turned to come back, Rob went up and looked at the horse's mouth. "Gettin' purty near of age. Say, who's sparkin' Julia now-anybody?"

"Nobody 'cept some ol' Norwegians. She won't have them. Por wants her to, but she won't."

"Good f'r her. Nobody comes t' see her Sunday nights, eh?"

"Nope, only 'Tias Anderson an' Ole Hoover; but she goes off an' leaves 'em."

"Chk!" said Rob, starting old Jack across the field.

It was almost noon, and Jack moved reluctantly. He knew the time of day as well as the boy. He made this round after distinct protest.

In the meantime Julia, putting on her shoes and stockings, went to the fence and watched the man's shining white shirt as he moved across the cornfield. There had never been any special tenderness between them, but she had always liked him. They had been at school together. She wondered why he had come back at this time of the year, and wondered how long he would stay. How long had he stood looking at her? She flushed again at the thought of it. But he wasn't to blame; it was a public road. She might have known better.

She stood under a little popple tree, whose leaves shook musically at every zephyr, and her eyes through half-shut lids roved over the sea of deep-green glossy leaves, dappled here and there by cloud-shadows, stirred here and there like water by the wind, and out of it all a longing to be free from such toil rose like a breath, filling her throat, and quickening the motion of her heart. Must this go on forever, this life of heat and dust and labor? what did it all mean?

The girl laid her chin on her strong red wrists, and looked up into the blue spaces between the vast clouds—aerial mountains dissolving in a shoreless azure sea. How cool and sweet and restful they looked! li she might only lie out on the billowy, snow-white, sunlit edge! The voices of the driver and the plowman recalled her, and she fixed her eyes again upon the slowly nodding head of the patient horse, on the boy turned half about on the horse, talking to the white-sleeved man, whose derby hat bobbed up and down quite curiously, like the horse's head. Would she ask him to dinner? what would her people say?

"Phew! it's hot!" was the greeting the young fellow gave as he came up. He smiled in a frank, boyish way as he hung his hat on the top of a stake and looked up at her. "D' y' know, I kind o' enjoy getting at it again. Fact. It ain't no work for a girl, though," he added.

"When 'd you get back?" she asked, the flush not yet out of her face. Rob was looking at her thick, fine hair and full Scandinavian face, rich as a rose in color, and did not reply for a few seconds. She stood with her hideous sun bonnet pushed back on her shoulders. A kingbird was chattering overhead.

"Oh' a few days ago."

"How long y' goin' t' stay?"

"Oh, I d' know. A week, mebbe."

A far-off halloo came pulsing across the shimmering air. The boy screamed "Dinner!" and waved his hat with an answering whoop, then flopped off the horse like a turtle off a stone into water. He had the horse unhooked in an instant, and had flung his toes up over the horse's back, in act to climb on, when Rob said:

"H'yare, young feller! wait a minute. Tired?" he asked the girl with a tone that was more than kindly; it was almost tender.

"Yes," she replied in a low voice. "My shoes hurt me."

"Well, here y' go," he replied, taking his stand by the horse and holding out his hand like a step. She colored and smiled a little as she lifted her foot into his huge, hard, sunburned hand.

"Oop-a-daisy!" he called. She gave a spring and sat the horse like one at home there.

Rob had a deliciously unconscious, abstracted, businesslike air. He really left her nothing to do but enjoy his company, while he went ahead and did precisely as he pleased.

"We don't raise much corn out there, an' so I kind o' like to see it once more."

"I wish I didn't have to see another hill of corn as long as I live!" replied the girl bitterly.

"Don't know as I blame yeh a bit. But, all the same, I'm glad you was working in it today," he thought to hiniseif as he walked beside her horse toward the house.

"Will you stop to dinner?" she inquired bluntly, almost surmy. It was evident that there were reasons why she didn't mean to press. him to'. do so.

"You bet I will," he replied; "that is, if you want I should."

"You know how we live," she replied evasively. "I' you c'n stand it, why-" She broke off abruptly.

Yes, he remembered how they lived in that big, square, dirty, white frame house. It had been- three or four years since he had been ill it, but the smell of the cabbage and onions, the penetrating, peculiar mixture of odors, assailed his memory as something unforgettable.

"I guess I'll stop," he said as she hesitated. She said no more, but tried to act as if she were not in any way responsible for what came afterward.

"I guess I c'n stand fr one meal what you stand all the while," he added.

As she left them at the well and went to the house, he saw her limp painfully, and the memory of her face so close to his 1ips as he helped her down from the horse gave him pleasure, at the same time that he was touched by its tired and gloomy look. Mrs. Peterson came to the door of the kitchen, looking just the same as ever. Broadfaced, unwieldly, flabby, apparently wearing the same dress he remembered to have seen her in years before a dirty drab-colored thing-she looked as shapeless as a sack of wool. Her English was limited to "How de do, Rob?"

He washed at the pump, while the girl, in the attempt to be hospitable, held the clean towel for him.

"You're purty well used up, eh?" he said to her.

"Yes; it's awful hot out there."

"Can't you lay off this afternoon? It ain't right"

"No. He won't listen to that."

"Well, let me take your place."

"No; there ain't any use o' that."

Peterson, a brawny wide-bearded Norwegian, came up at this moment and spoke to Rob in a sullen, gruff way

"He ain't very glad to see me," said Rob, winking at Julia. "He ain't b'ilin' over with enthusiasm; but I c'n stand it, for your sake," he added with amazing assurance; but the girl had turned away, and it was wasted.

At the table he ate heartily of the "bean swaagen," which filled a large wooden bowl in the center of the table, and which was ladled into smaller wooden bowls at each plate. Julia had tried hard to convert her mother to Yankee ways, and had at last given it up in despair. Rob kept on safe subjects, mainly asking questions about the crops of Peterson, and when addressing the girl, inquired of the schoolmates. By skillful questioning, he kept the subject of marriage uppermost, and seemingly was getting an inventory of the girls not yet married or engaged.

It was embarrassing for the girl. She was all too well aware of the difference between her home and the home of her schoolmates and friends, She. knew that it was not pleasant for her "Yankee" friends to come to visit her when they could not feel sure of a welcome from the tireless, silent, and grim-visaged old Norse, if, indeed, they could escape insult. Julia ate her food mechanically, and it could hardly be said that she enjoyed the brisk talk of the young man, his eyes were upon her so constantly and his smile so obviously addressed to her, She rose as soon as possible and, going outside, took a seat on a chair under the trees in the yard. She was not a coarse or dull girl. In fact, she had developed so rapidly by contact with the young people of the neighborhood that she no longer found pleasure, in her own home. She didn't believe in keeping up the old-fashioned Norwegian customs, and her life with her mother was not one to breed love or confidence. She was more like a hired hand. The love of the mother for her "Yulyie" was sincere though rough and inarticulate, and it was her jealousy of the young "Yankees" that widened the chasm between the girl and herself—an inevitable result.

Rob followed the girl out into the yard, and threw himself on the grass at her feet, perfectly unconscious of the fact that this attitude was exceedingly graceful and becoming to them both. He did it because he wanted to talk to her, and the grass was cool and easy; there wasn't any other chair, anyway.

"Do they keep up the ly-ceum and the sociables same as ever?"

"Yes. The others go a good 'eal, but I don't. We're gettin' such a stock round us, and father thinks he needs me s' much, I don't get out often. I'm gettin' sick of it."

"I sh'd think y' would," he replied, his eyes on her face,

"I c'd stand the churnin' and housework, but when it comes it comes t' workin' outdoors in the dirt an' hot sun, gettin' all sunburned and chapped up, it's another thing. An' then it seems as if he gets stingier 'n' stingier every year. I ain't had a new dress in—I d'-know-how-long. He says it's all nonsense, an' Mother's just about as bad. She don't want a new dress, an' so she thinks I don't."

The girl was feeling the influence of a sympathetic listener and was making up for her long silence. "I've tried t' go out t' work, but they won't let me. They'd have t' pay a hand twenty dollars a month f'r the work I do, an' they like cheap help; but I'm not goin' t' stand it much longer, I can tell you that."

Rob thought she was very handsome as she sat there with her eyes fixed on the horizon, while these rebellious thoughts found utterance in her quivering, passionate voice.

"Yulie! Nom heat!" roared the old man from the well. A frown of anger and pain came into her face. She looked at Rob. "That means more work."

"Say! let me go out in your place. Come, now; what's the use-"

"No; it wouldn't do no good. It ain't t'day s' much; it's every day, and-"

"Yulie!" called Peterson again with a string of impatient Norwegian.

"Well, all right, only I'd like to"

"Well, goodbye," she said, with a little touch of feeling. "When d'ye go back?"

"I don't know. I'll see y' again before I go. Goodbye." He stood watching her slow, painful pace till she reached the well, where Otto was standing with the horse. He stood watching them as they moved out into the road and turned down toward the field. He felt that she had sent him away; but still there was a look in her eyes which was not altogether—

He gave it up in despair at last. He was not good at analyses of this nature; he was used to plain, blunt expressions. There was a woman's subtlety here quite beyond his reach.

He sauntered slowly off up the road after his talk with Julia. His head was low on his breast; he was thinking as one who is about to take a decided and important step.

He stopped at length, and turning, watched the girl moving along in the deeps of the corn. Hardly a leaf was stirring; the untempered sunlight fell in a burning flood upon the field; the grasshoppers rose, snapped, buzzed, and fell; the locust uttered its dry, heat-intensifying cry. The man lifted his head.

"It's a d-n shame!" he said, beginning rapidly to retrace his steps. He stood leaning on the fence, awaiting the girl's coming very much as she had waited his on the round he had made before dinner. He grew impatient at the slow gait of the horse and drummed on their rail while he whistled. Then he took off his hat and dusted it nervously. As the horse got a little nearer he wiped his face carefully, pushed his hat back on his head, and climbed over the fence, where he stood with elbows on the middle rail as the girl and boy and horse came to the end of the furrow.

"Hot, ain't it?" he said as she looked up.

"Jimminy Peters, it's awful!" puffed the boy. The girl did not reply and she swung the plow about after the horse, and set it upright into the next row. Her powerful body had a superb swaying motion at the waist as she did this-a motion which affected Rob vaguely but massively.

"I thought you'd gone," she said gravely, pushing hack her bonnet, and he could see her face dewed with sweat and pink as a rose. She had the high cheekbones of her race, but she had also their exquisite fairess of color.

"Say, Otto," asked Rob alluringly, "wan' to go swimming?"

"You bet!" replied Otto.

"Well, I'll go a round if-"

The boy dropped off the horse, not waiting to hear any more. Rob grinned; but the girl dropped her eyes, then looked away.

"Got rid o' him mighty quick. Say, Julyie, I hate like thunder t' see you out here; it ain't right. I wish you'd—I wish—"

She could not look at him now, and her bosom rose and fell with a motion that was not due to fatigue. Her moist hair matted around her forehead gave her a boyish look.

Rob nervously tried again, tearing splinters from the fence. "Say, now, I'll tell yeh what I came back here fer t' git married; and if you're willin', I'll do it tonight. Come, now, whaddy y' say?"

"What 've I got t' do 'bout it?" she finally asked, the color flooding her face and a faint smile coming to her lips. "Go ahead. I ain't got anything-"

Rob put a splinter in his mouth and faced her. "Oh, looky here, now, Julyie! you know what I mean. I've got a good claim out near Boomtown-a rattlin' good claim; a shanty on it fourteen by sixteen-no tarred paper about it; and a suller to keep butter in; and a hundred acres wheat just about ready to turn now. I need a wife."

Here he straightened up, threw away the splinter, and took off his hat. He was a very pleasant figure as the girl stole a look at him. His black laughing eyes were especially earnest just now. His voice had a touch of pleading. The popple tree over their heads murmured applause at his eloquence, then hushed to listen. A cloud dropped a silent shadow down upon them, and it sent a little thrill of fear through Rob, as if it were an omen of failure. As the girl remained silent, looking away, he began, man-fashion, to desire her more and more as he feared to lose her. He put his hat on the post again and took out his jackknife. Her calico dress draped her supple and powerful figure simply but naturally. The stoop in her shoulders, given by labor, disappeared as she partly leaned upon the fence. The curves of her muscular arms showed through her sleeve.

"It's all-fired lonesome fr me out there on that claim, and it ain't no picnic f'r you here. Now, if you'll come out there with me, you needn't do anything but cook f'r me, and after harvest we can git a good layout o' furniture, an' I'll lath and plaster the house, an' put a little hell [ell] in the rear." He smiled, and so did she. He felt encouraged to say: "An' there we be, as snug as y' please. We're close t' Boomtown, an' we can go down there to church sociables an' things, and they're a jolly lot there."

The girl was still silent, but the man's simple enthusiasm came to her charged with passion and a sort of romance such as her hard life had known little of. There was something enticing about this trip to the West.

"What 'li my folks say?" she said at last.

A virtual surrender, but Rob was not acute enough to see it. He pressed on eagerly:

"I don't care. Do you? They'll jest keep y' plowin' corn and milkin' cows till the day of judgment. Come, Julyie, I ain't got no time to fool away. I've got t' get back t' that grain. It's a whoopin' old crop, sure's y'r born, an' that means som'pin' purty scrumptious in furniture this fall. Come, now." He approached her and laid his hand on her shoulder very much as he would have touched Albert Seagraves or any other comrade. "Whady y' say?"

She neither started, nor shrunk, nor looked at him. She simply moved a step away. "They'd never let me ge," she replied bitterly. "I'm too cheap a hand. I do a man's work an' get no pay at all."

"You'll have half o' all I c'n make," he put in.

"How long c'n you wait?" she asked, looking down at her dress.

"Just two minutes," he said, pulling out his watch. "It ain't no use t' wait. The old man 'li be jest as mad a week from now as he is today. why not go now?"

"I'm of age day after tomorrow," she mused, wavering, calculating.

"You c'n be of age tonight if you'll jest call on old Square Hatfield with me."

"All right, Rob," the girl said, turning and holding out her hand.

"That's the talk!" he exclaimed, seizing it. "An' now a kiss, to bind the bargain, as the fellah says."

"I guess we c'n get along without that."

"No, we can't. It won't seem like an engagement without it."

"It ain't goin' to seem much like one anyway," she answered with a sudden realization of how far from her dreams of courtship this reality was.

"Say, now, Julyie, that ain't fair; it ain't treatin' me right. You don't seem to understand that I like you, but I do."

Rob was carried quite out of himself by the time, the place, and the girl. He had said a very moving thing.

The tears sprang involuntarily to the girl's eyes. "Do you mean it? If y' do, you may."

She was trembling with emotion for the first time. The sincerity of the man's voice had gone deep.

He put his arm around her almost timidly and kissed her on the cheek, a great love for her springing up in his heart. "That setties it," he said. "Don't cry, Jalyie. You'll never be sorry for it. Don't cry. It kind o' hurts me to see it."

He didn't understand her feelings. He was only aware that she was crying, and tried in a bungling way to soothe her. But now that she had given way, she sat down in the grass and wept bitterly.

"Yulyie!" yelled the old Norwegian, like a distant fog-horn.

The girl sprang up; the habit of obedience was strong.

"No; you set right there, and I'll go round," he said. "Otto!"

The boy came scrambling out of the wood half dressed. Rob tossed him upon the horse, snatched Julia's sun-bonnet, put his own hat on her head, and moved off down the corn rows, leaving the girl smiling through her tears as he whistled and chirped to the horse. Farmer Peterson, seeing the familiar sunbonnet above the corn rows, went back to his work, with a sentence of Norwegian trailing after him like the tail of a kite-something about lazy girls who didn't earn the crust of their bread, etc.

Rob was wild with delight. "Git up there Jack! Hay, you old corncrib! Say, Otto, can you keep your mouth shut if it puts money in your pocket?"

"Jest try me 'n' see," said the keen-eyed little scamp. "Well, you keep quiet about my being here this alter-noon, and I'll put a dollar on y'r tongue—hay?—what?—understand?"

"Show me y'r dollar," said the boy, turning about and showing his tongue.

"All right. Begin to practice now by not talkin' to me."

Rob went over the whole situation on his way back, and when he got in sight of the girl his plan was made. She stood waiting for him with a new look on her face. Her sullenness had given way to a peculiar eagerness and anxiety to believe in him. She was already living that free life in a far-off wonderful country. No more would her stern father and sullen mother force her to tasks which she hated. She'd be a member of a new firm. She'd work, of course, but it would be because she wanted to, and not because she was forced to. The independence and the love promised grew more and more attractive. She laughed back with a softer light in her eyes when she saw the smiling face of Rob looking at her from her sun-bonnet

"Now you mustn't do any more o' this," he said. "You go back to the house an' tell y'r mother you're too lame to plow any more today, and it's too late, anyhow. To-night!" he whispered quickly. "Eleven! Here!"

The girl's heart leaped with fear. "I'm afraid."

"Not of me, are yeh?"

"No, I'm not afraid of you, Rob."

"I'm glad o' that. I-I want you to-to like me, Julyie; won't you?"

"I'll try," she answered with a smile.

"Tonight, then," he said as she moved away.

"Tonight. Goodbye."

"Goodbye."

He stood and watched her till her tall figure was lost among the drooping corn leaves. There was a singular choking feeling in his throat. The girl's voice and face had brought up so many memories of parties and picnics and excursions on far-off holidays, and at the same time such suggestions of the future. He already felt that it was going to be an unconscionably long time before eleven o'clock.

He saw her go to the house, and then he turned and walked slowly up the dusty road. Out of the May weed the grasshoppers sprang, buzzing and snapping their dull red wings. Butterflies, yellow and white, fluttered around moist places in the ditch, and slender striped water snakes glided across the stagnant pools at sound of footsteps.

But the mind of the man was far away on his claim, building a new house, with a woman's advice and presence.

* * * * * *

It was a windless night. The katydids and an occasional cricket were the only sounds Rob could hear as he stood beside his team and strained his ear to listen. At long intervals a little breeze ran through the corn like a swift serpent, bringing to the nostrils the sappy smell of the growing corn. The horses stamped uneasily as the mosquitoes settled on their shining limbs. The sky was full of stars, but there was no moon.

"What if she don't come?" he thought. "Or can't come? I can't stand that. I'll go to the old man an' say, 'Looky here-' Sh!"

He listened again. There was a rustling in the corn. It was not like the fitful movement of the wind; it was steady, slower, and approaching. It ceased. He whistled the wailing, sweet cry of the prairie chicken. Then a figure came out into the road—a woman—Julia!

He took her in his arms as she came panting up to him.

"Rob!"

"Julyie!"

* * * * * *

A few words, the dull tread of swift horses, the rising of a silent train of dust, and then the wind wandered in the growing corn. The dust fell, a dog barked down the road and the katydids sang to the liquid contralto of the river in its shallows.

4. THE RETURN OF A PRIVATE

On the road leading "back to God's country" and wile and babies.

I

The nearer the train drew toward La Crosse, the soberer the little group of "vets" became. On the long way from New Orleans they had beguiled tedium with jokes and friendly chaff; or with planning with elaborate detail what they were going to do now, after the war. A long journey, slowly, irregularly, yet persistently pushing northward. when they entered on Wisconsin Territory they gave a cheer, and another when they reached Madison, but after that they sank into a dumb expectancy. Comrades dropped off at one or two points beyond, until there were only four or five left who were bound for La Crosse County

Three of them were gaunt and brown, the fourth was gaunt and pale, with signs of fever and ague upon him. One had a great scar down his temple; one limped; and they all had unnaturally large bright eyes, showing emaciation. There were no bands greeting them at the stations, no banks of gaily dressed ladies waving hand-kerchiefs and shouting "Bravo!" as they came in on the caboose of a freight tram into the towns that had cheered and blared at them on their way to war. As they looked out or stepped upon the platform for a moment, as the train stood at the station, the loafers looked at them indifferently. Their blue coats, dusty and grimy, were too familiar now to excite notice, much less a friendly word. They were the last of the army to return, and the loafers were surfeited with such sights.

The train jogged forward so slowly that it seemed likely to be midnight before they should reach La Crosse. The little squad of "vets" grumbled and swore, but it was no use, the train would not hurry; and as a matter of fact, rt was nearly two o'clock when the engine whistled "down brakes."

Most of the group were farmers, living in districts several miles out of the town, and all were poor.

"Now, boys," said Private Smith, he of the fever and ague, "we are landed in La Crosse in the night. We've got to stay somewhere till mornin'. Now, I ain't got no two dollars to waste on a hotel. I've got a wife and children, so I'm goin' to roost on a bench and take the cost of a bed out of my hide."

"Same here," put in one of the other men. "Hide'll grow on again, dollars come hard. It's goin' to be mighty hot skirmishin' to find a dollar these days."

"Don't think they'll be a deputation of citizens waitin' to 'scort us to a hotel, eh?" said another. His sarcasm was too obvious to require an answer.

Smith went on: "Then at daybreak we'll start f'r home; at least I will."

"Well, I'll be dummed if I'll take two dollars out o' my hide," one of the younger men said. "I'm goin' to a hotel, ef I don't never lay up a cent."

"That'll do f'r you," said Smith; "but if you had a wife an' three young 'uns dependin' on yeh-"

"Which I ain't, thank the Lord! and don't intend havin' while the court knows itself."

The station was deserted, chill, and dark, as they came into it at exactly a quarter to two in the morning. Lit by the oil lamps that flared a dull red light over the dingy benches, the waiting room was not an inviting place. The younger man went off to look up a hotel, while the rest remained and prepared to camp down on the floor and benches. Smith was attended to tenderly by the other men, who spread their blankets on the bench for him, and by robbing themselves made quite a comfortable bed, though the narrowness of the bench made his sleeping precarious.

It was chill, though August, and the two men sitting with bowed heads grew stiff with cold and weariness, and were forced to rise now and again, and walk about to warm their stiffened limbs It didn't occur to them, probably, to contrast their coming home with their going forth, or with the coming home of the generals, colonels, or even captains-but to Private Smith, at any rate, there came a sickness at heart almost deadly, as he lay there on his hard bed and went over his situation.

In the deep of the night, lying on a board in the town where he had enlisted three years ago, all elation and enthusiasm gone out of him, he faced the fact that with the joy of homecoming was mingled the bitter juice of care. He saw himself sick, worn out, taking up the work on his half-cleared farm, the inevitable mortgage standing ready with open jaw to swallow half his earnings. He had given three years of his life for a mere pittance of pay, and now—

Morning dawned at last, slowly, with a pale yellow dome of light rising silently above the bluffs which stand like some huge battlemented castle, just east of the city. Out to the left the great river swept on its massive yet silent way to the south. Jays called across the river from hillside to hillside, through the clear, beautiful air, and hawks began to skim the tops of the hills. The two vets were astir early, but Private Smith had fallen at last into a sleep, and they went out without waking him. He lay on his knapsack, his gaunt face turned toward the ceiling, his hands clasped on his breast, with a curious pathetic effect of weakness and appeal.

An engine switching near woke him at last, and he slowly sat up and stared about. He looked out of the window and saw that the sun was lightening the hills across the river. He rose and brushed his hair as well as he could, folded his blankets up, and went out to find his companions. They stood gazing silently at the river and at the hills.

"Looks nat'cherl, don't it?" they said as he came out.

"That's what it does," he replied. "An' it looks good. D'yeh see that peak?" He pointed at a beautiful symmetrical peak, rising like a slightly truncated cone, so high that it seemed the very highest of them all. It was lighted by the morning sun till it glowed like a beacon, and a light scarf of gray morning fog was rolling up its shadowed side.

"My farm's just beyond that. Now, ef I can only ketch a ride, we'll be home by dinnertime."

"I'm talkin' about breakfast," said one of the others.

"I guess it's one more meal o' hardtack f'r me," said Smith.

They foraged around, and finally found a restaurant with a sleepy old German behind the counter, and procured some coffee, which they drank to wash down their hardtack.

"Time'll come," said Smith, holding up a piece by the corner, "when this'll be a curiosity."

"I hope to God it will! I bet I've chawed hardtack enough to shingle every house in the coulee. I've chawed it when my lampers was down, and when they wasn't. I've took it dry, soaked, and mashed. I've had it wormy, musty, sour, and blue-moldy. I've had it in little bits and big bits; 'fore coffee an' after coffee. I'm ready f'r a change. I'd like t' git hol't jest about now o' some of the hot biscuits my wife c'n make when she lays herself out f'r company."

"Well, if you set there gablin', you'll never see yer wife."

"Come on," said Private Smith. "Wait a moment, boys; less take suthin'. It's on me." He led them to the rusty tin dipper which hung on a nail beside the wooden water pail, and they grinned and drank. (Things were primitive in La Crosse then.) Then, shouldering their blankets and muskets, which they were "taking home to the boys," they struck out on their last march.

"They called that coffee 'Jayvy,'" grumbled one of them, "but it never went by the road where government Jayvy resides. I reckon I know coffee from peas."

They kept together on the road along the turnpike, and up the winding road by the river, which they followed for some miles. The river was very lovely, curving down along its sandy beds, pausing now and then under broad basswood trees, or running in dark, swift, silent currents under tangles of wild grapevines, and drooping alders, and haw trees. At one of these lovely spots the three vets sat down on the thick green sward to rest, "on Smith's account." The leaves of the trees were as fresh and green as in June, the jays called cheery greetings to them, and kingfishers darted to and fro, with swooping, noiseless flight.

"I tell yeh, boys, this knocks the swamps of Loueesiana into kingdom come."

"You bet. All they c'n raise down there is snakes, niggers, and p'rticler hell."

"An' fightin' men," put in the older man.

"An' fightin' men. If I had a good hook an' line I'd sneak a pick'rel out o' that pond. Say, remember that time I shot that alligator-"

"I guess we'd better be crawlin' along," interrupted Smith, rising and shouldering his knapsack, with considerable effort, which he tried to hide.

"Say, Smith, lemme give you a lift on that."

"I guess I c'n manage," said Smith grimly.

"'Course. But, yeh see, I may not have a chance right off to pay yeh back for the times ye've carried my gun and hull caboodie. Say, now, girne that gun, anyway."

"All right, if yeh feel like it, Jim," Smith replied, and they trudged along doggedly in the sun, which was getting higher and hotter each half mile.

"Ain't it queer there ain't no teams comin' along."

"Well, no, seem's it's Sunday."

"By jinks, that's a fact! It is Sunday. I'll git home in time fr dinner, sure. She don't hev dinner usually till-about one on Sundays." And he fell into a muse, in which he smiled.

"Well, I'll git home jest about six o'clock, jest about when the boys are milkin' the cows," said old Jim Cranby. "I'll step into the barn an' then I'll say, 'Heah! why ain't this milkin' done before this time o' day? An' then won't they yell!" he added, slapping his thigh in great glee.

Smith went on. "I'll jest go up the path. Old Rover'll come down the road to meet me. He won't bark; he'll know me, an' he'll come down waggin' his tail an' shonin' his teeth. That's his way of laughin'. An' so I'll walk up to the kitchen door, an' I'll say 'Dinner fr a hungry man!' An' then she'll jump up, an'-"

He couldn't go on. His voice choked at the thought of it. Saunders, the third man, hardly uttered a word. He walked silently behind the others. He had lost his wife the first year he was in the army. She died of pneumonia caught in the autumn rains, while working in the fields in his place.

They plodded along till at last they came to a parting of the ways. To the right the road continued up the main valley; to the left it went over the ridge.

"Well, boys," began Smith as they grounded their muskets and looked away up the valley, "here's where we shake hands. We've marched together a good many miles, an' now I s'pose we're done."

"Yes, I don't think we'll do any more of it fr a while. I don't want to, I know."

"I hope I'll see yeh once in a while, boys, to talk over old times."

"Of course," said Saunders, whose voice trembled a little, too. "It ain't exactly like dyin'."

"But we'd ought'r go home with you," said the younger man. "You never'll climb that ridge with all them things on yer back."

"Oh, I'm all right! Don't worry about me. Every step takes me nearer home, yeh see. Well, goodbye, boys."

They shook hands. "Goodbye. Good luck!"

"Same to you. Lemme know how you find things at home."

He turned once before they passed out of sight and waved his cap, and they did the same, and all yelled. Then all marched away with their long, steady, loping, veteran step. The solitary climber in blue walked on for a time, with his mind filled with the kindness of his comrades, and musing upon the many jolly days they had had together in camp and field.

He thought of his chum, Billy Tripp. Poor Billy! A "mime" ball fell into his breast one day, fell wailing like a cat, and tore a great ragged hole in his heart. He looked forward to a sad scene with Billy's mother and sweet-heart. They would want to know all about it. He tried to recall all that Billy had said, and the particulars of it, but there was little to remember, just that wild wailing sound high in the air, a dull slap, a short, quick, expulsive groan, and the boy lay with his face in the dirt in the plowed field they were marching across.

That was all. But all the scenes he had since been through had not dimmed the horror, the terror of that moment, when his boy comrade fell, with only a breath between a laugh and a death groan. Poor handsome Billy! Worth millions of dollars was his young wife.

These somber recollections gave way at length to more cheerful feelings as he began to approach his home coulee. The fields and houses grew familiar, and in one or two he was greeted by people seated in the doorway. But he was in no mood to talk, and pushed on steadily, though he stopped and accepted a drink of milk once at the well-side of a neighbor.

The sun was getting hot on that slope, and his step grew slower, in spite of his iron resolution. He sat down several times to rest. Slowly he crawled up the rough, reddish-brown road, which wound along the hillside, under great trees, through dense groves of jack oaks, with treetops' far below him on his left hand, and the hills far above him on his right. He crawled along like some minute wingless variety of fly.

He ate some hardtack, sauced with wild berries, when he reached the summit of the ridge, and sat there for some time, looking down into his home coulee.

Somber, pathetic figure! His wide, round, gray eyes gazing down into the beautiful valley, seeing and not seeing, the splendid cloud-shadows sweeping over the western hills and across the green and yellow wheat far below. His head drooped forward on his palm, his shoulders took on a tired stoop, his cheekbones showed painfully. An observer might have said, "He is looking down upon his own grave."

II

Sunday comes in a Western wheat harvest with such sweet and sudden relaxation to man and beast that it would be holy for that reason, if for no other. And Sundays are usually fair in harvest time. As one goes out into the field in the hot morning sunshine, with no sound abroad save the crickets and the indescribably pleasant, silken rustling of the ripened grain, the reaper and the very sheaves in the stubble seem to be resting, dreaming.

Around the house, in the shade of the trees, the men sit, smoking, dozing, or reading the papers, while the women, never resting, move about at the housework. The men eat on Sundays about the same as on other days; and breakfast is no sooner over and out of the way than dinner begins.

But at the Smith farm there were no men dozing or reading. Mrs. Smith was alone with her three children, Mary, nine, Tommy, six, and littie Ted, just past four. Her farm, rented to a neighbor, lay at the head of a coulee or narrow galley, made at some far-off postglacial period by the vast and angry floods of water which gullied these tremendous furrows in the level prairie-furrows so deep that undisturbed portions of the original level rose like hills on either side rose to quite considerable mountains.

The chickens wakened her as usual that Sabbath morning from dreams of her absent husband, from whom she had not heard for weeks. The shadows drifted over the hills, down the slopes, across the wheat, and up the opposite wall in leisurely way, as if, being Sunday, they could "take it easy," also. The fowls clustered about the housewife as she went out into the yard. Fuzzy little chickens swarmed out from the coops where their clucking and perpetually disgruntled mothers tramped about, petulantly thrusting their heads through the spaces between the slats.

A cow called in a deep, musical bass, and a call answered from a little pen nearby, and a pig scurried guiltily out of the cabbages. Seeing all this, seeing the pig in the cabbages, the tangle of grass in the garden, the broken fence which she had mended again and again—the little woman, hardly more than a girl, sat down and cried. The bright Sabbath morning was only a mockery without him!

A few years ago they had bought this farm, paying part, mortgaging the rest in the usual way. Edward Smith was a man of terrible energy. He worked "nights and Sundays," as the saying goes, to clear the farm of its brush and of its insatiate mortgage. In the midst of his Herculean struggle came the call for volunteers, and with the grim and unselfish devotion to his country which made the Eagle Brigade able to "whip its weight in wildcats," he threw down his scythe and his grub ax, turned his cattle loose, and became a blue-coated cog in a vast machine for killing men, and not thistles. While the millionnaire sent his money to England for safekeeping, this man, with his girl-wife and three babies, left them on a mortgaged farm and went away to fight for an idea. It was foolish, but it was sublime for all that.

That was three years before, and the young wife, sitting on the well curb on this bright Sabbath harvest morning, was righteously rebellious. It seemed to her that she had borne her share of the country's sorrow. Two brothers had been killed, the renter in whose hands her husband had left the farm had proved a villain, one year the farm was without crops, and now the overripe grain was waiting the tardy hand of the neighbor who had rented it, and who was cutting his own grain first.

About six weeks before, she had received a letter saying, "We'll be discharged in a little while." But no other word had come from him. She had seen by the papers that his army was being discharged, and from day to day other soldiers slowly percolated in blue streams back into the state and county, but still her private did not return.

Each week she had told the children that he was coming' and she had watched the road so long that it had become unconscious, and as she stood at the well, or by the kitchen door, her eyes were fixed unthinkingly on the road that wound down the coulee. Nothing wears on the human soul like waiting. If the stranded mariner, 'searching the sun-bright seas, could once give up hope of a ship, that horrible grinding on his brain would cease. It was this waiting, hoping, on the edge of despair, that gave Emma Smith no rest.

Neighbors said, with kind intentions, "He's sick, maybe, an' can't start North just yet. He'll come along one o' these days."

"Why don't he write?" was her question, which silenced them all. This Sunday morning it seemed to her as if she couldn't stand it any longer. The house seemed intolerably lonely. So she dressed the little ones in their best calico dresses and homemade jackets, and closing up the house, set off down the coulee to old Mother Gray's.

"Old Widder Gray" lived at the "mouth of the coulee." She was a widow woman with a large family of stalwart boys and laughing girls. She was the visible incarnation of hospitality and optimistic poverty. With Western open-heartedness she fed every mouth that asked food of her, and worked herself to death as cheerfully as her girls danced in the neighborhood harvest dances.

She waddled down the path to meet Mrs. Smith with a smile on her face that would have made the countenance of a convict expand.

"Oh, you little dears! Come right to yer granny. Gimme a kiss! Come right in, Mis' Smith. How are yeh, anyway? Nice mornin', ain't it? Come in an' set down. Every-thing's in a clutter, but that won't scare you any."

She led the way into the "best room," a sunny, square room, carpeted with a faded and patched rag carpet, and papered with a horrible white-and-green-striped wallpaper, where a few ghastly effigies of dead members of the family hung in variously sized oval walnut frames. The house resounded with singing, laughter, whistling, tramping of boots, and scufflings. Half-grown boys came to the door and crooked their fingers at the children, who ran out, and were soon heard in the midst of the fun.

"Don't s'pose you've heard from Ed?" Mrs. Smith shook her head. "He'll turn up some day, when you ain't look-in' for 'm." The good old soul had said that so many times that poor Mrs. Smith derived no comfort from it any longer.

"Liz heard from Al the other day. He's comin' some, day this week. Anyhow, they expect him."

"Did he say anything of-"

"No, he didn't," Mrs. Gray admitted. "But then it was only a short letter, anyhow. Al ain't much for ritin', anyhow. But come out and see my new cheese. I tell yeh, I don't believe I ever had hetter luck in my life. If Ed should come, I want you should take him up a piece of this cheese."

It was beyond human nature to resist the influence of that noisy, hearty, loving household, and in the midst of the singing and laughing the wife forgot her anxiety, for the time at least, and laughed and sang with the rest.

About eleven o'clock a wagonload more drove up to the door, and Bill Gray, the widow's oldest son, and his whole family from Sand Lake Coulee piled out amid a good-natured uproar, as characteristic as it was ludicrous. Everyone talked. at once, except Bill, who sat in the wagon with his wrists on his knees, a straw in his mouth, and an amused twinkle in his blue eyes.

"Ain't heard nothin' o' Ed, I s'pose?" he asked in a kind of bellow. Mrs. Smith shook her head. Bill, with a delicacy very striking in such a great giant, rolled his quid in his mouth and said:

"Didn't know but you had. I hear two or three of the Sand Lake boys are comm'. Left New Orleenes some time this week. Didn't write nothin' about Ed, but no news is good news in such cases, Mother always says."

"Well, go put out yer team," said Mrs. Gray, "an' go'n bring me in some taters, an', Sim, you go see if you c'n find some corn. Sadie, you put on the water to b'ile. Come now, hustle yer boots, all o' yeh. If I feed this yer crowd, we've got to have some raw materials. If y' think.I'm goin' to feed yeh on pie-"

The children went off into the fields, the girls put dinner on to "b'ile," and then went to change their dresses and fix their hair. "Somebody might come," they said.

"Land sakes, l hope not! I don't know where in time I'd set 'em, 'less they'd eat at the secont table," Mrs. Gray laughed in pretended dismay.

The two older boys, who had served their time in the army, lay out on the grass before the house, and whittied and talked desultorily about the war and the crops, and planned buying a threshing machine. The older girls and Mrs. Smith helped enlarge the table and put on the dishes, talking all the time in that cheery, incoherent, and meaningful way a group of such women have-a conversation to be taken for its spirit rather than for its letter, though Mrs. Gray at last got the ear of them all and dissertated at length on girls.

"Girls in love ain't no use in the whole blessed week," she said. "Sundays they're a-lookin' down the road, expectin' he'll come. Sunday afternoons they can't think o' nothin' else, 'cause he's here. Monday mornin's they're sleepy and kind o' dreamy and slimpsy, and good fr nothin' on Tuesday and Wednesday. Thursday they git absent-minded, an' begin to look off toward Sunday agin, an' mope aroun' and let the dishwater git cold, right under their noses. Friday they break dishes, and go off in the best room an' snivel, an' look out o' the winder. Saturdays they have queer spurts o' workin' like all p'ssessed, an spurts o' frizzin' their hair. An' Sunday they begin it all over agin."

The girls giggled and blushed all through this tirade from their mother, their broad faces and powerful frames anything but suggestive of lackadaisical sentiment. But Mrs. Smith said:

"Now, Mrs. Gray, I hadn't ought to stay to dinner. You've got-"

"Now you set right down! If any of them girls' beaus comes, they'll have to take what's left, that's all. They ain't s'posed to have much appetite, nohow. No, you're goin' to stay if they starve, an' they ain't no danger o' that."

At one o'clock the long table was piled with boiled potatoes, cords of boiled corn on the cob, squash and pumpkin pies, hot biscuit, sweet pickles, bread and butter, and honey. Then one of the girls took down a conch shell from a nail and, going to the door, blew a long, fine, free blast, that showed there was no weakness of lungs in her ample chest.

Then the children came out of the forest of corn, out of the crick, out of the loft of the barn, and out of the garden. The men shut up their jackknives, and surrounded the horse trough to souse their faces in the cold, hard water, and in a few moments the table was filled with a merry crowd, and a row of wistful-eyed youngsters circled the kitchen wail, where they stood first on one leg and then on the other, in impatient hunger.

"They come to their feed f'r all the world jest like the pigs when y' hoilder 'poo-ee!' See 'em scoot!" laughed Mrs. Gray, every wrinkle on her face shining with delight. "Now pitch in, Mrs. Smith," she said, presiding over the table. "You know these men critters. They'll eat every grain of it, if yeh give 'em a chance. I swan, they're made o' Indian rubber, their stomachs is, I know it."

"Haft to eat to work," said Bill, gnawing a cob with a swift, circular motion that rivaled a corn sheller in results.

"More like workin' to eat," put in one of the girls with a giggle. "More eat 'n' work with you."

"You needn't say anything, Net. Anyone that'll eat seven ears-"

"I didn't, no such thing. You piled your cobs on my plate."

"That'll do to tell Ed Varney. It won't go down here, where we know yeh."

"Good land! Eat all yeh want! They's plenty more in the fiel's, but I can't afford to give you young 'uns tea. The tea is for us womenfolks, and 'specially fr Mis' Smith an' Bill's wife. We're agoin' to tell fortunes by it."

One by one the men filled up and shoved back, and one by one the children slipped into their places, and by two o'clock the women alone remained around the debris-covered table, sipping their tea and telling fortunes.

As they got well down to the grounds in the cup, they shook them with a circular motion in the hand, and then turned them bottom-side-up quickly in the saucer, then twirled them three or four times one way, and three or four times the other, during a breathless pause. Then Mrs. Gray lifted the cup and, gazing into it with profound gravity, pronounced the impending fate.

It must be admitted that, to a critical observer, she had abundant preparation for hitting close to the mark; as when she told the girls that "somebody was coming." "It is a man," she went on gravely. "He is cross-eyed-"

"Oh, you hush!"

"He has red hair, and is death on b'iled corn and hot biscuit."

The others shrieked with delight.

"But he's goin' to get the mitten, that redheaded feller is, for I see a feller comin' up behind him."

"Oh, lemme see, lemme see!" cried Nettle.

"Keep off," said the priestess with a lofty gesture. "His hair is black. He don't eat so much, and he works more."

The girls exploded in a shriek of laughter and pounded their sister on the back.

At last came Mrs. Smith's turn, and she was trembling with excitement as Mrs. Gray again composed her jolly face to what she considered a proper solemnity of expression.

"Somebody is comin' to you," she said after a long pause. "He's got a musket on his back. He's a soldier. He's almost here. See?"

She pointed at two little tea stems, which formed a faint suggestion of a man with a musket on his back. He had climbed nearly to the edge of the cup. Mrs. Smith grew pale with excitement. She trembled so she could hardly hold the cup in her hand as she gazed into it.

"It's Ed," cried the old woman. "He's on the way home. Heavens an' earth! There he is now!" She turned and waved her hand out toward the road. They rushed to the door and looked where she pointed.

A man in a blue coat, with a musket on his back, was toiling slowly up the hill, on the sun-bright, dusty road, toiling slowly, with bent head half-hidden by a heavy knapsack. So tired it seemed that walking was indeed a process of falling. So eager to get home he would not stop, would not look aside, but plodded on, amid the cries of the locusts, the welcome of the crickets, and the rustle of the yellow wheat. Getting back to God's country, and his wife and babies!

Laughing, crying, trying to call him and the children at the same time, the little wife, almost hysterical, snatched her hat and ran out into the yard. But the soldier had disappeared over the hill into the hollowy beyond, and, by the time she had found the children, he was too far away for her voice to reach him. And besides, she was not sure it was her husband, for he had not turned his head at their shouts. This seemed so strange. Why didn't he stop to rest at his old neighbor's house? Tortured by hope and doubt, she hurried up the coulee as fast as she could push the baby wagon, the blue coated figure just ahead pushing steadily, silently forward up the coulee.

When the excited, panting little group came in sight of the gate, they saw the blue-coated figure standing, leaning upon the rough rail fence, his chin on his palms, gazing at the empty house. His knapsack, canteen, blankets, and musket lay upon the dusty grass at his feet.

He was like a man lost in a dream. His wide, hungry eyes devoured the scene. The rough lawn, the little unpainted house, the field of clear yellow wheat behind it, down across which streamed the sun, now almost ready to touch the high hill to the west, the crickets crying merrily, a cat on the fence nearby, dreaming, unmindful of the stranger in blue.

How peaceful it all was. O God! How far removed from all camps, hospitals, battlelines. A little cabin in a Wisconsin coulee, but it was majestic in its peace. How did he ever leave it for those years of tramping, thirsting, killing?

Trembling, weak with emotion, her eyes on the silent figure, Mrs. Smith hurried up to the fence. Her feet made no noise in the dust and grass, and they were close upon him before he knew of them. The oldest boy ran a little ahead. He will never forget that figure, that face. It will always remain as something epic, that return of the private. He fixed his eyes on the pale face, covered with a ragged beard.

"Who are you, sir?" asked the wife, or, rather, started to ask, for he turned, stood a moment, and then cried:

"Emma!"

"Edward!"

The children stood in a curious row to see their mother kiss this bearded, strange man, the elder girl sobbing sympathetically with her mother. Illness had left the soldier partly deaf, and this added to the strangeness of his manner.

But the boy of six years stood away, even after the girl had recognized her father and kissed him. The man turned then to the baby and said in a curiously unpaternal tone:

"Come here, my little man; don't you know me?" But the baby backed away under the fence and stood peering at him critically.

"My little man!" What meaning in those words! This baby seemed like some other woman's child, and not the infant he had left in his wife's arms. The war had come between him and his baby-he was only "a strange man, with big eyes, dressed in blue, with Mother hanging to his arm, and talking in a loud voice.

"And this is Tom," he said, drawing the oldest boy to him. "He'll come and see me. He knows his poor old pap when he comes home from the war."

The mother heard the pain and reproach in his voice and hastened to apologize.

"You've changed so, Ed. He can't know yeh. This is Papa, Teddy; come and kiss him-Tom and Mary do, Come, won't you?" But Teddy still peered through the fence with solemn eyes, well out of reach. He resembled a half-wild kitten that hesitates, studying the tones of one's voice.

"I'll fix him," said the soldier, and sat down to undo his knapsack, out of which he drew three enormous and very red apples. After giving one to each of the older children, he said:

"Now I guess he'll come. Eh, my little man? Now come see your pap."

Teddy crept slowly under the fence, assisted by the overzealous Tommy, and a moment later was kick-ing and squalling in his father's arms. Then they entered the house, into the sitting room, poor, bare, art-forsaken little room, too, with its rag carpet, its square clock, and its two or three chromos and pictures from Harper's Weekly pinned about.

"Emma, I'm all tired out," said Private Smith as he flung himself down on the carpet as he used to do, while his wife brought a pillow to put under his head, and the children stood about, munching their apples.

"Tommy, you run and get me a pan of chips; and Mary, you get the teakettle on, and I'll go and make some biscuit."

And the soldier talked. Question after question he poured forth about the crops, the cattle, the renter, the neighbors. He slipped his heavy government brogan shoes off his poor, tired, blistered feet, and lay out with utter, sweet relaxation. He was a free man again, no longer a soldier under command. At supper he stopped once, listened, and smiled. "That's old Spot. I know her voice. I s'pose that's her calf out there in the pen. I can't milk her tonight, though, I'm too tired; but I tell you, I'd like a drink o' her milk. What's become of old Rove?"

"He died last winter. Poisoned, I guess." There was a moment of sadness for them all. It was some time before the husband spoke again, in a voice that trembled a little.

"Poor old feller! He'd a known me a half a mile away. I expected him to come down the hill to meet me. It 'ud 'a' been more like comin' home if I could 'a' seen him comm' down the road an' waggin' his tail, an' laugh-in' that way he has. I tell yeh, it kin' o' took hold o' me to see the blinds down an' the house shut up."

"But, yeh see, we-we expected you'd write again 'fore you started. And then we thought we'd see you if you did come," she hastened to explain.

"Well, I ain't worth a cent on writin'. Besides, it's just as well yeh didn't know when I was comm'. I tell yeh, it sounds good to hear them chickens out there, an' turkeys, an' the crickets. Do you know they don't have just the same kind o' crickets down South. Who's Sam hired t' help cut yer grain?"

"The Ramsey boys."

"Looks like a good crop; but I'm afraid I won't do much gettin' it cut. This cussed fever an' ague has got me down pretty low. I don't know when I'll get red of it. I'll bet I've took twenty-five pounds of quinine, if I've taken a bit. Gimme another biscuit. I tell yeh, they taste good, Emma. I ain't had anything like it-Say, if you'd a heard me braggin' to th' boys about your butter 'n' biscuits, I'll bet your ears 'ud 'a' burnt."

The private's wife colored with pleasure. "Oh, you're always a-braggin' about your things. Everybody makes good butter."

"Yes; old lady Snyder, for instance."

"Oh, well, she ain't to be mentioned. She's Dutch."

"Or old Mis' Snively. One more cup o' tea, Mary. That's my girl! I'm feeling better already. I just b'lieve the matter with me is, I'm starved."

This was a delicious hour, one long to be remembered. They were like lovers again. But their tenderness, like that of a typical American, found utterance in tones, rather than in words. He was praising her when praising her biscuit, and she knew it. They grew soberer when he showed where he had been struck, one ball burning the back of his hand, one cutting away a lock of hair from his temple, and one passing through the calf of his leg. The wife shuddered to think how near she had come to being a soldier's widow. Her waiting no longer seemed hard. This sweet, glorious hour effaced it all.

Then they rose and all went out into the garden and down to the barn. He stood beside her while she milked old Spot. They began to plan fields and crops for next year. Here was the epic figure which Whitman has in mind, and which he calls the "common American soldier." With the livery of war on his limbs, this man was facing his future, his thoughts holding no scent of battle. Clean, clear-headed, in spite of physical weakness, Edward Smith, private, turned future-ward with a sublime courage.

His farm was mortgaged, a rascally renter had run away with his machinery, "departing between two days," his children needed clothing, the years were coming upon him, he was sick and emaciated, but his heroic soul did not quail. With the same courage with which he faced his southern march, be entered upon a still more hazardous future.

Oh, that mystic hour! The pale man with big eyes standing there by the well, with his young wife by his side. The vast moon swinging above the eastern peaks; the cattle winding down the pasture slopes with jangling bells; the crickets singing; the stars blooming out sweet and far and serene; the katydids rhythmically calling; the little turkeys crying querulously as they settled to roost in the poplar tree near the open gate. The voices at the well drop lower, the little ones nestle in their father's arms at last, and Teddy falls asleep there.

The common soldier of the American volunteer army had returned. His war with the South was over, and his fight, his daily running fight, with nature and against the injustice of his fellow men was begun again. In tlie dusk of that far-off valley his figure looms vast, his personal peculiarities fade away, he rises into a magnificent type.

He is a gray-haired man of sixty now, and on the brown hair of his wife the white is also showing. They are fighting a hopeless battle, and must fight till God gives them furlough.

5. UNDER THE LION'S PAW

"Along the main-travelled road trailed an endless line of prairie schooners. Coming into sight at the east, and passing out of sight over the swell to the west. We children used to wonder where they were going and why they went."

IT was the last of autumn and first day of winter coming together. All day long the ploughmen on their prairie farms had moved to and fro in their wide level fields through the falling snow, which melted as it fell, wetting them to the skin all day, notwithstanding the frequent squalls of snow, the dripping, desolate clouds, and the muck of the furrows, black and tenacious as tar.

Under their dripping harness the horses swung to and fro silently with that marvellous uncomplaining patience which marks the horse. All day the wild geese, honking wildly, as they sprawled sidewise down the wind, seemed to be fleeing from an enemy behind, and with neck outthrust and wings extended, sailed down the wind, soon lost to sight.

Yet the ploughman behind his plough, though the snow lay on his ragged great-coat, and the cold clinging mud rose on his heavy boots, fettering him like gyves, whistled in the very beard of the gale. As day passed, the snow, ceasing to melt, lay along the ploughed land, and lodged in the depth of the stubble, till on each slow round the last furrow stood out black and shining as jet between the ploughed land and the gray stubble.

When night began to fall, and the geese, flying low, began to alight invisibly in the near corn-field, Stephen Council was still at work "finishing a land." He rode on his sulky plough when going with the wind, but walked when facing it. Sitting bent and cold but cheery under his slouch hat, he talked encouragingly to his four-in-hand.

"Come round there, boys! Round agin! We got t' finish this land. Come in there, Dan! Stiddy, Kate, stiddy! None o' y'r tantrums, Kittie. It's purty tuff, but got a be did. Tchk! tchk! Step along, Pete! Don't let Kate git y'r single-tree on the wheel. Once more!"

They seemed to know what he meant, and that this was the last round, for they worked with greater vigor than before. "Once more, boys, an' then, sez I, oats an' a nice warm stall, an' sleep f'r all."

By the time the last furrow was turned on the land it was too dark to see the house, and the snow was changing to rain again. The tired and hungry man could see the light from the kitchen shining through the leafless hedge, and he lifted a great shout, "Supper f'r a half a dozen!"

It was nearly eight o'clock by the time he had finished his chores and started for supper. He was picking his way carefully through the mud, when the tall form of a man loomed up before him with a premonitory cough.

"Waddy ye want?" was the rather startled question of the farmer.

"Well, ye see," began the stranger, in a deprecating tone, "we'd like t' git in f'r the night. We've tried every house f'r the last two miles, but they hadn't any room f'r us. My wife's jest about sick, 'n' the children are cold and hungry— "

"Oh, y' want 'o stay all night, eh,?"

"Yes, sir; it 'ud be a great accom— "

"Waal, I don't make it a practice t' turn anybuddy way hungry, not on sech nights as this. Drive right in. We ain't got much, but sech as it is—"

But the stranger had disappeared. And soon his steaming, weary team, with drooping heads and swinging single-trees, moved past the well to the block beside the path. Council stood at the side of the "schooner" and helped the children out two little half- sleeping children and then a small woman with a babe in her arms.

"There ye go!" he shouted jovially, to the children. "Now we're all right! Run right along to the house there, an' tell Mam' Council you wants sumpthin' t' eat. Right this way, Mis' keep right off t' the right there. I'll go an' git a lantern. Come," he said to the dazed and silent group at his side.

"Mother'" he shouted, as he neared the fragrant and warmly lighted kitchen, "here are some wayfarers an' folks who need sumpthin' t' eat an' a place t' snoot." He ended by pushing them all in.

Mrs. Council, a large, jolly, rather coarse-looking woman, too the children in her arms. "Come right in, you little rabbits. 'Mos asleep, hey? Now here's a drink o' milk f'r each o' ye. I'll have sam tea in a minute. Take off y'r things and set up t' the fire."

While she set the children to drinking milk, Council got out his lantern and went out to the barn to help the stranger about his team, where his loud, hearty voice could be heard as it came and went between the haymow and the stalls.

The woman came to light as a small, timid, and discouraged looking woman, but still pretty, in a thin and sorrowful way.

"Land sakes! An' you've travelled all the way from Clear Lake' t'-day in this mud! Waal! Waal! No wonder you're all tired out Don't wait f'r the men, Mis'— " She hesitated, waiting for the name.

"Haskins."

"Mis' Haskins, set right up to the table an' take a good swig o tea whilst I make y' s'm toast. It's green tea, an' it's good. I tell Council as I git older I don't seem to enjoy Young Hyson n'r Gunpowder. I want the reel green tea, jest as it comes off'n the vines. Seems t' have more heart in it, some way. Don't s'pose it has. Council says it's all in m' eye."

Going on in this easy way, she soon had the children filled with bread and milk and the woman thoroughly at home, eating some toast and sweet-melon pickles, and sipping the tea.

"See the little rats!" she laughed at the children. "They're full as they can stick now, and they want to go to bed. Now, don't git up, Mis' Haskins; set right where you are an' let me look after 'em. I know all about young ones, though I'm all alone now. Jane went an' married last fall. But, as I tell Council, it's lucky we keep our health. Set right there, Mis' Haskins; I won't have you stir a finger."

It was an unmeasured pleasure to sit there in the warm, homely kitchen. the jovial chatter of the housewife driving out and holding at bay the growl of the impotent, cheated wind.

The little woman's eyes filled with tears which fell down upon the sleeping baby in her arms. The world was not so desolate and cold and hopeless, after all.

"Now I hope. Council won't stop out there and talk politics all night. He's the greatest man to talk politics an' read the Tribune—How old is it?"

She broke off and peered down at the face of the babe.

"Two months 'n' five days," said the mother, with a mother's exactness.

"Ye don't say! I want 'o know! The dear little pudzy-wudzy!" she went on, stirring it up in the neighborhood of the ribs with her fat forefinger.

"Pooty tough on 'oo to go gallivant'n' 'cross lots this way—"

"Yes, that's so; a man can't lift a mountain," said Council, entering the door. "Mother, this is Mr. Haskins, from Kansas. He's been eat up 'n' drove out by grasshoppers."

"Glad t' see yeh! Pa, empty that wash-basin 'n' give him a chance t' wash." Haskins was a tall man, with a thin, gloomy face. His hair was a reddish brown, like his coat, and seemed equally faded by the wind and sun, and his sallow face, though hard and set, was pathetic somehow. You would have felt that he had suffered much by the line of his mouth showing under his thin, yellow mustache.

"Hadn't Ike got home yet, Sairy?"

"Hadn't seen 'im."

"W-a-a-l, set right up, Mr. Haskins; wade right into what we've got; 'taint much, but we manage to live on it she gits fat on it," laughed Council, pointing his thumb at his wife.

After supper, while the women put the children to bed, Haskins and Council talked on, seated near the huge cooking-stove, the steam rising from their wet clothing. In the Western fashion Council told as much of his own life as he drew from his guest. He asked but few questions, but by and by the story of Haskins' struggles and defeat came out. The story was a terrible one, but he told it quietly, seated with his elbows on his knees, gazing most of the time at the hearth.

"I didn't like the looks of the country, anyhow," Haskins said, partly rising and glancing at his wife. "I was ust t' northern Ingyannie, where we have lots o' timber 'n' lots o' rain, 'n' I didn't like the looks o' that dry prairie. What galled me the worst was goin' s' far away acrosst so much fine land layin' all through here vacant.

"And the 'hoppers eat ye four years, hand runnin', did they?" "Eat! They wiped us out. They chawed everything that was green. They jest set around waitin' f'r us to die t' eat us, too. My God! I ust t' dream of 'em sittin' 'round on the bedpost, six feet long, workin' their jaws. They eet the fork-handles. They got worse 'n' worse till they jest rolled on one another, piled up like snow in winter Well, it ain't no use. If I was t' talk all winter I couldn't tell nawthin'. But all the while I couldn't help thinkin' of all that land back here that nobuddy was usin' that I ought 'o had 'stead o' bein' out there in that cussed country."

"Waal, why didn't ye stop an' settle here?" asked Ike, who had come in and was eating his supper.

"Fer the simple reason that you fellers wantid ten 'r fifteen dollars an acre fer the bare land, and I hadn't no money fer that kind o' thing."

"Yes, I do my own work," Mrs. Council was heard to say in the pause which followed. "I'm a gettin' purty heavy t' be on m'laigs all day, but we can't afford t' hire, so I keep rackin' around somehow, like a foundered horse. S' lame I tell Council he can't tell how lame I am, f'r I'm jest as lame in one laig as t' other." And the good soul laughed at the joke on herself as she took a handful of flour and dusted the biscuit-board to keep the dough from sticking.

"Well, I hadn't never been very strong," said Mrs. Haskins. "Our folks was Canadians an' small-boned, and then since my last child I hadn't got up again fairly. I don't like t' complain. Tim has about all he can bear now but they was days this week when I jest wanted to lay right down an' die."

"Waal, now, I'll tell ye," said Council, from his side of the stove silencing everybody with his good-natured roar, "I'd go down and see Butler, anyway, if I was you. I guess he'd let you have his place purty cheap; the farm's all run down. He's teen anxious t' let t' somebuddy next year. It 'ud be a good chance fer you. Anyhow, you go to bed and sleep like a babe. I've got some ploughing t' do, anyhow, an' we'll see if somethin' can't be done about your case. Ike, you go out an' see if the horses is all right, an' I'll show the folks t' bed."

When the tired husband and wife were lying under the generous quilts of the spare bed, Haskins listened a moment to the wind in the eaves, and then said, with a slow and solemn tone,

"There are people in this world who are good enough t' be angels, an' only haff t' die to be angels."

Jim Butler was one of those men called in the West "land poor. " Early in the history of Rock River he had come into the town and started in the grocery business in a small way, occupying a small building in a mean part of the town. At this period of his life he earned all he got, and was up early and late sorting beans, working over butter, and carting his goods to and from the station. But a change came over him at the end of the second year, when he sold a lot of land for four times what he paid for it. From that time forward he believed in land speculation as the surest way of getting rich. Every cent he could save or spare from his trade he put into land at forced sale, or mortgages on land, which were "just as good as the wheat," he was accustomed to say.

Farm after farm fell into his hands, until he was recognized as one of the leading landowners of the county. His mortgages were scattered all over Cedar County, and as they slowly but surely fell in he sought usually to retain the former owner as tenant.

He was not ready to foreclose; indeed, he had the name of being one of the "easiest" men in the town. He let the debtor off again and again, extending the time whenever possible.

"I don't want y'r land," he said. "All I'm after is the int'rest on my money that's all. Now, if y' want 'o stay on the farm, why, I'll give y' a good chance. I can't have the land layin' vacant. " And in many cases the owner remained as tenant.

In the meantime he had sold his store; he couldn't spend time in it—he was mainly occupied now with sitting around town on rainy days smoking and "gassin' with the boys," or in riding to and from his farms. In fishing-time he fished a good deal. Doc Grimes, Ben Ashley, and Cal Cheatham were his cronies on these fishing excursions or hunting trips in the time of chickens or partridges. In winter they went to Northern Wisconsin to shoot deer.

In spite of all these signs of easy life Butler persisted in saying he "hadn't enough money to pay taxes on his land," and was careful to convey the impression that he was poor in spite of his twenty farms. At one time he was said to be worth fifty thousand dollars, but land had been a little slow of sale of late, so that he was not worth so much.

A fine farm, known as the Higley place, had fallen into his hands in the usual way the previous year, and he had not been able to find a tenant for it. Poor Higley, after working himself nearly to death on it in the attempt to lift the mortgage, had gone off to Dakota, leaving the farm and his curse to Butler.

This was the farm which Council advised Haskins to apply for; and the next day Council hitched up his team and drove down to see Butler.

"You jest let me do the talkin'," he said. "We'll find him wearin' out his pants on some salt barrel somew'ers; and if he thought you wanted a place he'd sock it to you hot and heavy. You jest keep quiet, I'll fix 'im."

Butler was seated in Ben Ashley's store telling fish yarns when Council sauntered in casually.

"Hello, But; lyin' agin, hey?"

"Hello, Steve! How goes it?"

"Oh, so-so. Too clang much rain these days. I thought it was goin' t freeze up f r good last night. Tight squeak if I get m' ploughin' done. How's farmin' with you these days?"

"Bad. Ploughin' ain't half done."

"It 'ud be a religious idee f r you t' go out an' take a hand y'rself."

"I don't haff to," said Butler, with a wink.

"Got anybody on the Higley place?"

"No. Know of anybody?"

"Waal, no; not eggsackly. I've got a relation back t' Michigan who's ben hot an' cold on the idea o' comin' West f r some time. Might come if he could get a good lay-out. What do you talk on the farm?"

"Well, I d' know. I'll rent it on shares or I'll rent it money rent."

"Waal, how much money, say?"

"Well, say ten per cent, on the price two-fifty."

"Wall, that ain't bad. Wait on 'im till 'e thrashes?"

Haskins listened eagerly to this important question, but Council was coolly eating a dried apple which he had speared out of a barrel with his knife. Butler studied him carefully.

"Well, knocks me out of twenty-five dollars interest."

"My relation'll need all he's got t' git his crops in," said Council, in the same, indifferent way.

"Well, all right; say wait," concluded Butler.

"All right; this is the man. Haskins, this is Mr. Butler no relation to Ben the hardest-working man in Cedar County."

On the way home Haskins said: "I ain't much better off. I'd like that farm; it's a good farm, but it's all run down, an' so 'm I. I could make a good farm of it if I had half a show. But I can't stock it n'r seed it."

"Waal, now, don't you worry," roared Council in his ear. "We'll pull y' through somehow till next harvest. He's agreed t' hire it ploughed, an' you can earn a hundred dollars ploughin' an' y' c'n git the seed o' me, an' pay me back when y' can."

Haskins was silent with emotion, but at last he said, "I ain't got nothin' t' live on."

"Now, don't you worry 'bout that. You jest make your headquarters at ol' Steve Council's. Mother'll take a pile o' comfort in havin' y'r wife an' children 'round.

Y' see, Jane's married off lately, an' Ike's away a good 'eal, so we'll be darn glad t' have y' stop with us this winter. Nex' spring we'll see if y' can't git a start agin." And he chirruped to the team, which sprang forward with the rumbling, clattering wagon.

"Say, looky here, Council, you can't do this. I never saw " shouted Haskins in his neighbor's ear.

Council moved about uneasily in his seat and stopped his stammering gratitude by saying: "Hold on, now; don't make such a fuss over a little thing. When I see a man down, an' things all on top of 'm, I jest like t' kick 'em off an' help 'm up. That's the kind of religion I got, an' it's about the only kind."

They rode the rest of the way home in silence. And when the red light of the lamp shone out into the darkness of the cold and windy night, and he thought of this refuge for his children and wife, Haskins could have put his arm around the neck of his burly companion and squeezed him like a lover. But he contented himself with saying, "Steve Council, you'll git y'r pay f'r this some day."

"Don't want any pay. My religion ain't run on such business principles."

The wind was growing colder, and the ground was covered with a white frost, as they turned into the gate of the Council farm, and the children came rushing out, shouting, "Papa's come!" They hardly looked like the same children who had sat at the table the night before. Their torpidity, under the influence of sunshine and Mother Council, had given way to a sort of spasmodic cheerfulness, as insects in winter revive when laid on the hearth.

Haskins worked like a fiend, and his wife, like the heroic woman that she was, bore also uncomplainingly the most terrible burdens. They rose early and toiled without intermission till the darkness fell on the plain, then tumbled into bed, every bone and muscle aching with fatigue, to rise with the sun next morning to the same round of the same ferocity of labor.

The eldest boy drove a team all through the spring, ploughing and seeding, milked the cows, and did chores innumerable, in most ways taking the place of a man.

An infinitely pathetic but common figure this boy on the American farm, where there is no law against child labor. To see him in his coarse clothing, his huge boots, and his ragged cap, as he staggered with a pail of water from the well, or trudged in the cold and cheerless dawn out into the frosty field behind his team, gave the city-bred visitor a sharp pang of sympathetic pain. Yet Haskins loved his boy, and would have saved him from this if he could, but he could not.

By June the first year the result of such Herculean toil began to show on the farm. The yard was cleaned up and sown to grass, the garden ploughed and planted, and the house mended.

Council had given them four of his cows.

"Take 'em an' run 'em on shares. I don't want 'o milk s' many. Ike's away s' much now, Sat'd'ys an' Sund'ys, I can't stand the bother anyhow."

Other men, seeing the confidence of Council in the newcomer, had sold him tools on time; and as he was really an able farmer, he soon had round him many evidences of his care and thrift. At the advice of Council he had taken the farm for three years, with the privilege of re-renting or buying at the end of the term.

"It's a good bargain, an' y' want 'o nail it," said Council. "If you have any kind ov a crop, you c'n pay y'r debts, an' keep seed an' bread."

The new hope which now sprang up in the heart of Haskins and his wife grew almost as a pain by the time the wide field of wheat began to wave and rustle and swirl in the winds of July. Day after day he would snatch a few moments after supper to go and look at it.

"'Have ye seen the wheat t'-day, Nettie?" he asked one night as he rose from supper.

"No, Tim, I ain't had time."

"Well, take time now. Le's go look at it."

She threw an old hat on her head Tommy's hat and looking almost pretty in her thin, sad way, went out with her husband to the hedge.

"Ain't it grand, Nettie? Just look at it."

It was grand. Level, russet here and there, heavy-headed, wide as a lake, and full of multitudinous whispers and gleams of wealth, it stretched away before the gazers like the fabled field of the cloth of gold.

"Oh, I think I hope we'll have a good crop, Tim; and oh, how good the people have been to us!"

"Yes; I don't know where we'd be t'-day if it hadn't teen f'r Council and his wife."

"They're the best people in the world," said the little woman, with a great sob of gratitude.

"We'll be in the field on Monday sure," said Haskins, gripping the rail on the fences as if already at the work of the harvest.

The harvest came, bounteous, glorious, but the winds came and blew it into tangles, and the rain matted it here and there close to the ground, increasing the work of gathering it threefold.

Oh, how they toiled in those glorious days! Clothing dripping with sweat, arms aching, filled with briers, fingers raw and bleeding, backs broken with the weight of heavy bundles, Haskins and his man toiled on. Tummy drove the harvester, while his father and a hired man bound on the machine. In this way they cut ten acres every day, and almost every night after supper, when the hand went to bed, Haskins returned to the field shocking the bound grain in the light of the moon. Many a night he worked till his anxious wife came out at ten o'clock to call him in to rest and lunch. At the same time she cooked for the men, took care of the children, washed and ironed, milked the cows at night, made the butter, and sometimes fed the horses and watered them while her husband kept at the shocking.

No slave in the Roman galleys could have toiled so frightfully and lived, for this man thought himself a free man, and that he was working for his wife and babes.

When he sank into his bed with a deep groan of relief, too tired to change his grimy, dripping clothing, he felt that he was getting nearer and nearer to a home of his own, and pushing the wolf of want a little farther from his door.

There is no despair so deep as the despair of a homeless man or woman. To roam the roads of the country or the streets of the city, to feel there is no rood of ground on which the feet can rest, to halt weary and hungry outside lighted windows and hear laughter and song within, these are the hungers and rebellions that drive men to crime and women to shame.

It was the memory of this homelessness, and the fear of its coming again, that spurred Tnothy Haskins and Nettie, his wife, to such ferocious labor during that first year.

"'M, yes; 'm, yes; first-rate," said Butler, as his eye took in the neat garden, the pig-pen, and the well-filled barnyard. "You're gitt'n' quite a stock around yeh. Done well, eh?" Haskins was showing Butler around the place. He had not seen it for a year, having spent the year in Washington and Boston with Ashley, his brother-in-law, who had been elected to Congress.

"Yes, I've laid out a good deal of money durin' the last three years. I've paid out three hundred dollars f'r fencin'."

"Um h'm! I see, I see," said Butler, while Haskins went on:

"The kitchen there cost two hundred; the barn ain't cost much in money, but I've put a lot o' time on it. I've dug a new well, and I— "

"Yes, yes, I see. You've done well. Stock worth a thousand dollars, " said Butler, picking his teeth with a straw.

"About that," said Haskins, modestly. "We begin to feel's if we was gitt'n' a home f'r ourselves; but we've worked hard. I tell you we begin to feel it, Mr. Butler, and we're goin' t' begin to ease up purty soon. We've been kind o' plannin' a trip back t' her folks after the fall ploughin's done."

"Eggs-actly!" said Butler, who was evidently thinking of something else. "I suppose you've kind o' calc'lated on stayin' here three years more?"

"Well, yes. Fact is, I think I c'n buy the farm this fall, if you'll give me a reasonable show."

"Um m! What do you call a reasonable show?"

"Well, say a quarter down and three years' time."

Butler looked at the huge stacks of wheat, which filled the yard, over which the chickens were fluttering and crawling, catching grasshoppers, and out of which the crickets were singing innumerably. He smiled in a peculiar way as he said, "Oh, I won't be hard on yeh. But what did you expect to pay f'r the place?"

"Why, about what you offered it for before, two thousand five hundred, or possibly three thousand dollars," he added quickly, as he saw the owner shake his head.

"This farm is worth five thousand and five hundred dollars," said Butler, in a careless and decided voice.

"What!" almost shrieked the astounded Haskins. "What's that? Five thousand? Why, that's double what you offered it for three years ago."

"Of course, and it's worth it. It was all run down then—now it's in good shape. You've laid out fifteen hundred dollars in improvements, according to your own story."

"But you had nothin' t' do about that. It's my work an' my money. "

"You bet it was; but it's my land."

"But what's to pay me for all my— "

"Ain't you had the use of 'em?" replied Butler, smiling calmly into his face.

Haskins was like a man struck on the head with a sandbag; he couldn't think; he stammered as he tried to say: "But I never'd git the use You'd rob me! More'n that: you agreed you promised that I could buy or rent at the end of three years at— "

"That's all right. But I didn't say I'd let you carry off the improvements, nor that I'd go on renting the farm at two-fifty. The land is doubled in value, it don't matter how; it don't enter into the question; an' now you can pay me five hundred dollars a year rent, or take it on your own terms at fifty-five hundred, or git out."

He was turning away when Haskins, the sweat pouring from his face, fronted him, saying again:

"But you've done nothing to make it so. You hadn't added a cent. I put it all there myself, expectin' to buy. I worked an' sweat to improve it. I was workin' for myself an' babes— "

"Well, why didn't you buy when I offered to sell? What y' kickin' about?"

"I'm kickin' about payin' you twice f'r my own things, my own fences, my own kitchen, my own garden."

Butler laughed. "You're too green t' eat, young feller. Your improvements! The law will sing another tune."

"But I trusted your word."

"Never trust anybody, my friend. Besides, I didn't promise not to do this thing. Why, man, don't look at me like that. Don't take me for a thief. It's the law. The reg'lar thing. Everybody does it."

"I don't care if they do. It's stealin' jest the same. You take three thousand dollars of my money the work o' my hands and my wife's." He broke down at this point. He was not a strong man mentally. He could face hardship, ceaseless toil, but he could not face the cold and sneering face of Butler.

"But I don't take it," said Butler, coolly "All you've got to do is to go on jest as you've been a-coin', or give me a thousand dollars down, and a mortgage at ten per cent on the rest."

Haskins sat down blindly on a bundle of oats near by, and with staring eyes and drooping head went over the situation. He was under the lion's paw. He felt a horrible numbness in his heart and limbs. He was hid in a mist, and there was no path out.

Butler walked about, looking at the huge stacks of grain, and pulling now and again a few handfuls out, shelling the heads in his hands and blowing the chaff away. He hummed a little tune as he did so. He had an accommodating air of waiting.

Haskins was in the midst of the terrible toil of the last year. He was walking again in the rain and the mud behind his plough - he felt the dust and dirt of the threshing. The ferocious husking- time, with its cutting wind and biting, clinging snows, lay hard upon him. Then he thought of his wife, how she had cheerfully cooked and baked, without holiday and without rest.

"Well, what do you think of it?" inquired the cool, mocking, insinuating voice of Butler.

"I think you're a thief and a liar!" shouted Haskins, leaping up. "A black-hearted houn'!" Butler's smile maddened him; with a sudden leap he caught a fork in his hands, and whirled it in the air. "You'll never rob another man, damn ye!" he grated through his teeth, a look of pitiless ferocity in his accusing eyes.

Butler shrank and quivered, expecting the blow; stood, held hypnotized by the eyes of the man he had a moment before despised a man transformed into an avenging demon. But in the deadly hush between the lift of the weapon and its fall there came a gush of faint, childish laughter and then across the range of his vision, far away and dim, he saw the sun-bright head of his baby girl, as, with the pretty, tottering run of a two-year-old, she moved across the grass of the dooryard. His hands relaxed: the fork fell to the ground; his head lowered.

"Make out y'r deed an' mor'gage, an' git off'n my land, an' don't ye never cross my line agin; if y' do, I'll kill ye."

Butler backed away from the man in wild haste, and climbing into his buggy with trembling limbs drove off down the road, leaving Haskins seated dumbly on the sunny pile of sheaves, his head sunk into his hands.

6. THE CREAMERY MAN

"Along these woods in storm and sun the busy people go."

THE tin-peddler has gone out of the West. Amiable gossip and sharp trader that he was, his visits once brought a sharp business grapple to the farmer's wife and daughters, after which, as the man of trade was repacking his unsold wares, a moment of cheerful talk often took place. It was his cue, if he chanced to be a tactful peddler, to drop all attempts at sale and become distinctly human and neighborly.

His calls were not always well received, but they were at their best pleasant breaks of a monotonous round of duties. But he is no longer a familiar spot on the landscape. He has passed into the limbo of the things no longer necessary. His red wagon may be rumbling and rattling through some newer region, but the "coulee country" knows him no more.

'The creamery man" has taken his place. Every afternoon, rain or shine, the wagons of the North Star Creamery in "Dutcher's Coulee" stop at the farmers' windmills to skim the cream from the "submerged cans." His wagon is not gay; it is generally battered and covered with mud and filled with tall cans; but the driver himself is generally young and sometimes attractive. The driver in Molasses Gap, which is a small coulee leading into Dutcher's Coulee was particularly good-looking and amusing.

He was aware of his good looks, and his dress not only showed that he was single, but that he hoped to be married soon. He wore brown trousers, which fitted him very well, and a dark-blue shirt, which had a gay lacing of red cord in front, and a pair of suspenders that were a vivid green. On his head he wore a Chinese straw helmet; which was as ugly as anything could conceivably be, but he was as proud of it as he was of his green suspenders. In summer he wore no coat at all, and even in pretty cold weather he left his vest on his wagon seat, not being able to bring himself to the point of covering up the red and green of his attire.

It was noticeable that the women of the neighborhood always came out, even on washday, to see that Claude (his name was Claude Willlams) measured the cream properly. There was much banter about this. Mrs. Kennedy always said she wouldn't trust him "fur's you can fling a yearlin' bull by the tail."

"Now that's the difference between us," he would reply. "I'd trust you anywhere. Anybody with such a daughter as your'n"

He seldom got further, for Lucindy always said (in substance), "Oh, you go 'long."

There need be no mystery in the matter. 'Cindy was the girl for whose delight he wore the green and red. He made no secret of his love, and she made no secret of her scorn. She laughed at his green 'spenders and the "red shoestring" in his shirt; but Claude considered himself very learned in women's ways, by reason of two years' driving the creamery wagon, and be merely winked at Mrs.

Kennedy when the girl was looking, and kissed his hand at 'Cindy when her mother was not looking.

He looked forward every afternoon to these little exchanges of wit, and was depressed when for any reason the womenfolks were away. There were other places pleasanter than the Kennedy farm-some of "the Dutchmen" had fine big brick houses and finer and bigger barns, but their women were mostly homely and went around barefooted and barelegged, with ugly blue dresses hanging frayed and greasy round their lank ribs and big joints.

"Some way their big houses have a look like a stable when you get close to 'em," Claude said to 'Cindy once. "Their women work so much in the field they don't have any time to fix up-the way you do. I don't believe in women workin' in the fields." He said this looking 'Cindy in the face. "My wife needn't set her foot outdoors 'less she's a mind to."

"Oh, you can talk," replied the girl scornfully, "but you'd be like the rest of 'em." But she was glad that she had on a clean collar and apron-if it was ironing day.

What Claude would have said further 'Cindy could not divine, for her mother called her away, as she generally did when she saw her daughter lingering too long with the creamery man. Claude was not considered a suitable match for Lucindy Kennedy, whose father owned one of the finest farms in the coulee. Worldly considerations hold in Molasses Gap as well as in Bluff Siding and Tyre.

But Claude gave little heed to these moods in Mrs. Kennedy. If 'Cindy sputtered, he laughed; and if she smiled, he rode on whistling till he came to old man Haldeman's, who owned the whole lower half of Molasses Gap, and had one unmarried daughter, who thought Claude one of the handsomest men in the world. She was always at the gate to greet him as he drove up, and forced sections of cake and pieces of gooseberry pie upon him each day.

"She's good enough-for a Dutchman," Claude said of her, "but I hate to see a woman go around looking as if her clothes would drop off if it rained on her. And on Sundays, when she dresses up, she looks like a boy rigged out in some girl's cast-off duds."

This was pretty hard on Nina. She was tall and lank and sandy, with small blue eyes, her limbs were heavy, and she did wear her Sunday clothes badly, but she was a good, generous soul and very much in love with the creamery man. She was not very clean, but then she could not help that; the dust of the field is no respecter of sex. No, she was not lovely, but she was the only daughter of old Ernest Haldeman, and the old man was not very strong.

Claude was the daily bulletin of the Gap. He knew whose cow died the night before, who was at the strawberry dance, and all about Abe Anderson's night in jail up at the Siding. If his coming was welcome to the Kennedy's, who took the Bluff Siding Gimlet and the county paper, how much the more cordial ought his greeting to be at Haldeman's, where they only took the Milwaukee Weekly Freiheit.

Nina in her poor way had longings and aspirations. She wanted to marry "a Yankee," and not one of her own kind. She had a little schooling obtained at the small brick shed under the towering cottonwood tree at the corner of her father's farm; but her life had been one of hard work and mighty little play. Her parents spoke in German about the farm, and could speak English only very brokenly. Her only brother had adventured into the foreign parts of Pine County and had been killed in a sawmill. Her life was lonely and hard.

She had suitors among the Germans, plenty of them, but she had a disgust of them-considered as possible husbands-and though she went to their beery dances occasionally, she had always in her mind the ease, lightness, and color of Claude. She knew that the Yankee girls did not work in the fields-even the Norwegian girls seldom did so now, they worked out in town-but she had been brought up to hoe and pull weeds from her childhood, and her father and mother considered it good for her, and being a gentle and obedient child, she still continued to do as she was told. Claude pitied the girl, and used to talk with her, during his short stay, in his cheeriest manner.

"Hello, Nina! How you vass, ain't it? How much cream already you got this morning? Did you hear the news, not?"

"No, vot hass happened?"

"Everything. Frank Mcvey's horse stepped through the bridge and broke his leg, and he's going to sue the county-mean Frank is, not the horse."

"Iss dot so?"

"Sure! and Bill Hetner had a fight, and Julia Dooriliager's got home."

"Vot wass Bill fightding apoudt?"

"Oh, drunk-fighting for exercise. Hain't got a fresh pie cut?"

Her face lighted up, and she turned so suddenly to go that her bare leg showed below her dress. Her unstockinged feet were thrust into coarse working shoes. Claude wrinkled his nose in disgust, but he took the piece of green currant pie on the palm of his hand and bit the acute angle from it.

"First-rate. You do make lickin' good pies," he said Out of pure kindness of heart, and Nina was radiant.

"She wouldn't be so bad-lookin' if they didn't work her in the fields like a horse," he said to himself as he drove away.

The neighbors were well aware of Nina's devotion, and Mrs. Smith, who lived two or three houses down the road, said, "Good evening, Claude. Seen Nina today?"

"Sure! and she gave me a piece of currant pie-her own make."

"Did you eat it?"

"Did I? I guess yes. I ain't refusin' pie from Nina-not while her pa has five hundred acres of the best land in Molasses Gap."

Now, it was this innocent joking on his part that started all Claude's trouble. Mrs. Smith called a couple of days later and had her joke with 'Cindy.

"'Cindy, your cake's all dough."

"Why, what's the matter now?"

"Claude come along t'other day grinnin' from ear to ear, and some currant pie in his musstache. He had jest fixed it up with Nina. He jest as much as said he was after the old man's acres."

"Well, let him have 'em. I don't know as it interests me," replied 'Cindy, waving her head like a banner. "If he wants to sell himself to that greasy Dutchwoman why, let him, that's all! I don't care."

Her heated manner betrayed her to Mrs. Smith, who laughed with huge enjoyment.

"Well, you better watch out!"

The next day was very warm, and when Claude drove up under the shade of the big maples he was ready for a chat while his horses rested, but 'Cindy was nowhere to be seen. Mrs. Kennedy came out to get the amount of the skimming and started to re-enter the house without talk.

"Where's the young folks?" asked Claude carelessly.

"If you mean Lucindy, she's in the house."

"Ain't sick or nothin', is she?"

"Not that anybody knows of. Don't expect her to be here to gass with you every time, do ye?"

"Well, I wouldn't mind"' replied Claude. He was too keen not to see his chance. "In fact, I'd like to have her with me all the time, Mrs. Kennedy," he said with engaging frankness.

"Well, you can't have her," the mother replied ungraciously.

"What's the matter with me?"

"Oh, I like you well enough, but 'Cindy'd be a big fool to marry a man without a roof to cover his head."

"That's where you take your inning, sure," Claude replied. "I'm not much better than a hired hand. Well, now, see here, I'm going to make a strike one of these days, and then-look out for me! You don't know but what I've invested in a gold mine. I may be a Dutch lord in disguise. Better not be brash."

Mrs. Kennedy's sourness could not stand against sueb sweetness and drollery. She smiled in wry fashion. "You'd better be moving, or you'll be late."

"Sure enough. If I only had you for a mother-in-law-that's why I'm so poor. Nobody to keep me moving. If I had someone to do the talking for me, I'd work." He grinned broadly and drove out.

His irritation led him to say some things to Nina which he would not have thought of saying the day before. She had been working in the field and had dropped her hoe to see him.

"Say, Nina, I wouldn't work outdoors such a day as this if I was you. I'd tell the old man to go to thunder, and I'd go in and wash up and look decent Yankee women don't do that kind of work, and your old dad's rich; no use of your sweatin' around a cornfield with a hoe in your hands. I don't like to see a woman goin' round without stockin's and her hands all chapped and calloused. It ain't accordin' to Hoyle. No, sir! I wouldn't stand it. I'd serve an injunction on the old man right now."

A dull, slow flush crept into the girl's face, and she put one hand over the other as they rested on the fence. One looked so much less monstrous than two.

Claude went on, "Yes, sir! I'd brace up and go to Yankee meeting instead of Dutch; you'd pick up a Yankee beau like as not."

He gathered his cream while she stood silently by, and when he looked at her again she was in deep thought.

"Good day," he said cheerily.

"Goodbye," she replied, and her face flushed again.

It rained that night, and the roads were very bad, and he was late the next time he arrived at Haldeman's. Nina came out in her best dress, but he said nothing about it, supposing she was going to town or something Like that, and he hurried through with his task and had mounted his seat before he realized that anything was wrong.

Then Mrs. Haldeman appeared at the kitchen door and hurled a lot of unintelligible German at him. He knew she was mad, and mad at him, and also' at Nina, for she shook her fist at them alternately.

Singular to tell, Nina paid no attention to her mother's sputter. She looked at Claude with a certain timid audacity.

"How you like me today?"

"That's better," he said as he eyed her critically. "Now you're talkin'! I'd do a little reading of the newspaper myself, if I was. you. A woman's business ain't to work out in the hot sun-it's to cook and fix up things round the house, and then put on her clean dress and set in the shade and read or sew on something. Stand up to 'em! Doggone me if I'd paddle round that hot cornfield with a mess o' Dutchmen-it ain't decent!"

He drove off with a chuckle at the old man, who was seated at the back of the house with a newspaper in his hand. He was lame, or pretended he was, and made his wife and daughter wait upon him. Claude had no conception of what was working in Nina's mind, but he could not help observing the changes for the better in her appearance. Each day he called she was neatly dressed and wore her shoes laced up to the very top hook.

She was passing through tribulation on his account, but she said nothing about it. The old man, her father, no longer spoke to her, and the mother sputtered continually, but the girl seemed sustained by some inner power. She calmly went about doing as she pleased, and no fury of words could check her or turn her aside.

Her hands grew smooth and supple once more, and her face lost the parboiled look it once had.

Claude noticed all these gains and commented on them with the freedom of a man who had established friendly relations with a child.

"I tell you what, Nina, you're coming along, sure. Next ground hop you'll be wearin' silk stockin's and high-heeled shoes. How's the old man? Still mad?"

"He don't speak to me no more. My mudder says I am a big fool."

"She does? Well, you tell her I think you're just getting sensible."

She smiled again, and there was a subtle quality in the mixture of boldness and timidity of her manner. His praise was so sweet and stimulating.

"I sold my pigs," she said. "The old man, he wass madt, but I didn't mind. I bought me a new dress with the money."

"That's right! I like to see a woman have plenty Of new dresses," Claude replied. He was really enjoying the girl's rebellion and growing womanliness.

Meanwhile his own affairs with Lucindy were in a bad way. He seldom saw her now. Mrs. Smith was careful to convey to her that Claude stopped longer than was necessary at Haldeman's, and so Mrs. Kennedy attended to the matter of recording the cream. Kennedy hersell was always in the field, and Claude had no opportunity for a conversation with him, as he very much wished to have. Once, when he saw 'Cindy in the kitchen at work, he left his team to rest in the shade and sauntered to the door and looked in.

She was kneading out cake dough, and she looked the loveliest thing he had ever seen. Her sleeves were rolled up. Her neat brown dress was covered with a big apron, and her collar was open a little at the throat, for it was warm in the kitchen. She frowned when she saw him.

He began jocularly. "Oh, thank you, I can wait till it bakes. No trouble at all."

"Well, it's a good deal of trouble to me to have you standin' there gappin' at me!"

"Ain't gappin' at you. I'm waitin' for the pie."

"'Tain't pie; it's cake."

"Oh, well, cake'll do for a change. Say, 'Cindy-"

"Don't call me 'Cindy!"

"Well, Lucindy. It's mighty lonesome when I don't see you on my trips."

"Oh, I guess you can stand it with Nina to talk to."

"Aha! jealous, are you?"

"Jealous of that Dutchwoman! I don't care who you talk to, and you needn't think it."

Claude was learned in woman's ways, and this pleased him mightily.

"Well, when shall I speak to your daddy?"

"I don't know what you mean, and I don't care."

"Oh, yes, you do. I'm going to come up here next Sunday in my best bib and tucker, and I'm going to say, 'Mr. Kennedy'-'~

The sound of Mrs. Kennedy's voice and footsteps approaching made Claude suddenly remember his duties.

"See ye later," he said with a grin. "I'll call for the cake next time."

"Call till you split your throat, if you want to," said 'Cindy.

Apparently this could have gone on indefinitely, but it didn't. Lucindy went to Minneapolis for a few weeks to stay with her brother, and that threw Claude deeper into despair than anything Mrs. Kennedy might do or any word Lucindy might say. It was a dreadful blow to him to have her pack up and go so suddenly and without one backward look at him, and, besides, he had planned taking her to Tyre on the Fourth of July.

Mr. Kennedy, much better-natured than the mother, told Claude where she had gone.

"By mighty! That's a knock on the nose for me. When did she go?"

"Yistady. I took her down to the Siding."

"When's she coming back?"

"Oh, after the hot weather is over; four or five weeks."

"I hope I'll be alive when she returns," said Claude gloomily.

Naturally he had a little more time to give to Nina and her remarkable doings, which had set the whole neighborhood to wondering "what had come over the girl."

She no longer worked in the field. She dressed better, and had taken to going to the most fashionable church in town. She was a woman transformed. Nothing was able to prevent her steady progression and bloom. She grew plumper and fairer and became so much more attractive that the young Germans thickened round her, and one or two Yankee boys looked her way. Through it all Claude kept up his half-humorous banter and altogether serious daily advice, without once realizing that any-thing sentimental connected him with it all. He knew she liked him, and sometimes he felt a little annoyed by her attempts to please him, but that she was doing all that she did and ordering her whole life to please him never entered his self-sufficient head.

There wasn't much room left in that head for anyone else except Lucindy, and his plans for wining her. Plan as he might, he saw no way of making more than the two dollars a day he was earning as a cream collector.

Things ran along thus from week to week till it was nearly time for Lucindy to return. Claude was having his top buggy repainted and was preparing for a vigorous campaign when Lucindy should be at home again. He owned his team and wagon and the buggy-nothing more.

One Saturday Mr. Kennedy said, "Lucindy's coming home. I'm going down after her tonight."

"Let me bring her up," said Claude with suspicious eagerness.

Mr. Kennedy hesitated. "No, I guess I'll go myself. I want to go to town, anyway."

Claude was in high spirits as he drove into Haldeman's yard that afternoon.

Nina was leaning over the fence singing softly to herself, but a fierce altercation was going on inside the house. The walls resounded. It was all Dutch to Claude, but he knew the old people were quarreling.

Nina smiled and colored as Claude drew up at the side gate. She seemed not to hear the eloquent discussion inside.

"What's going on?" asked Claude.

"Dey tink I am in house."

"How's that?"

"My mudder she lock me up."

Claude stared. "Locked you up? What for?"

"She tondt like it dot I come out to see you."

"Oh, she don't?" said Claude. "What's the matter o' me? I ain't a dangerous chap. I ain't eatin' up little. girls."

Nina went on placidly. "She saidt dot you was goin' to marry me undt' get the farm."

Claude grinned, then chuckied, and at last roared and whooped with the delight of it. He took off his hat and said:

"She said that, did she? Why, bless her old cabbage head-"

The opening of the door and the sudden irruption of Frau Haldeman interrupted him. She came rushing toward him like a she grizzly bear, uttering a torrent of German expletives, and hurled herself upon him, clutching at his hair and throat. He leaped aside and struck down her hands with a sweep of his hard right arm. As she turned to come again he shouted,

"Keep off! or I'll knock you down!"

But before the blow came Nina seized the infuriated woman from behind and threw her down, and held her till the old man came hobbling to the rescue. He seemed a little dazed by it all and made no effort to assault Claude.

The old woman, who was already black in the face with rage, suddenly fell limp, and Nina, kneeling beside her, grew white with fear.

"Oh, vat is the matter! I hat kildt her!"

Claude rushed for a bucket of water and dashed it in the old woman's face. He flooded her with slashings of it, especially after he saw her open her eyes, ending by emptying the bucket in her face. He was a little malicious about that.

The mother sat up soon, wet, scared, bewildered, gasping.

"Mein Gott! Mein Gotd Ich bin ertrinken!"

"What does she say-she's been drinkin'? Well, that looks reasonable."

"No, no-she thinks she is trouned."

"Oh, drowned!" Claude roared again. "Not much she ain't. She's only just getting cooled off."

He helped the girl get her mother to the house and stretch her out on a bed. The old woman seemed to have completely exhausted herself with her effort and submitted like a child to be waited upon. Her sudden fainting had subdued her.

Claude had never penetrated so far into the house before, and was much pleased with the neatness and good order of the rooms, though they were bare of furniture and carpets.

As the girl came out with him to the gate he uttered the most serious word he had ever had with her

"Now, I want you to notice," he said, "that I did nothing to call out the old lady's rush at me. I'd 'a' hit her, sure, if she'd 'a' clinched me again. I don't believe in striking a woman, but she was after my hide for the time bein', and I can't stand two such clutches in the same place. You don't blame me, I hope."

"No. You done choost ride."

"What do you suppose the old woman went for me for?"

Nina looked down uneasily.

"She know you an' me lige one anudder, an' she is afrait you marry me, an' den ven she tie you get the farm a-ready."

Claude whisfied. "Great Jehosaphat! She really thinks that, does she? Well, dog my cats! What put that idea into her head?"

"I told her," said Nina calmly.

"You told her?" Claude turned and stared at her. She looked down, and her face slowly grew to a deep red. She moved uneasily from one foot to the' other, like an awkward, embarrassed child. As he looked at her standing like a culprit before him, his first impulse was to laugh. He was not specially refined, but he was a kindly man, and it suddenly occurred to 'him that the girl was suffering.

"Well, you were mistaken," he said at last, gently enough. "I don't know why you should think so, but I never thought of marrying you-never thought of it."

The flush faded from her face, and she stopped swaying. She lifted her eyes to his in a tearful, appealing stare.

"I t'ought so-you made me t'ink so."

"I did? How? I never said a word to you about-liking you or-marrying-or anything like that. I-" He was going to tell her he intended to marry Lucindy, but he checked himself.

Her lashes fell again, and the tears began to stream down her cheeks. She knew the worst now. His face had convinced her. She could not tell him the grounds of her belief-that every time he had said, "I don't like to see a woman do -this or that," or, "I like to see a woman fix up around the house," she had considered his words in the light of courtship, believing that in such ways the Yankees made love. So she stood suffering dumbly while he loaded his cream can and stood by the wheel ready to mount his wagon.

He turned. "I'm mighty sorry about it," he said. "Mebbe I was to blame. I didn't mean nothing by it-not a thing. It was all a mistake. Let's shake hands over it and call the whole business off."

He held his hand out to her, and with a low cry she seized it and laid her cheek upon it. He started back in amazement and drew his hand away. She fell upon her knees in the path and covered her face with her apron, while he hastily mounted his seat and drove away.

Nothing so profoundly moving had come into his life since the death of his mother, and as he rode on down the road he did a great deal of thinking. First it gave him a pleasant sensation to think a woman should care so much for him. He had lived a homeless life for years and had come into intimate relations with few women, good or bad. They had always laughed with him (not at him, for Claude was able to take care of himself), and no woman before had taken him seriously, and there was a certain charm about the realization.

Then he fell to wondering what he had said or done to give the girl such a notion of his purposes. Perhaps he had been too free with his talk. He was so troubled that he hardly smiled once during the rest of his circuit, and at night he refrained from going up town, and sat under the trees back of the creamery and smoked and pondered on the astounding situation.

He came at last to the resolution that it was his duty to declare himself to Lucindy and end all uncertainty, so that no other woman would fall into Nina's error. He was as good as an engaged man, and the world should know it.

The next day, with his newly painted buggy flashing in the sun, and the extra dozen ivory rings he had purchased for his harnesses clashing together, he drove up the road as a man of leisure and a resolved lover. It was a beautiful day in August.

Lucindy was getting a light tea for some friends up from the Siding, when she saw Claude drive up.

"Well, for the land sake!" she broke out, using one of her mother's phrases, "if here isn't that creamery man!" In that phrase lay the answer to Claude's question-if he had heard it. He drove in, and Mr. Kennedy, with impartial hospitality, went out and asked him to 'light and put his team in the barn.

He did so, feeling very much exhilarated. He never before had gone courting in this direct and aboveboard fashion. He mistook the father's hospitality for compliance in his designs. He followed his host into the house and faced, with very fair composure, two girls who smiled broadly as they shook hands with him. Mrs. Kennedy gave him a lax hand and a curt how-de-do, and Lucindy fairly scowled in answer to his radiant smile.

She was much changed, he could see. She wore a dress with puffed sleeves, and her hair was dressed differently. She seemed strange and distant, but he thought she was "putting that on" for the benefit of others. At the table the three girls talked of things at the Siding and ignored him so that he was obliged to turn to Farmer Kennedy for refuge. He kept his courage up by thinking, "Wait till we are alone."

After supper, when Lucindy explained that the dishes would have to be washed, he offered to help her in his best manner.

"Thank you, I don't need any help," was Lucindy's curt reply.

Ordinarily he was a man of much facility and ease in addressing women, but be was vastly disconcerted by her manner. He sat rather silently waiting for the room to clear. When the visitors intimated that they must go, he rose with cheerful alacrity.

"I'll get your horse for you."

He helped hitch the horse into the buggy, and helped the girls in with a return of easy gallantry, and watched them drive off with joy. At last the field was clear.

They returned to the sitting room, where the old folks remained for a decent interval, and then left the young people alone. His courage returned then, and he turned toward her with resolution in his voice and eyes.

"Lucindy," he began.

"Miss Kennedy, please," interrupted Lucindy with cutting emphasis.

"I'll be darned if I do," he replied hotly. "What's the matter with you? Since going to Minneapolis you put on a lot of city airs, it seems to me."

"If you don't like my airs, you know what you can do!"

He saw his mistake.

"Now see here, Lucindy, there's no sense in our quarreling."

"I don't want to quarrel; I don't want anything to do with you. I wish I'd never seen you."

"Oh, you don't mean that! After all the good talks we've had."

She flushed red. "I never had any such talks with you."

He pursued his advantage.

"Oh, yes, you did, and you took pains that I should see you."

"I didn't; no such thing. You came poking into the kitchen where you'd no business to be."

"Say, now, stop fooling. You like me and-"

"I don't. I hate you, and if you don't clear out I'll call father. You're one o' these kind o' men that think if a girl looks at 'em that they want to marry 'em. I tell you I don't want anything more to do with you, and I'm engaged to another man, and I wish you'd attend to your own business. So there! I hope you're satisfied."

Claude sat for nearly a minute in silence, then he rose. "I guess you're right. I've made a mistake. I've made a mistake in the girl." He spoke with a curious hardness in his voice. "Good evening, Miss Kennedy."

He went out with dignity and in good order. His retreat was not ludicrous. He left the girl with the feeling that she had lost her temper and with the knowledge that she had uttered a lie.

He put his horses to the buggy with a mournful self-pity as he saw the wheels glisten. He had done all this for a scornful girl who could not treat him decently. 'As he drove slowly down the road he mused deeply. It was a knock-down blow, surely. He was a just man, so far as he knew, and as he studied the situation over he could not blame the girl. In the light of her convincing wrath he comprehended that the sharp things she had said to him in the past were not make-believe-not love taps, but real blows. She had not been coquetting with him; she had tried to keep him away. She considered herself too good for a hired man. Well, maybe she' was. Anyhow, she had gone out of his reach, hopelessly.

As he came past the Haldemans' he saw Nina sitting out under the trees in the twilight. On the impulse he pulled in. His mind took another turn. Here was a woman who was open and aboveboard in her affection. Her words meant what they stood for. He remembered how she had bloomed out the last few months. She has the making of a handsome woman in her, he thought.

She saw him and came out to the gate, and while he leaned out of his carriage she rested her arms on the gate and looked up at him. She looked pale and sad, and he was touched.

"How's the old lady?" he asked.

"Oh, she's up! She is much change-ed. She is veak and quiet"

"Quiet, is she? Well, that's good."

"She t'inks God strike her fer her vickedness. Never before did she fainted like dot."

"Well, don't spoil that notion in her. It may do her a world of good."

"Der priest come. He saidt it wass a punishment. She saidt I should marry who I like."

Claude looked at her searchingly. She was certainly much improved. All she needed was a little encouragement and advice, and she would make a handsome wife. If the old lady had softened down, her son-in-law could safely throw up the creamery job and become the boss of the farm. The old man was used up, and the farm needed someone right away.

He straightened up suddenly. "Get your hat," he said, "and we'll take a ride."

She started erect, and he could see her pale face glow with joy.

"With you?"

"With me. Get your best hat. We may turn up at the minister's and get married-if a Sunday marriage is legal."

As she hurried up the walk he said to himself, "I'll bet it gives Lucindy a shock!"

And the thought pleased him mightily.

7. A DAY'S PLEASURE

"Mainly it is long and weariful, and has a home o' toil at one end and a dull little town at the other."

WHEN Markham came in from shoveling his last wagon-load of corn into the crib, he found that his wife had put the children to bed, and was kneading a batch of dough with the dogged action of a tired and sullen woman.

He slipped his soggy boots off his feet and, having laid a piece of wood on top of the stove, put his heels on it comfortably. His chair squeaked as he leaned back on its hind legs, but he paid no attention; he was used to it, exactly as he was used to his wife's lameness and ceaseless toil.

"That closes up my corn," he said after a silence. "I guess I'll go to town tomorrow to git my horses shod."

"I guess I'll git ready and go along," said his wife in a sorry attempt to be firm and confident of tone.

"What do you want to go to town fer?" he grumbled. "What does anybody want to go to town fer?" she burst out, facing him. "I ain't been out o' this house fer six months, while you go an' go!"

"Oh, it ain't six months. You went down that day I got the mower."

"When was that? The tenth of July, and you know it."

"Well, mebbe 'twas. I didn't think it was so long ago. I ain't no objection to your goin', only I'm goin' to take a load of wheat."

"Well, jest leave off a sack, an' that'll balance me an' the baby," she said spiritedly.

"All right," he replied good-naturedly, seeing she was roused. "Only that wheat ought to be put up tonight if you're goin'. You won't have any time to hold sacks for me in the morning with them young ones to get off to school."

"Well, let's go do it then," she said, sullenly resolute.

"I hate to go out agin; but I s'pose we'd better."

He yawned dismally and began pulling his boots on again, stamping his swollen feet into them with grunts of pain. She put on his coat and one of the boy's caps, and they went out to the granary. The night was cold and clear.

"Don't look so much like snow as it did last night," said Sam. "It may turn warm."

Laying out the sacks in the light of the lantern, they sorted out those which were whole, and Sam climbed into the bin with a tin pail in his hand, and the work began.

He was a sturdy fellow, and he worked desperately fast; the shining tin pail dived deep into the cold wheat and dragged heavily on the woman's tired hands as it came to the mouth of the sack, and she trembled with fatigue, but held on and dragged the sacks away when filled, and brought others, till at last Sam climbed out, puffing and wheezing, to tie them up.

"I guess I'll load 'em in the morning," he said. "You needn't wait fer me. I'll tie 'em up alone."

"Oh, I don't mind," she replied, feeling a little touched by his unexpectedly easy acquiescence to her request. When they went back to the house the moon had risen.

It had scarcely set when they were wakened by the crowing roosters. The man rolled stiffly out of bed and began rattling at the stove in the dark, cold kitchen.

His wife arose lamer and stiffer than usual and began twisting her thin hair into a knot.

Sam did not stop to wash, but went out to the barn. The woman, however, hastily soused her face into the hard limestone water at the sink and put the kettle on. Then she called the children. She knew it was early, and they would need several callings. She pushed breakfast forward, running over in her mind the things she must have: two spools of thread, six yards of cotton flannel, a can of coffee, and mittens for Kitty. These she must have-there were oceans of things she needed.

The children soon came scudding down out of the darkness of the upstairs to dress tumultuously at the kitchen stove. They humped and shivered, holding up their bare feet from the cold floor, like chickens in new fallen snow. They were irritable, and snarled and snapped and struck like cats and dogs. Mrs. Markham stood it for a while with mere commands to "hush up," but at last her patience gave out, and she charged down on the struggling mob and cuffed them right and left.

They ate their breakfast by lamplight, and when Sam went back to his work around the barnyard it was scarcely dawn. The children, left alone with their mother, began to tease her to let them go to town also.

"No, sir-nobody goes but baby. Your father's goin' to take a load of wheat."

She was weak with the worry of it all when she had sent the older children away to school, and the kitchen work was finished. She went into the cold bedroom off the little sitting room and put on her best dress. It had never been a good fit, and now she was getting so thin it hung in wrinkled folds everywhere about the shoulders and waist. She lay down on the bed a moment to ease that dull pam in her back. She had a moment's distaste for going out at all. The thought of sleep was more alluring. Then the thought of the long, long day, and the sickening sameness of her life, swept over her again, and she rose. and prepared the baby for the journey.

It was but little after sunrise when Sam drove out into the road and started for Belleplain. His wife sat perched upon the wheat sacks behind him, holding the baby in her lap, a cotton quilt under her, and a cotton horse blanket over her knees.

Sam was disposed to be very good-natured, and he talked back at her occasionally, though she could only under-stand him when he turned his face toward her. The baby stared out at the passing fence posts and wiggled his hands out of his mittens at every opportunity. He was merry, at least.

It grew warmer as they went on, and a strong south wind arose. The dust settled upon the woman's shawl and hat. Her hair loosened and blew unkemptly about her face. The road which led across the high, level prairie was quite smooth and dry, but still it jolted her, and the pam in her back increased. She had nothing to lean against, and the weight of the child grew greater, till she was forced to place him on the sacks beside her, though she could not loose her hold for a moment.

The town drew in sight-a cluster of small frame houses and stores on the dry prairie beside a railway station. There were no trees yet which could be called shade trees. The pitilessly severe light of the sun flooded everything. A few teams were hitched about, and in the lee of the stores a few men could be seen seated comfortably, their broad hat rims flopping up and down, their faces brown as leather.

Markham put his wife out at one of the grocery stores and drove off down toward the elevators to sell his wheat.

The grocer greeted Mrs. Markham in. a perfunctorily kind manner and offered her a chair, which she took gratefully. She sat for a quarter of an hour almost without moving, leaning against the back of the high chair. At last the child began to get restless and troublesome, and she spent half an hour helping him amuse himself around the nail kegs.

At length she rose and went out on the walk, carrying the baby. She went into the dry-goods store and took a seat on one of the little revolving stools. A woman was buying some woolen goods for a dress. It was worth twenty-seven cents a yard, the clerk said, but he would knock off two cents if she took ten yards. It looked warm, and Mrs. Markham wished she could afford it for Mary.

A pretty young girl came in, and laughed and chatted with the clerk, and bought a pair of gloves. She was the daughter of the grocer. Her happiness made the wife and mother sad. When Sam came back she asked him for some money.

"Want you want to do with it?" he asked.

"I want to spend it," she said.

She was not to be trifled with, so he gave her a dollar.

"I need a dollar more."

"Well, I've got to go take up that note at the bank."

"Well, the children's got to have some new underclo'es," she said.

He handed her a two-dollar bill and then went out to pay his note.

She bought her cotton flannel and mittens and thread, and then sat leaning against the counter. It was noon, and she was hungry. She went out to the wagon, got the lunch she had brought, and took it into the grocery to eat it-where she could get a drink of water.

The grocer gave the baby a stick of candy and handed the mother an apple.

"It'll kind o' go down with your doughnuts," he said. After eating her lunch she got up and went out. She felt ashamed to sit there any longer. She entered another dry-goods store, but when the clerk came toward her saying, "Anything today, Mrs.-?" she answered, "No, I guess not," and turned away with foolish face.

She walked up and down the street, desolately home-less. She did not know what to do with herself. She knew no one except the grocer. She grew bitter as she saw a couple of ladies pass, holding their demitrains in the latest city fashion. Another woman went by pushing a baby carriage, in which sat a child just about as big as her own. It was bouncing itself up and down on the long slender springs and laughing and shouting. Its clean round face glowed from its pretty fringed hood. She looked down at the dusty clothes and grimy face of her own little one and walked on savagely.

She went into the drugstore where the soda fountain was, but it made her thirsty to sit there, and she went out on the street again. She heard Sam laugh and saw him in a group of men over by the blacksmith shop. He was having a good time and had forgotten her.

Her back ached so intolerably that she concluded to go in and rest once more in the grocer's chair. The baby was growing cross and fretful. She bought five cents' worth of candy to take home to the children and gave baby a little piece to keep him quiet. She wished Sam would come. It must be getting late. The grocer said it was not much after one. Time seemed terribly long. She felt that she ought to do something while she was in town. She ran over her purchases-yes, that was all she had planned to buy. She fell to figuring on the things she needed. It was terrible. It ran away up into twenty or thirty dollars at the least. Sam, as well as she, needed underwear for the cold winter, but they would have to wear the old ones, even if they were thin and ragged. She would not need a dress, she thought bitterly, because she never went anywhere. She rose, and went out on the street once more, and wandered up and down, looking at everything in the hope of enjoying something.

A man from Boon Creek backed a load of apples up to the sidewalk, and as he stood waiting for the grocer he noticed Mrs. Markham and the baby, and gave the baby an apple. This was a pleasure. He had such a hearty way about him. He on his part saw an ordinary farmer's wife with dusty dress, unkempt hair, and tired face. He did not know exactly whey she appealed to him, but he tried to cheer her up.

The grocer was familiar with these bedraggled and weary wives. He was accustomed to see them sit for hours in his big wooden chair and nurse tired and fretful children. Their forlorn, aimless, pathetic wandering up and down the street was a daily occurrence, and had never possessed any special meaning to him.

II

In a cottage around the corner from the grocery store two men and a woman were finishing a dainty luncheon. The woman was dressed in cool, white garments, and she seemed to make the day one of perfect comfort.

The home of the Honorable Mr. Hall was by no means the costliest in the town, but his wife made it the most attractive. He was one of the leading lawyers of the county and a man of culture and progressive views. He was entertaining a friend who had lectured the night before in the Congregational church.

They were by no means in serious discussion. The talk was rather frivolous. Hall had the ability to caricature men with a few gestures and attitudes, and was giving to his Eastern friend some descriptions of the old-fashioned Western lawyers he had met in his practice. He was very amusing, and his guest laughed heartily for a time.

But suddenly Hall became aware that Otis was not listening. Then he perceived that he was peering out of the window at someone, and that on his face a look of bitter sadness was falling.

Hall stopped. "What do you see, Otis?"

Otis replied, "I see a forlorn, weary woman."

Mrs. Hall rose and went to the window. Mrs. Markham was walking by the house, her baby in her arms. Savage anger and weeping were in her eyes and on her lips, and there was hopeless tragedy in her shambling walk and weak back.

In the silence Otis went on: "I saw the poor, dejected creature twice this morning. I couldn't forget her."

"Who is she?" asked Mrs. Hall very softly.

"Her name is Markham; she's Sam Markham's wife," said Hall.

The young wife led the way into the sitting room, and the men took seats and lit their cigars. Hall was meditating a diversion when Otis resumed suddenly:

"That woman came to town today to get a change, to have a little play spell, and she's wandering around like a starved and weary cat. I wonder if there is a woman in this town with sympathy enough and courage enough to go out and help that woman? The saloonkeepers, the politicians, and the grocers make it pleasant for the man-so pleasant that he forgets his wife. But the wife is left without a word."

Mrs. Hall's work dropped, and on her pretty face was a look of pain. The man's harsh words had wounded her-and wakened her. She took up her hat and hurried out on the walk. The men looked at each other, and then the husband said:

"It's going to be a little sultry for the men around these diggings. Suppose we go out for a walk."

Delia felt a hand on her arm as she stood at the corner. "You look tired, Mrs. Markham; won't you come in a little while? I'm Mrs. Hall."

Mrs. Markham turned with a scowl on her face and a biting word on her tongue, but something in the sweet, round little face of the other woman silenced her, and her brow smoothed out.

"Thank you kindly, but it's most time to go home. I'm looking fer Mr. Markham now."

"Oh, come in a little while; the baby is cross and tried out; please do."

Mrs. Markham yielded to the friendly voice, and together the two women reached the gate just as two men hurriedly turned the other corner.

"Let me relieve you," said Mrs. Hall.

The mother hesitated: "He's so dusty."

"Oh, that won't matter. Oh, what a big fellow he is! I haven't any of my own," said Mrs. Hall, and a look passed like an electric spark between the two women, and Delia was her willing guest from that moment.

They went into the little sitting room, so dainty and lovely to the farmer's wife, and as she sank into an easy-chair she was faint and drowsy with the pleasure of it. She submitted to being brushed. She gave the baby into the hands of the Swedish girl, who washed its face and hands and sang it to sleep, while its mother sipped some tea. Through it all she lay back in her easychair, not speaking a word, while the ache passed out of her back, and her hot, swollen head ceased to throb.

But she saw everything-the piano, the pictures, the curtains, the wallpaper, the little tea stand. They were almost as grateful to her as the food and fragrant tea. Such housekeeping as this she had never seen. Her mother had worn her kitchen floor thin as brown paper in keeping a speckless house, and she had been in houses that were larger and costlier, but something of the charm of her hostess was in the arrangement of vases, chairs, or pictures. It was tasteful.

Mrs. Hall did not ask about her affairs. She talked to her about the sturdy little baby and about the things upon which Delia's eyes dwelt. If she seemed interested in a vase she was told what it was and where it was made. She was shown all the pictures and books. Mrs. Hall seemed to read her visitor's mind. She kept as far from the farm and her guest's affairs as possible, and at last she opened the piano and sang to her-not slow-moving hymns, but catchy love songs full of sentiment, and then played some simple melodies, knowing that Mrs. Markham's eyes were studying her hands, her rings, and the flash of her fingers on the keys-seeing more than she heard-and through it all Mrs. Hall conveyed the impression that she, too, was having a good time.

The rattle of the wagon outside roused them both. Sam was at the gate for her. Mrs. Markham rose hastily. "Oh, it's almost sundown!" she gasped in astonishment as she looked out of the window.

"Oh, that won't kill anybody," replied her hostess. "Don't hurry. Carrie, take the baby out to the wagon for Mrs. Markham while I help her with her things."

"Oh, I've had such a good time," Mrs. Markham said as they went down the little walk.

"So have I," replied Mrs. Hall. She took the baby a moment as her guest climbed in. "Oh, you big, fat fellow!" she cried as she gave him a squeeze. "You must bring your wife in oftener, Mr. Markham," she said as she handed the baby up.

Sam was staring with amazement

"Thank you, I will," he finally managed to say.

"Good night," said Mrs. Markham.

"Good night, dear," called Mrs. Hall, and the wagon began to rattle off.

The tenderness and sympathy in her voice brought the tears to Delia's eyes not hot nor bitter tears, but tears that cooled her eyes and cleared her mind.

The wind had gone down, and the red sunlight fell mistily over the world of corn and stubble. The crickets were strn chirping, and the feeding cattle were drifting toward the farmyards. The day had been made beautiful by human sympathy.

8. MRS. RIPLEY'S TRIP

"And in winter the winds sweep the snows across it."

The night was in windy November, and the blast, threatening rain, roared around the poor little shanty of "Uncle Ripley," set like a chicken trap on the vast Iowa prairie. Uncle Ethan was mending his old violin, with many York State "dums!" and "I gal darns!" totally oblivious of his tireless old wife, who, having "finished the supper dishes," sat knitting a stocking, evidently for the little grandson who lay before the stove like a cat. Neither of the old people wore glasses, and their light was a tallow candle; they couldn't afford "none o' them newfangled lamps." The room was small, the chairs wooden, and the walls bare- a home where poverty was a never-absent guest. The old lady looked pathetically little, wizened, and hopeless in her ill-fitting garments (whose original color had long since vanished), intent as she was on the stocking in her knotted, stiffened fingers, but there was a peculiar sparkle in her little black eyes, and an unusual resolution in the straight line of her withered and shapeless lips. Suddenly she paused, stuck a needle in the spare knob of hair at the back of her head, and looking at Ripley, said decisively: "Ethan Ripley, you'll haff to do your own cooking from now on to New Year's; I'm goin' back to Yaark State."

The old man's leather-brown face stiffened into a look of quizzical surprise for a moment; then he cackled in-credulously: "Ho! Ho! har! Sho! be y', now? I want to know if y' be."

"Well, you'll find out."

"Goin' to start tomorrow, Mother?"

"No, sir, I ain't; but I am on Thursday. I want to get to Sally's by Sunday, sure, an' to Silas's on Thanksgivin'."

There was a note in the old woman's voice that brought genuine stupefaction into the face of Uncle Ripley. Of course, in this case, as in all others, the money consideration was uppermost.

"Howgy 'xpect to get the money, Mother? Anybody died an' left yeh a pile?"

"Never you mind where I get the mony so 's 't tiy don't haff to bear it. The land knows, if I'd a-waited for you to pay my way-"

"You needn't twit me of bein' poor, old woman," said Ripley, flaming up after the manner of many old people. "I've done my part t' get along. I've worked day in and day out-"

"Oh! I ain't done no work, have I?" snapped she, laying down the stocking and leveling a needle at him, and putting a frightful emphasis on "I."

"I didn't say you hadn't done no work."

"Yes, you did!"

"I didn't, neither. I said

"I know what you said."

"I said I'd done my part!" roared the husband, dominating her as usual by superior lung power. "I didn't say you hadn't done your part," he added with an unfortunate touch of emphasis on "say."

"I know y' didn't say it, but y' meant it. I don't know what y' call doin' my part, Ethan Ripley; but if cookin' for a drove of harvest hands and thrashin' hands, takin' care o' the eggs and butter, 'n' diggin' taters an' milkin' ain't my part, I don't never expect to do my part, 'n' you might as well know it fust 's last. I'm sixty years old," she went on with a little break in her harsh voice, dominating him now by woman's logic, "an' I've never had a day to my-self, not even Fourth o' July. If I've went a-visitin' 'r to a picnic, I've had to come home an' milk 'n' get supper for you menfolks. I ain't been away t' stay overnight for thirteen years in this house, 'n' it was just so in Davis County for ten more. For twenty-three years, Ethan Ripley, I've stuck right to the stove an' churn without a day or a night off." Her voice choked again, but she rarned and continued impressively, "And now I'm a-goin' back to Yaark State."

Ethan was vanquished. He stared at her in speechless surprise, his jaw hanging. It was incredible.

"For twenty-three years," she went on musingly, "I've just about promised myself every year I'd go back an' see my folks." She was distinctly talking to herself now, and her voice had a touching, wistful cadence. "I've wanted to go back an' see the old folks, an' the hills where we played, an' eat apples off the old tree down by the old well. I've had them trees an' hills in my mind days and days-nights, togan' the girls I used to know, an' my own folks-"

She fell into a silent muse, which lasted so long that the ticking of the clock grew loud as the gong in the man's ears, and the wind outside seemed to sound drearier than usual. He returned to the money problem, kindly, though.

"But how y' goin' t' raise the money? I ain't got no extra cash this time. Agin Roach is paid an' the mortgage interest paid we ain't got no hundred dollars to spare, Jane, not by a jugful."

"Waal, don't you lay awake nights studyin' on where I'm a-goin' to get the money," said the old woman, taking delight in mystifying him. She had him now, and he couldn't escape. He strove to show his indifference, however, by playing a tune or two on the violin.

"Come, Tukey, you better climb the wooden hill," Mrs. Ripley said a half hour later to the little chap on the floor, who was beginning to get drowsy under the influence of his grandpa's fiddling. "Pa, you had orta 'a put that string in the clock today-on the 'larm side the string is broke," she said upon returning from the boy's bedroom. "I orta get up extry early tomorrow to get some sewin' done. Land knows, I can't fix up much, but they is a leetle I c'n do. I want to look decent."

They were alone now, and they both sat expectantly. "You 'pear to think, Mother, that I'm agin yer goin'." "Waal, it would kinder seem as if y' hadn't hustled yerself any t' help me git off."

He was smarting under the sense of being wronged. "Waal, I'm jest as willin' you should go as I am for myself; but if I ain't got no money, I don't see how I'm goin' to send-"

"I don't want ye to send; nobody ast ye to, Ethan Ripley. I guess if I had what I've earnt since we came on this farm, I'd have enough to go to Jericho with."

"You've got as much out of it as I have. You talk about your gom' back. Ain't I been wantin' to go back myself? And ain't I kep' still 'cause I see it wa'n't no use? I guess I've worked jest as long and as hard as you, an' in storms an' mud an' heat, ef it comes t' that."

The woman was staggered, but she wouldn't give up; she must get m one more thrust.

"Waal, if you'd 'a managed as well as I have, you'd have some money to go with." And she rose, and went to mix her bread, and set it "raisin'." He sat by the fire twanging his fiddle softly. He was plainly thrown into gloomy retrospection, something quite unusual for him. But his fingers picking out the bars of a familiar tune set him to smiling, and, whipping his bow across the strings, he forgot all about his wife's resolutions and his own hardships. Trouble always slid off his back like "punkins off a haystack" anyway.

The old man still sat fiddling softly after his wife disappeared in the hot and stuffy little bedroom off the kitchen. His shaggy head bent lower over his violin. He heard her shoes drop-one, two. Pretty soon she called:

"Come, put up that squeakin' old fiddle and go to bed. Seems as if you orta have sense enough not to set there keepin' everybody in the house awake."

"You hush up," retorted he. "I'll come when I git ready, not till. I'll be glad when you're gone-"

"Yes, I warrant that."

With which amiable good night they went off to sleep, or at least she did, while he lay awake, pondering on "where under the sun she was goin' t' raise that money."

The next day she was up bright and early, working away on her own affairs, ignoring Ripley totally, the fixed look of resolution still on her little old wrinkled face. She killed a hen and dressed and baked it She fried up a pan of doughnuts and made a cake. She was engaged on the doughnuts when a neighbor came in, one of those women who take it as a personal affront when anyone in the neighborhood does anything without asking their advice. She was fat, and could talk a man blind in three minutes by the watch.

"What's this I hear, Mis' Ripley?"

"I dun know. I expect you hear about all they is goin' on in this neighborhood," replied Mrs. Ripley with crushing bluntness; but the gossip did not flinch.

"Well, Sett Turner told me that her husband told her that Ripley told him that you was goin' back East on a visit."

"Waal, what of it?"

"Well, air yeh?"

"The Lord willin' an' the weather permitin', I expect to be."

"Good land, I want to know! Well, well! I never was so astonished in my life. I said, says I, 'It can't be.' 'Well,' ses 'e, 'tha's what she told me,' ses 'e. 'But,' ses I, 'she is the last woman in the world to go gallivantin' off East,' ses I. An' ses he, 'But it comes from good authority,' ses he. 'Well, then, it must be so,' ses I. But, land sakes! do tell me all about it. How come you to make up y'r mind? Ail these years you've been kind a-talkin' it over, an' now y'r actshelly goin'-Waal, I never! 'I s'pose Ripley furnishes the money,' ses I to him. 'Well, no,' ses 'e. 'Ripley says he'll be blowed if he sees where the money's comin' from,' ses 'e; and ses I, 'But maybe she's jest jokin',' ses I. 'Not much,' he says. S' 'e: 'Ripley believes she's goin' fast enough. He's jest as anxious to find out as we be-'"

Here Mrs. Doudney paused for breath; she had walked so fast and had rested so little that her interminable flow of "ses I's" and "ses he's" ceased necessarily. She had reached, moreover, the point of most vital interest-the money.

"An' you'll find out jest 'bout as soon as he does," was the dry response from the figure hovering over the stove, and with all her maneuvering that was all she got.

All day Ripley went about his work exceedingly thoughtful for him. It was cold, blustering weather. The wind rustled among the cornstalks with a wild and mournful sound, the geese and ducks went sprawling down the wind, and horses' coats were ruffled and backs raised.

The old man was husking corn alone in the field, his spare form rigged out in two or three ragged coats, his hands inserted in a pair of gloves minus nearly all the fingers, his thumbs done up in "stalls," and his feet thrust into huge coarse boots. During the middle of the day the frozen ground thawed, and the mud stuck to his boots, and the "down ears" wet and chapped his hands, already worn to the quick. Toward night it grew colder and threatened snow. In spite of all these attacks he kept his cheerfulness, and though he was very tired, he was softened in temper.

Having plenty of time to think matters over, he had come to the conclusion "that the old woman needed a play spell. I ain't likely to be no richer next year than I am this one; if I wait till I'm able to send her she won't never go. I calc'late I c'n git enough out o' them shoats to send her. I'd kind a 'lotted on eat'n' them pigs done up into sassengers, but if the ol' woman goes East, Tukey an' me'll kind a haff to pull through without 'em. We'll. have a turkey f'r Thanksgivin', an' a chicken once 'n a while. Lord! But we'll miss the gravy on the flapjacks. Amen!" (He smacked his lips over the thought of the lost dainty.) "But let 'er rip! We can stand it. Then there is my buffalo overcoat. I'd kind a calc'lated on havin' a buffalo-but that's gone up the spout along with them sassengers."

These heroic sacrifices having been determined upon, he put them into effect at once.

This he was able to do, for his corn rows ran alongside the road leading to Cedarville, and his neighbors were passing almost all hours of the day.

It would have softened Jane Ripley's heart could she have seen his bent and stiffened form amid the corn rows, the cold wind piercing to the bone through his threadbare and insufficient clothing. The rising wind sent the snow rattling among the moaning stalks at intervals. The cold made his poor dim eyes water, and he had to stop now and then to swing his arms about his chest to warm them. His voice was hoarse with shouting at the shivering team.

That night, as Mrs. Ripley was clearing the dishes away, she got to thinking about the departure of the next day, and she began to soften. She gave way to a few tears when little Tewksbury Gilchrist, her grandson, came up and stood beside her.

"Gran'ma, you ain't goin' to stay away always, are yeh?"

"Why, course not, Tukey. What made y' think that?"

"Well, y' ain't told us nawfliln' 'tall about it. An' yeb kind o' look 'sif yeh was mad."

"Well, I ain't mad; I'm jest a-thinkin', Tukey. Y'see, I come away from them hills when I was a little glrl a'most; before I married y'r grandad. And I ain't never been back. 'Most all my folks is there, souny, an' we've been s' poor all these years I couldn't seem t' never get started. Now, when I'm 'most ready t' go, I feel kind a queer-'sif I'd cry."

And cry she did, while little Tewksbury stood patting her trembling hands. Hearing Ripley's step on the porch, she rose hastily and, drying her eyes, plunged at the work again. Ripley came in with a big armful of wood, which he rolled into the woodbox with a thundering crash. Then he pulled off his mittens, slapped them together to knock off the ice and snow, and laid them side by side under the stove. He then removed cap, coat, blouse, and boots, which last he laid upon the woodbox, the soles turned toward the stovepipe.

As he sat down without speaking, he opened the front doors of the stove and held the palms of his stiffened hands to the blaze. The light brought out a thoughtful look on his large, uncouth, yet kindly visage. Life had laid hard lines on his brown skin, but it had not entirely soured a naturally kind and simple nature. It had made him penurious and dull and iron-muscled; had stifled all the slender flowers of his nature; yet there was warm soil somewhere hid in his heart.

"It's snowin' like all p'sessed," he remarked finally. "I guess we'll have a sleigh ride tomorrow. I calc'late t' drive y' daown in scrumptious style. If yeh must leave, why, we'll give yeh a whoopin' old send-off-won't we, Tukey?

"I've ben a4hinkin' things over kind o' t'day, Mother, an' I've come t' the conclusion that we have been kind a hard on yeh, without knowin' it, y' see. Y' see, I'm kind a easygoin, 'an' little Tuke he's only a child, an' we ain't c'nsidered how you felt."

She didn't appear to be listening, but she was, and he didn't appear, on his part, to be talking to her, and he kept his voice as hard and dry as he could.

"An' I was tellin' Tukey t'day that it was a dum shame our crops hadn't, turned out better. An' when I saw ol' Hatfield go by, I hailed him an' asked him what he'd gimme for two o' m' shoats. Waal, the upshot is, I sent t' town for some things I calc'lated ye'd heed. An' here's a ticket to Georgetown, and ten dollars. Why, Ma, what's up?"

Mrs. Ripley broke down, and with her hands all wet with dishwater, as they were, covered her face and sobbed. She felt like kissing him, but she didn't. Tewksbury began to whimper, too; but the old man was astonished. His wife had not wept for years (before him). He rose and walked clumsily up to her and timidly touching her hair—

"Why, Mother! What's the matter? What 'v' I done now? I was calc'latln' to sell them pigs anyway. Hatfield jest advanced the money on' em."

She hopped up and dashed into the bedroom, and in a few minutes returned with a yarn mitten, tied around the wrist, which she laid on the table with a thump, saying:

"I don't want yer money. There's money enough to take me where I want to go."

"Whee-w! Thunder and jimson root! Wher'd ye git that? Didn't dig it out of a hole?"

"No. I jest saved it-a dime at a time-see?"

Here she turned it out on the table-some bills, but mostly silver dimes and quarters.

"Thunder and scissors! Must be two er three hundred dollars there," stared he.

"They's jest seventy-five dollars and thirty cents; jest about enough to go back on. Tickets is fifty-five dollars, goin' an' comin'. That leaves twenty dollars for other expenses, not countin' what I've already spent, which is six-fifty," said she, recovering her self-possession. "It's plenty."

"But y' ain't calc'lated on no sleepers nor hotel bills."

"I ain't goin' on no sleeper. Mis' Doudney says it's jest scandalous the way things is managed on them cars. I'm goin' on the old-fashioned cars, where they ain't no half-dressed men runain' around."

"But you needn't be afraid of them, Mother; at your age-"

"There! you needn't throw my age an' homeliness into my face, Ethan Ripley. If I hadn't waited an' tended on you so long, I'd look a little more's I did when I married yeh."

Ripley gave it up in despair. He didn't realize fully enough how the proposed trip had unsettled his wife's nerves. She didn't realize it herself.

"As for the hotel bills, they won't be none. I a-goin' to pay them pirates as much for a day's board as we'd charge for a week's, an' have nawthin' to eat but dishes. I'm goin' to take a chicken an' some hard-boiled eggs, an' I'm goin' right through to Georgetown."

"Well, all right; but here's the ticket I got."

"I don't want yer ticket."

"But you've got to take it."

"Wall, I hain't."

"Why, yes, ye have. It's bought, an' they won't take it back."

"Won't they?" She was staggered again.

"Not much they won't. I ast 'em. A ticket sold is sold."

"Waal, if they won't-"

"You bet they won't."

"I s'pose I'll haff to use it"; and that ended in -They were a familiar sight as they rode down the road toward town next day. As usual, Mrs. Ripley sat up straight and stiff as "a half-drove wedge in a white-oak log." The day was cold and raw. There was some snow on the ground, but not enough to warrant the use of sleighs. It was "neither sleddin' nor wheelin'." The old people sat on a board laid across the box, and had an old quilt or two drawn up over their knees. Tewksbury lay in the back part of the box (which was filled with hay), where he jounced up and down, in company with a queer old trunk and a brand-new imitation-leather handbag, There is no ride quite so desolate and uncomfortable as a ride in a lumber wagon on a cold day in autumn, when the ground is frozen and the wind is strong and raw with threatening snow. The wagon wheels grind along in the snow, the cold gets in under the seat at the calves of one's legs, and the ceaseless bumping of the bottom of the box on the feet is frightful.

There was not much talk on the way down, and what little there was related mainly to certain domestic regulations to be strictly followed regarding churning, pickles, pancakes, etc. Mrs. Ripley wore a shawl over her head and carried her queer little black bonnet in her hand. Tewksbury was also wrapped in a shawl. The boy's teeth were pounding together like castanets by the time they reached Cedarville, and every muscle ached with the fatigue of shaking. After a few purchases they drove down to the railway station, a frightful little den (common in the West) which was always too hot or too cold. It happened to be hot just now-a fact which rejoiced little Tewksbury.

"Now git my trunk stamped 'r fixed, 'r whatever they call it," she said to Ripley in a commanding tone, which gave great delight to the inevitable crowd of loafers begliming to assemble. "Now remember, Tukey, have Granddad kill that biggest turkey night before Thanksgiving, an' then you run right over to Mis' Doudney's-she's got a nawful tongue, but she can bake a turkey first-rate-an' she'll fix up some squash pies for yeh. You can warm up one s' them mince pies. I wish ye could be with me, but ye can't, so do the best ye can."

Ripley returning now, she said: "Waal, now, I've fixed things up the best I could. I've baked bread enough to last a week, an' Mis' Doudney has promised to bake for yeh."

"I don't like her bakin'."

"Waal, you'll haff to stand it till I get back, 'n' you'll find a jar o' sweet pickles an' some crabapple sauce down suller, 'n' you'd better melt up brown sugar for 'lasses, 'n' for goodness' sake don't eat all them mince pies up the fust week, 'n' see that Tukey ain't froze goin' to school. An' now you'd better get out for home. Good-bye, an' remember them pies.

As they were riding home, Ripley roused up after a long silence.

"Did she-a-kiss you goodbye, Tukey?"

"No, sir," piped Tewksbury.

"Thunder! didn't she?" After a silence. "She didn't me, neither. I guess she kind of sort a forgot it, bein' so frustrated, y' know."

One cold, windy, intensely bright day, Mrs. Stacey, who lives about two miles from Cedarville, looking out of the window, saw a queer little figure struggling along the road, which was blocked here and there with drifts. It was an old woman laden with a good half-dozen parcels, any one of which was a load, which the wind seemed determined to wrench from her. She was dressed in black, with a full skirt, and her cloak being short, the wind had excellent opportunity to inflate her garments and sail her off occasionally into the deep snow outside the track, but she held on bravely till she reached the gate. As she turned in, Mrs. Stacey cried:

"Why! it's Gran'ma Ripley, just getting back from her trip. Why! how do you do? Come in. Why! you must be nearly frozen. Let me take off your hat and veil."

"No, thank ye kindly, but I can't stop. I must be gittin' back to Ripley. I expec' that man has jest let ev'rything go six ways f'r Sunday."

"Oh, you must sit down just a minute and warm."

"Waal, I will, but I've got to git home by sundown. Sure I don't s'pose they's a thing in the house to eat."

"Oh dear! I wish Stacey was here, so he could take you home. An' the boys at school."

"Don't need any help, if 'twa'n't for these bundles an' things. I guess I'll jest leave some of 'em here an'- Here! take one of these apples. I brought 'em from Lizy Jane's suller, back to Yaark State."

"Oh! they're delicious! You must have had a lovely time."

"Pretty good. But I kep' thinkin' o' Ripley an' Tukey all the time. I s'pose they have had a gay time of it" (she meant the opposite of gay). "Waal, as I told Lizy Jane, I've had my spree, an' now I've got to git back to work. They ain't no rest for such as we are. As I told Lizy Jane, them folks in the big houses have Thanksgivin' dinners every day uv their lives, and men an' women in splendid do's to wait on 'em, so't Thanksgivin' don't mean anything to 'em; but we poor critters, we make a great to-do if we have a good dinner oncet a year. I've saw a pile o' this world, Mrs. Stacey-a pile of it! I didn't think they was so many big houses in the world as I saw b'tween here an' Chicago. Waal, I can't set here gabbin'; I must get home to Ripley. Jest kinder stow them bags away. I'll take two an' leave them three others. Goodbye. I must be gittin' home to Ripley. He'll want his supper on time." And off up the road the indomitable little figure trudged, head held down to the cutting blast. Little snow fly, a speck on a measureless expanse, crawling along with painful breathing and slipping, sliding steps- "Gittin' home to Ripley an' the boy."

Ripley was out to the barn when she entered, but Tewksbury was building a fire in the old cookstove. He sprang up with a cry of joy and ran to her. She seized him and kissed him, and it did her so much good she hugged him close and kissed him again and again, crying hysterically.

"Oh, gran'ma, I'm so glad to see you! We've had an awful time since you've been gone."

She released him and looked around. A lot of dirty dishes were on the table, the tablecloth was a "sight to behold," and so was the stove-kettle marks all over the tablecloth, splotches of pancake batter all over the stove.

"Waal, I sh'd say as much," she dryly vouchsafed, untying her bonnet strings.

When Ripley came in she had on her regimentals, the stove was brushed, the room swept, and she was elbow-deep in the dishpan. "Hullo, Mother! Got back, hev yeh?"

"I sh'd say it was about time," she replied briefly with-out looking up or ceasing work. "Has ol' 'Cruuipy' dried up yit?" This was her greeting.

Her trip was a fact now; no chance could rob her of it. She had looked forward twenty-three years toward it, and now she could look back at it accomplished. She took up her burden again, never more thinking to lay it down.

9. UNCLE ETHAN RIPLEY

"Like the Main-Travelled Road of Life, it is traversed by many classes of people."

UNCLE ETHAN had a theory that a man's character could be told by the way he sat in a wagon seat.

"A mean man sets right plumb in the middle o' the seat, as much as to say, 'Walk, goldarn yeh, who cares!' But a man that sets in the corner o' the seat, much as to say, 'Jump in-cheaper t' ride 'n to walk,' you can jest tie to."

Uncle Ripley was prejudiced in favor of the stranger, therefore, before he came opposite the potato patch, where the old man was "bugging his vines." The stranger drove a jaded-looking pair of calico ponies, hitched to a clattering democrat wagon, and he sat on the extreme end of the seat, with the lines in his right hand, while his left rested on his thigh, with his little finger gracefully crooked and his elbows akimbo. He wore a blue shirt, with gay-colored armlets just above the elbows, and his vest hung unbuttoned down his lank ribs. It was plain he was well pleased with himself.

As he pulled up and threw one leg over the end of the seat, Uncle Ethan observed that the left spring was much more worn than the other, which proved that it was not accidental, but that it was the driver's habit to sit on that end of the seat.

"Good afternoon," said the stranger pleasantly.

"Good afternoon, sir."

"Bugs purty plenty?"

"Plenty enough, I gol! I don't see where they all come fum."

"Early Rose?" inquired the man, as if referring to the bugs.

"No; Peachblows an' Carter Reds. My Early Rose is over near the house. The old woman wants 'em near. See the darned things!" he pursued, rapping savagely on the edge of the pan to rattle the bugs back.

"How do yeh kill 'em-scald 'em?"

"Mostly. Sometimes!"

"Good piece of oats," yawned the stranger listessly.

"That's barley."

"So 'tis. Didn't notice."

Uncle Ethan was wondering who the man was. He had some pots of black paint in the wagon and two or three square boxes.

"What do yeh think o' Cleveland's chances for a second term?" continued the man, as if they had been talking politics all the while.

Uncle Ripley scratched his head. "Waal-I dunn bein' a Republican-I think-"

"That's so-it's a purty scaly outlook. I don't believe in second terms myself," the man hastened to say.

"Is that your new barn acrosst there?" be asked, pointing with his whip.

"Yes, sir, it is," replied the old man proudly. After years of planning and hard work he had managed to erect a little wooden barn, costing possibly three hundred dollars. It was plain to be seen he took a childish pride in the fact of its newness.

The stranger mused. "A lovely place for a sign," he said as his eyes wandered across its shining yellow broadside.

Uncle Ethan stared, unmindful of the bugs crawling over the edge of his pan. His interest in the pots of paint deepened.

"Couldn't think o' lettin' me paint a sign on that barn?" the stranger continued, putting his locked hands around one knee and gaining away across the pigpen at the building.

"What kind of a sign? Goldarn your skins!" Uncle Ethan pounded the pan with his paddle and scraped two or three crawling abominations off his leathery wrist.

It was a beautiful day, and the man in the wagon seemed unusually loath to attend to business. The tired ponies slept in the shade of the lombardies. The plain was draped in a warm mist and shadowed by vast, vaguely defined masses of clouds-a lazy June day.

"Dodd's Family Bitters," said the man, waking out of his abstraction with a start and resuming his working manner. "The best bitter in the market." He alluded to it in the singular. "Like to look at it? No trouble to show goods, as the fellah says," he went on hastily, seeing Uncle Ethan's hesitation.

He produced a large bottle of triangular shape, like a bottle for pickled onions. It had a red seal on top and a strenuous caution in red letters on the neck, "None genuine unless 'Dodd's Family Bittem' is blown in the bottom."

"Here's what it cures," pursued the agent, pointing at the side, where; in an inverted pyramid, the names of several hundred diseases were arranged, running from "gout" to "pulmonary complaints," etc.

"I gol! She cuts a wide swath, don't she?" exclaimed Uncle Ethan, profoundly impressed with the list.

"They ain't no better bitter in the world," said the agent with a conclusive inflection.

"What's its speshy-ality? Most of 'em have some speshy-ality."

"Well-summer complaints-an'-an'-spring an' fall troubles-tones ye up, sort of."

Uncle Ethan's forgotten pan was empty of his gathered bugs. He was deeply interested in this man. There was something he liked about him.

"What does it sell fur?" he asked after a pause.

"Same price as them cheap medicines-dollar a bottle-big bottles, too. Want one?"

"Wal, mother ain't to home, an' I don't know as she'd like this kind. We ain't been sick f'r years. Still, they's no tellln'," he added, seeing the answer to his objection in the agent's eyes. "Times is purty close too, with us, y' see; we've just built that stable-"

'Say I'll tell yeh what I'll do," said the stranger, waking up and speaking in a warnily generous tone. "I'll give you ten bottles of the bitter if you'll let me paint a sign on that barn. It won't hurt the barn a bit, and if you want 'o you can paint it Out a year from date. Come, what d'ye say?"

"I guess I hadn't better."

The agent thought that Uncle Ethan was after more pay, but in reality he was thinking of what his little old wife would say.

"It simply puts a family bitter in your home that may save you fifty dollars this comin' fall. You can't tell."

Just what the man said after that Uncle Ethan didn't follow. His voice had a confidential purring sound as he stretched across the wagon seat and talked on, eyes half shut. He straightened up at last and concluded in the tone of one who has carried his point:

"So! If you didn't want to use the whole twenty five bottles y'rself, why! sell it to your neighbors. You can get twenty dollars out of it easy, and still have five bottles of the best family bitter that ever went into a bottle."

It was the thought of this opportunity to get a buffalo skin coat that consoled Uncle Ethan as he saw the hideous black letters appearing under the agent's lazy brush.

It was the hot side of the barn, and painting was no light work. The agent was forced to mop his forehead with his sleeve.

"Say, hain't got a cookie or anything, and a cup o' milk, handy?" he said at the end of the first enormous word, which ran the whole length of the barn.

Uncle Ethan got him the milk and cookie, which he ate with an exaggeratedly dainty action of his fingers, seated meanwhile on the staging which Uncle Ripley had helped him to build. This lunch infused new energy into him, and in a short time "DODD'S FAMILY BITTERS, Best in the Market," disfigured the sweet-smelling pine boards.

Ethan was eating his self-obtained supper of bread and milk when his wife came home.

"Who's been a-paintin' on that barn?" she demanded, her beadlike eyes flashing, her withered little face set in an ominous frown. "Ethan Ripley, what you been doin'?"

"Nawthin'," he replied feebly.

"Who painted that sign on there?"

"A man come along an' he wanted to paint that on there, and I let 'im; and it's my barn anyway. I guess I can do what I'm a min' to with it," he ended defiantly; but his eyes wavered.

Mrs. Ripley ignored the defiance. "What under the sun p'sessed you to do such a thing as that, Ethan Ripley? I declare I don't see! You git fooler an' fooler cv'ry day you live, I do believe."

Uncle Ethan attempted a defense.

"Wal, he paid me twenty-five dollars f'r it, anyway."

"Did 'e?" She was visibly affected by this news.

"Wal, anyhow, it amounts to that; he give me twenty-five bottles-"

Mrs. Ripley sank back in her chair. "Wal, I swan to Bungay! Ethan Ripley-wal, you beat all I ever see!" she added in despair of expression. "I thought you had some sense left; but you hain't, not one blessed scimpton. Where is the stuff?"

"Down cellar, an' you needn't take on no airs, ol' woman. I've known you to buy things you didn't need time an' time an' agin-tins an' things, an' I guess you wish you had back that ten dollars you paid for that illustrated Bible,"

"Go 'long an' bring that stuff up here. I never see such a man in my life. It's a wonder he didn't do it f'r two bottles." She glared out at the 'sign, which faced directly upon the kitchen window.

Uncle Ethan tugged the two cases up and set them down on the floor of the kitchen. Mrs. Ripley opened a bottle and smelled of it like a cautious cat.

"Ugh! Merciful sakes, what stuff! It ain't fit f'r a hog to take. What'd you think you was goin' to do with it?" she asked in poignant disgust.

"I expected to take it-if I was sick. Whaddy ye s'pose?" He defiantly stood his ground, towering above her like a leaning tower.

"The hull cartload of it?"

"No. I'm goin' to sell part of it an' git me an overcoat-"

"Sell it!" she shouted. "Nobuddy'il buy that sick'nin' stuff but an old numskull like you. Take that slop out o' the house this 'minute! Take it right down to the sinkhole an' smash every bottle on the stones."

Uncle Ethan and the cases of medicine disappeared, and the old woman addressed her concluding remarks to little Tewksbury, her grandson, who stood timidly on one leg in the doorway, like an intruding pullet.

"Everything around this place 'ud go to rack an' ruin if I didn't keep a watch on that soft-pated old dummy. I thought that lightnin'-rod man had glve him a lesson he'd remember; but no, he must go an' make a reg'lar-"

She subsided in a tumult of banging pans, which helped her out in the matter of expression and reduced her to a grim sort of quiet. Uncle Ethan went about the house like a convict on shipboard. Once she caught him looking out of the window.

"I should think you'd feel proud o' that."

Uncle Ethan had never been sick a day in his life. He was bent and bruised with never-ending toil, but he had nothing especial the matter with him.

He did not smash the medicine, as Mrs. Ripley commanded, because he had determined to sell it. The next Sunday morning, after his chores were done, he put on his best coat of faded diagonal, and was brushing his hair into a ridge across the center of his high, narrow head when Mrs. Ripley carne in from feeding the calves.

"Where you goin' now?"

"None o' your business," he replied. "It's darn funny if I can't stir without you wantin' to know all about it. Where's Tukey?"

"Feedin' the chickens. You ain't goin' to take him off this mornin' now! I don't care where you go."

"Who's a-goin' to take him off? I ain't said nothin' about takin' him off."

"Wal, take y'rseif off, an' if y' ain't here f'r dinner, I ain't goin' to get no supper."

Ripley took a water pail, and put four bottles of "the bitter into it, and trudged away up the road with it in a pleasant glow of hope. All nature seemed to declare the day a time of rest and invited men to disassociate ideas of toil from the rustling green wheat, shining grass, and tossing blooms. Something of the sweetness and buoyancy of all nature permeated the old man's work-calloused body, and he whistled little snatches of the dance tunes he played on his fiddle.

But he found neighbor Johnson to be supplied with another variety of bitter, which was all he needed for the present. He qualified his refusal to buy with a cordial invitation to go out and see his shoats, in which he took infinite pride. But Uncle Ripley said: "I guess I'll haf t' be gom'; I want 'o git up to Jennings' before dinner."

He couldn't help feeling a little depressed when he found Jennings away. The next house along the pleasant lane was inhabited by a "newcomer." He was sitting on the horse trough, holding a horse's halter, while his hired man dashed cold water upon the galled spot on the animal's shoulder.

After some preliminary talk Ripley presented his medicine.

"Hell, no! What do I want of such stuff? When they's anything the matter with me, I take a lunkin' ol' swig of popple bark and bourbon! That fixes me."

Uncle Ethan moved off up the lane. He hardly felt like whistling now. At the next house he set his pail down in the weeds beside the fence and went in without it. Doudney came to the door in his bare feet, buttoning his suspenders over a clean boiled shirt. He was dressing to go out.

"Hello, Ripley. I was just goin' down your way. Jest wait a minute, an' I'll be out."

When he came out, fully dressed, Uncle Ethan grappled him.

"Say, what d' you think o' paytent med-"

"Some of 'em are boss. But y' want 'o know what y're gittin'."

"What d' ye think o, Dodd's-"

"Best in the market."

Uncle Ethan straightened up and his face lighted. Doudney went on:

"Yes, sir; best bitter that ever went into a bottle. I know, I've tried it. I don't go much on patent medicines, but when I get a good-"

"Don't want 'o buy a bottle?"

Doudney turned and faced him.

"Buy! No. I've got nineteen bottles I want 'o sell" Ripley glanced up at Doudney's new granary and there read "Dodd's Family Bitters." He was stricken dumb. Doudney saw it all and roared.

"Wal, that's a good one! We two tryin' to sell each other bitters. Ho-ho-ho-har, whoop! wal, this is rich! How many bottles did you git?"

"None o' your business," said Uncle Ethan as he turned and made off, while Doudney screamed with merriment.

On his way home Uncle Ethan grew ashamed of his burden. Doudney had canvassed the whole neighborhood, and he practically gave up the struggle. Everybody he met seemed determined to find out what he had been doing, and at last he began lying about it.

"Hello, Uncle Ripley, what y' got there in that pail?"

"Goose eggs f r settin'."

He disposed of one bottle to old Gus Peterson. Gus never paid his debts, and he would only promise fifty cents "on tick" for the bottle, and yet so desperate was Ripley that this questionable sale cheered him up not a little.

As he came down the road, tired, dusty, and hungry, he climbed over the fence in order to avoid seeing that sign on the barn and slunk into the house without looking back.

He couldn't have felt meaner about it if he had allowed a Democratic poster to be pasted there.

The evening passed in grim silence, and in sleep he saw that sign wriggling across the side of the barn like boa constrictors hung on rails. He tried to paint them out, but every time he tried it the man seemed to come back with a sheriff and savagely warned him to let it stay till the year was up. In some mysterious way the agent seemed to know every time he brought out the paint pot, and he was no longer the pleasant-voiced individual who drove the calico ponies.

As he stepped out into the yard next morning that abominable, sickening, scrawling advertisement was the first thing that claimed his glance-it blotted out the beauty of the morning.

Mrs. Ripley came to the window, buttoning her dress at the throat, a wisp of her hair sticking assertively from the little knob at the back of her head.

"Lovely, ain't it! An' J've got to see it all day long. I can't look out the winder, but that thing's right in my face." It seemed to make her savage. She hadn't been in such a temper since her visit to New York. "I hope you feel satisfied with it."

Ripley walked off to the barn. His pride in its clean sweet newness was gone. He slyly tried the paint to see if it couldn't be scraped off, but it was dried in thoroughly. Whereas before he had taken delight in having his neighbors turn and look at the building, now he kept out of sight whenever he saw a team coming. He hoed corn away in the back of the field, when he should have been bugging potatoes by the roadside.

Mrs. Ripley was in a frightful mood about it, but she held herself in check for several days. At last she burst forth:

"Ethan Ripley, I can't stand that thing any longer, and I ain't goin' to, that's all! You've got to go and paint that thing out, or I will. I'm just about crazy with it."

"But, Mother, I promised-"

"I don't care what you promised, it's got to be painted out. I've got the nightmare now, seein' it. I'm goin' to send for a pail o' red paint, and I'm goin' to paint that out if it takes the last breath I've got to do it."

"I'll tend to it, Mother, if you won't hurry me-"

"I can't stand it another day. It makes me boil every time I look out the winder."

Uncle Ethan hitched up his team and drove gloomily off to town, where he tried to find the agent. He lived in some other part of the county, however, and so the old man gave up and bought a pot of red paint, not daring to go back to his desperate wife without it.

"Goin' to paint y'r new barn?" inquired the merchant with friendly interest.

Uncle Ethan turned with guilty sharpness; but the merchant's face was grave and kindly.

"Yes, I thought I'd tech it up a little-don't cost much."

"It pays-always," the merchant said emphatically.

"Will it-stick jest as well put on evenings?" inquired Uncle Ethan hesitatingly.

"Yes-won't make any difference. Why? Ain't goin' to have-"

"Wal-I kind o' thought I'd do it odd times night an' mornin'-kind o' odd times—-"

He seemed oddly confused about it, and the merchant looked after him anxiously as he drove away.

After supper that night he went out to the barn, and Mrs. Ripley heard him sawing and hammering. Then the noise ceased, and he came in and sat down in his usual place.

"What y' be'n makin'?" she inquired. Tewksbury had gone to bed. She sat darning a stocking.

"I jest thought I'd git the stagin' ready f'r paintin'," he said evasively.

"Wal! I'll be glad when it's covered up." When she got ready for bed, he was still seated in his chair, and after she had dozed off two or three times she began to wonder why he didn't come When the clock struck ten, and she realized that he had not stirred, she began to get impatient. "Come, are y' goin' to sit there all night?" There was no reply. She rose up in bed and looked about the room. The broad moon flooded it with light, so that she could see he was not asleep in his chair, as she had supposed. There was something ominous in his disappearance.

"Ethan! Ethan Ripley, where are yeh?" There was no reply to her sharp call. She rose and distractedly looked about among the furniture, as if he inight somehow be a cat and be hiding in a corner somewhere. Then she went upstairs where the boy slept, her hard little heels making a curious tunking noise on the bare boards. The moon fell across the sleeping hoy like a robe of silver. He was alone.

She began to be alarmed. Her eyes widened in fear. An sorts of vague horrors sprang unbidden into her brain. She still had the mist of sleep in her brain.

She hurried down the stairs and out into the fragrant night. The katydids were singing in infinite peace under the solemn splendor of the moon. The cattle sniffed and sighed, jangling their bells now and then, and the chickens in the coop stirred uneasily as if overheated. The old woman stood there in her bare feet and long nightgown, horror-stricken. The ghastly story of a man who had hung himself in his barn because his wife deserted him came into her mind and stayed there with frightful persistency. Her throat filled chokingly.

She felt a wild rush of loneliness. She had a sudden realization of how dear that gaunt old figure was, with its grizzled face and ready smile. Her breath came quick and quicker, and she was at the point of bursting into a wild cry to Tewksbury when she heard a strange noise. It came from the barn, a creaking noise. She looked that way and saw in the shadowed side a deeper shadow moving to and fro. A revulsion to astonishment and anger took place in her.

"Land o' Bungay! If he ain't paintin' that barn, like a perfect old idiot, in the night."

Uncle Ethan, working desperately, did not hear her feet pattering down the path, and was startled by her shrill voice.

"Well, Ethan Ripley, whaddy y' think you're doin' now?"

He made two or three slapping passes with the brush and then snapped out, "I'm a-paintin' this barn-whaddy ye s'pose? II ye had eyes y' wouldn't ask."

"Well, you come right straight to bed. What d'you mean by actin' so?"

"You go back into the house an' let me be. I know what I'm a-doin'. You've pestered me about this sign jest about enough." He dabbed his brush to and fro as he spoke. His gaunt figure towered above her in shadow. His slapping brush had a vicious sound.

Neither spoke for some time. At length she said more gently, "Ain't you comin' in?"

"No-not till I get a-ready. You go 'long an' tend to y'r own business. Don't stan' there an' ketch cold."

She moved off slowly toward the house. His shout subdued her. Working alone out there had rendered him savage; he was not to be pushed any further. She knew by the tone of his voice that he must now be respected.

She slipped on her shoes and a shawl, and came back where he was working, and took a seat on a sawhorse.

"I'm goin' to set right here till you come in, Ethan Ripley," she said in a firm voice, but gentler than usual.

"Wal, you'll set a good while," was his ungracious reply, but each felt a furtive tenderness for the other. He worked on in silence. The boards creaked heavily as he walked to and fro, and the slapping sound of the paint brush sounded loud in the sweet harmony of the night. The majestic moon swung slowly round the corner of the barn and fell upon the old man's grizzled head and bent shoulders. The horses inside could be heard stamping the mosquitoes away and chewing their hay in pleasant chorus.

The little figure seated on the sawhorse drew the shawl closer about her thin shoulders. Her eyes were in shadow, and her hands were wrapped in her shawl. At last she spoke in a curious tone.

"Wal, I don't know as you was so very much to blame. I didn't want that Bible myself-I hold out I did, but I didn't."

Ethan worked on until the full meaning of this unprecedented surrender penetrated his head, and then he threw down his brush.

"Wal, I guess I'll let 'er go at that. I'ye covered up the most of it, anyhow. Guess we better go in."

10. GOD'S RAVENS

I

CHICAGO has three winds that blow upon it. One comes from the East, and the mind goes out to the cold gray-blue lake. One from the North, and men think of illimitable spaces of pinelands and maple-clad ridges which lead to the unknown deeps of the arctic woods.

But the third is the West of Southwest wind, dry, magnetic, full of smell of unmeasured miles of growing grain in summer, or ripening corn and wheat in autumn. When it comes in winter the air glitters with incredible brilliancy. The snow of the country dazzles and flames in the eyes; deep blue shadows everywhere stream like stains of ink. Sleigh bells wrangle from early morning till late at night, and every step is quick and alert. In the city, smoke dims its clarity, but it is welcome.

But its greatest moment of domination is spring. The bitter gray wind of the East has held unchecked rule for days, giving place to its brother the North wind only at intervals, till some day in March the wind of the southwest begins to blow. Then the eaves begin to drip. Here and there a fowl (in a house that is really a prison) begins to sang the song it sang on the farm, and toward noon its song becomes a chant of articulate joy.

Then the poor crawl out of their reeking hovels on the South and West sides to stand in the sun-the blessed sun-and felicitate themselves on being alive. Windows of sickrooms are opened, the merry small boy goes to school without his tippet, and men lay off their long ulsters for their beaver coats. Caps give place to hats, and men women pause to chat when they meet each other the street. The open door is the sign of the great change of wind.

There are imaginative souls who are stirred yet deeper by this wind-men like Robert Bloom, to whom come vague and very sweet reminiscences of farm life when the snow is melting and the dry ground begins to appear. To these people the wind comes from the wide unending spaces of the prairie West. They can smell the strange thrilling odor of newly uncovered sod and moist brown plowed lands. To them it is like the opening door of a prison.

Robert had crawled downtown and up to his office high in the Star block after a month's sickness. He had resolutely pulled a pad of paper under his hand to write, but the window was open and that wind coming in, and he could not write-he could only dream.

His brown hair fell over the thin white hand which propped his head. His face was like ivory with dull yellowish stains in it. His eyes did not see the mountainous roofs humped and piled into vast masses of brick and stone, crossed and riven by streets, and swept by masses of gray-white vapor; they saw a little valley circled by low-wooded bluffs-his native town in Wisconsin.

As his weakness grew his ambition fell away, and his heart turned back to nature and to the things he had known in his youth, to the kindly people of the olden time. It did not occur to him that the spirit of the country might have changed.

Sitting thus, he had a mighty longing come upon him to give up the struggle, to go back to the simplest life with his wife and two boys. Why should he tread in the mill, when every day was taking the lifeblood out of his heart?

Slowly his longing took resolution. At last he drew his desk down, and as the lock clicked it seemed like the shutting of a prison gate behind him.

At the elevator door he met a fellow editor. "Hello, Bloom! Didn't know you were down today."

"I'm only trying it. I'm going to take a vacation for a while."

"That's right, man. You look like a ghost."

"He hadn't the courage to tell him he never expected to work there again. His step on the way home was firmer than it had been for weeks. In his white face his wife saw some subtle change.

"What is it, Robert?"

"Mate, let's give it up."

"What do you mean?"

"The struggle is too hard. I can't stand it. I'm hungry for the country again. Let's get out of this."

"Where'll we go?"

"Back to my native town-up among the Wisconsin hills and coulees. Go anywhere, so that we escape this pressure-it's killing me. Let's go to Bluff Siding for a year. It will do me good-may bring me back to life. I can do enough special work to pay our grocery bill; and the Merrill place-so Jack tells me-is empty. We can get it for seventy-five dollars for a year. We can pull through some way."

"Very well, Robert."

"I must have rest. All the bounce has gone out of me, Mate," he said with sad lines in his face. "Any extra work here is out of the question. I can only shamble around-an excuse for a man."

The wife had ceased to smile. Her strenuous cheerfulness could not hold before his tragically drawn and bloodless face.

"I'll go wherever you think best, Robert It will be just as well for the boys. I suppose there is a school there?"

"Oh, yes. At any rate, they can get a year's schooling in nature."

"Well-no matter, Robert; you are the one to be considered." She had the self-sacrificing devotion of the average woman. She fancied herself hopelessly his inferior.

They had dwelt so long on the crumbling edge of poverty that they were hardened to its threat, and yet the failure of Robert's health had been of the sort which terrifies. It was a slow but steady sinking of vital force. It had its ups and downs, but it was a downward trail, always downward. The time for sell-deception had passed.

His paper paid him a meager salary, for his work was prized only by the more thoughtful readers of the Star.

In addition to his' regular work he occasionally hazarded a story for the juvenile magazines of the East. In this way he turned the antics of his growing boys to account, as he often said to his wife.

He had also passed the preliminary stages of literary success by getting a couple of stories accepted by an Eastern magazine, and he still confidently looked forward to seeing them printed.

His wife, a sturdy, practical little body, did her part in the bitter struggle by keeping their little home one of the most attractive on the West Side, the North Side being altogether too high for them.

In addition, her sorely pressed brain sought out other ways of helping. She wrote out all her husband's stories on the typewriter, and secretly she had tried composing others herself, the results being queer dry little chronicles of the doings of men and women, strung together without a touch of literary grace.

She proposed taking a large house and re-renting rooms, but Robert would not hear to it. "As long as I can crawl about we'll leave that to others."

In the month of preparation which followed he talked a great deal about their venture.

"I want to get there," he said, "just when the leaves are coming out on the trees. I want to see the cherry trees blossom on the hillside. The popple trees always get green first."

At other times he talked about the people. "It will be a rest just to get back among people who aren't ready to tread on your head in order to lift themselves up. I believe a year among those kind, unhurried people will give me all the material I'll need for years. I'll write a series of studies somewhat like Jefferies'—or Barrie's—only, of course, I'll be original. I'll just take his plan Of telling about the people I meet and their queer ways, so quaint and good."

"I'm tired of the scramble," he kept breaking out Of silence to say. "I don't blame the boys, but it's plain to me they see that my going will let them move up one. Mason cynically voiced the whole thing today: 'I can say, "Sorry to see you go, Bloom," because your going doesn't concern me. I'm not in line of succession, but some of the other boys don't feel so. There's no divinity doth hedge an editor; nothing but law prevents the murder of those above by those below.'"

"I don't like Mr. Mason when he talks like that," said the wife.

"Well-I don't." He didn't tell her what Mason said when Robert talked about the good simple life of the people in Bluff Siding:

"Oh, bosh, Bloom! You'll find the struggle of the outside world reflected in your little town. You'll find men and women just as hard and selfish in their small way. It'll be harder to bear, because it will all be so petty and pusillanimous."

It was a lovely day in late April when they took the train out of the great grimy terrible city. It was eight o'clock, but the streets were muddy and wet, a cold East wind blowing off the lake.

With clanging bell the train moved away, piercing the ragged gray formless mob of houses and streets (through which railways always run in a city). Men were hurrying to work, and Robert pitied them, poor fellows, condemned to do that thing forever.

In an hour they reached the prairies, already clothed upon faintly with green grass and tender springing wheat. The purple-brown squares reserved for the corn looked deliciously soft and warm to the sick man, and he longed to set his bare feet into it.

His boys were wild with delight. They had the natural love of the earth still in them, and correspondingly cared little for the city. They raced through the cars like colts. They saw everything. Every blossoming plant, every budding tree, was precious to them all.

All day they rode. Toward noon they left the sunny prairie land of northern Illinois and southern Wisconsin, and entered upon the hill land of Madison and beyond. As they went North, the season was less advanced, but spring was in the fresh wind and the warm sunshine.

As evening drew on, the hylas began to peep from the pools, and their chorus deepened as they came on toward Bluff Siding, which seemed very small, very squalid, and uninteresting, but Robert pointed at the circling wine-colored wall of hills and the warm sunset sky.

"We're in luck to find a hotel," said Robert. "They burn down every three months."

They were met by a middle-aged man and conducted across the road to a hotel, which had been a roller-skating rink in other days, and was not prepossessing. However, they were ushered into the parlor, which resembled the sitting room of a rather ambitious village home, and there they took seats, while the landlord consulted about rooms.

The wife's heart sank. From the window she could see several of the low houses, and far off just the hills which seemed to make the town so very small, very lonely. She was not given time to shed tears. The children clamored for food, tired and cross.

Robert went out into the office, where he signed his name under the close and silent scrutiny of a half dozen roughly clad men, who sat leaning against the wall. They were merely workingmen to him, but in Mrs. Bloom's eyes they were dangerous people.

The landlord looked at the name as Robert wrote. "Your boxes are all here," he said.

Robert looked up at him in surprise. "What boxes?"

"Your household goods. They came in on No.9."

Robert recovered himself. He remembered this was a village where everything that goes on-everything-is known.

The stairway rose picturesquely out of the office to the low second story, and up these stairs they tramped to' their tiny rooms, which were like cells.

"Oh, Mamma, ain't it queer?" cried the boys.

"Supper is all ready," the landlord's soft, deep voice announced a few moments later, and the boys responded with whoops of hunger.

They were met by the close scrutiny of every boarder as they entered, and they heard also the muttered comments and explanations.

"Family to take the Merrill house."

"He looks purty well fiaxed out, don't he?"

They were agreeably surprised to find everything neat and clean and wholesome. The bread was good and the butter delicious. Their spirits revived.

"That butter tastes like old times," said Robert. "Ii's fresh. It's really butter."

They made a hearty meal, and the boys, being filled up, grew sleepy. After they were put to bed Robert said, "Now, Mate, let's go see the house."

They walked out arm in arm like lovers. Her sturdy form steadied him, though he would not have acknowledged it. The red flush was not yet gone from the west, and the hills still kept a splendid tone of purple-black. It was very clear, the stars were out, the wind deliciously soft. "Isn't it still?" Robert almost whispered.

They walked on under the budding trees up the hill, till they came at last to the small frame house set under tall maples and locust trees, just showing a feathery fringe of foliage.

"This is our home," said Robert.

Mate leaned on the gate in silence. Frogs were peeping. The smell of spring was in the air. There was a magnificent repose in the hour, restful, recreating, impressive.

"Oh, it's beautiful, Robert! I know we shall like it."

"We must like it," he said.

II

First contact with the people disappointed Robert. In the work of moving in he had to do with people who work at day's work, and the fault was his more than theirs. He forgot that they did not consider their work degrading. They resented his bossing. The drayman grew rebellious.

"Look a-here, my Christian friend, if you'll go 'long in the house and let us alone it'll be a good job. We know what we're about."

This was not pleasant, and he did not perceive the trouble. In the same way he got foul of the carpenter and the man who plowed his garden. Some way his tone was not right. His voice was cold and distant. He generally found that the men knew better than he what was to be done and how to do it; and sometimes he felt like apologizing, but their attitude had changed till apology was impossible.

He had repelled their friendly advances because he considered them (without meaning to do so) as workmen, and not as neighbors. They reported, therefore, that he was cranky and rode a high horse.

"He thinks he's a little tin god on wheels," the drayman said.

"Oh, he'll get over that," said McLane. "I knew the boy's folks years ago-tip-top folks, too. He ain't well, and that makes him a little crusty."

"That's the trouble-he thinks he's an upper crust," said Jim Cullen, the drayman.

At the end of ten days they were settled, and nothing remained to do but plan a little garden and-get well. The boys, with their unspoiled natures, were able to melt into the ranks of the village-boy life at once, with no more friction than was indicated by a couple of rough-and-tumble fights. They were sturdy fellows, like their mother, and these fights gave them high rank.

Robert got along in a dull, smooth way with his neighbors. He was too formal with them. He met them only at the meat shop and the post office. They nodded genially and said, "Got settled yet?" And he replied, "Quite comfortable, thank you." They felt his coldness. Conversation halted when he came near and made him feel that he was the subject of their talk. As a matter of fact, he generally was. He was a source of great speculation with them. Some of them had gone so far as to bet he wouldn't live a year. They all seemed grotesque to him, so work-scarred and bent and hairy. Even the men whose names he had known from childhood were queer to him. They seemed shy and distant, too, not like his ideas of them.

To Mate they were almost caricatures. "What makes them look so-so 'way behind the times, Robert?"

"Well, I suppose they are," said Robert. "Life in these coulees goes on rather slower than in Chicago. Then there are a great many Welsh and Germans and Norwegians living way up the coulees, and they're the ones you notice. They're not all so." He could be generous toward them in general; it was in special cases where he failed to know them.

They had been there nearly two weeks without meeting any of them socially, and Robert was beginning to change his opinion about them. "They let us severely alone," he was saying one night to his wife.

"It's very odd. I wonder what I'd better do, Robert. I don't know the etiquette of these small towns. I never lived in one before, you know. Whether I ought to call first-and, good gracious, who'll I call on? I'm in the dark."

"So am I, to tell the truth. I haven't lived in one of these small towns since I was a lad. I have a faint recollection that introductions were absolutely necessary. They have an etiquette which is as binding as that of McAllister's Four Hundred, but what it is I don't know."

"Well, we'll wait."

"The boys are perfectly at home," said Robert with a little emphasis on boys, which was the first indication of his disappointment. The people he had failed to reach.

There came a knock on the door that startled them both. "Come in," said Robert in a nervous shout.

"Land sakes! did I scare ye? Seem so, way ye yelled," said a high-keyed nasal voice, and a tall woman came in, followed by an equally stalwart man.

"How d'e do, Mrs. Folsom? My wife, Mr. Folsom."

Folsom's voice was lost in the bustle of getting settled, but Mrs. Folsom's voice rose above the clamor. "I was tellin' him it was about time we got neighborly. I never let anybody come to town a week without callin' on 'em. It does a body a heap o' good to see a face outside the family once in a while, specially in a new place. How do you like up here on the hill?"

"Very much. The view is so fine."

"Yes, I s'pose it is. Still, it ain't my notion. I don't like to climb hills well enough. Still, I've heard of people buildin' just for the view. It's all in taste, as the old woman said that kissed the cow."

There was an element of shrewdness and sell-analysis in Mrs. Folsom which saved her from being grotesque. She knew she was queer to Mrs. Bloom, but she did not resent it. She was still young in form and face, but her teeth were gone, and, like so many of her neighbors, she was too poor to replace them from the dentist's. She wore a decent calico dress and a shawl and hat.

As she talked her eyes took in every article of furniture in the room, and every little piece of fancywork and bric-a-brac. In fact, she reproduced the pattern of one of the tidies within two days.

Folsom sat dumbly in his chair. Robert, who met him now as a neighbor for the first time, tried to talk with him, but failed, and turned himself gladly to Mrs. Folsom, who delighted him with her vigorous phrases.

"Oh, we're a-movin', though you wouldn't think it. This town is filled with a lot of old skinflints. Close ain't no name for 'em. Jest ask Folsom thar about 'em. He's been buildin' their houses for 'em. Still, I suppose they say the same thing o' me," she added with a touch of humor which always saved her. She used a man's phrases. "We're always ready to tax some other feller, but we kick like mules when the tax falls on us," she went on. "My land! the fight we've had to git sidewalks in this town!"

"You should be mayor."

"That's what I tell Folsom. Takes a woman to clean things up. Well, I must run along. Thought I'd jest call in and see how you all was. Come down when ye kin."

"Thank you, I will."

After they had gone Robert turned with a smile: "Our first formal call."

"Oh, dear, Robert, what can I do with such people?"

"Go see 'em. I like her. She's shrewd. You'll like her, too."

"But what can I say to such people? Did you hear her say 'we fellers' to me?"

Robert laughed. "That's nothing. She feels as much of a man, or 'feller,' as anyone. Why shouldn't she?"

"But she's so vulgar."

"I admit she isn't elegant, but I think she's a good wife and mother."

"I wonder if they're all like that?"

"Now, Mate, we must try not to offend them. We must try to be one of them."

But this was easier said than done. As he went down to the post office and stood waiting for his mail like the rest, he tried to enter into conversation with them, but mainly they moved away from him. William McTurg nodded at him and said, "How de do?" and McLane asked how he liked his new place, and that was about all.

He couldn't reach them. They suspected him. They had only the estimate of the men who had worked for him; and, while they were civil, they plainly didn't need him in the slightest degree, except as a topic of conversation.

He did not improve as he had hoped to do. The spring was wet and cold, the most rainy and depressing the valley had seen in many years. Day after day the rain clouds sailed in over the northern hills and deluged the flat little town with water, till the frogs sang in every street, till the main street mired down every team that drove into it.

The corn rotted in the earth, but the grass grew tall and yellow-green, the trees glistened through the gray air, and the hills were like green jewels of incalculable worth, when the sun shone, at sweet infrequent intervals.

The cold and damp struck through into the alien's heart. It seemed to prophesy his dark future. He sat at his desk and looked out into the gray rain with gloomy eyes-a prisoner when he had expected to be free.

He had failed in his last venture. He had not gained any power-he was really weaker than ever. The rain had kept him confined to the house. The joy he had anticipated of tracing out all his boyish pleasure haunts was cut off. He had relied, too, upon that as a source of literary power.

He could not do much more than walk down to the post office and back on the pleasantest days. A few people called, but he could not talk to them, and they did not call again.

In the meanwhile his little bank account was vanishing. The boys were strong and happy; that was his only comfort. And his wife seemed strong, too. She had little time to get lonesome.

He grew morbid. His weakness and insecurity made him jealous of the security and health of others.

He grew almost to hate the people as he saw them coming and going in the mud, or heard their loud hearty voices sounding from the street. He hated their gossip, their dull jokes. The flat little town grew vulgar and low and desolate to him.

Every little thing which had amused him now annoyed him. The cut of their beards worried him. Their voices jarred upon him. Every day or two he broke forth to his wife in long tirades of abuse.

"Oh, I can't stand these people! They don't know any-thing. They talk every rag of gossip into shreds. Taters, fish, hops; hops, fish, and taters. They've saved and pinched and toiled till their souls are pinched and ground away. You're right. They are caricatures. They don't read or think about anything in which I'm interested. This life is nerve-destroying. Talk about the health of the village life! it destroys body and soul. It debilitates me. It will warp us both down to the level of these people."

She tried to stop him, but he went on, a flush of fever on his cheek:

"They degrade the nature they have touched. Their squat little town is a caricature like themselves. Everything they touch they belittle. Here they sit while side-walks rot and teams mire in the streets."

He raged on like one demented-bitter, accusing, rebellious. In such a mood he could not write. In place of inspiring him, the little town and its people seemed to undermine his power and turn his sweetness of spirit into gall and acid. He only bowed to them now as he walked feebly among them, and they excused it by referring to his sickness. They eyed him each time with pitying eyes; "He's failin' fast," they said among themselves.

One day, as he was returning from the post office, he felt blind for a moment and put his hand to his head. The world of vivid green grew gray, and life receded from him into illimitable distance. He had one dim fading glimpse of a shaggy-bearded face looking down at him, and felt the clutch of an iron-hard strong arm under him, and then he lost hold even on so much consciousness.

He came back slowly, rising out of immeasurable deeps toward a distant light which was like the mouth of a well filled with clouds of misty vapor. Occasionally he saw a brown big hairy face floating in over this lighted horizon, to smile kindly and go away again. Others came with shaggy beards. He heard a cheery tenor voice which he recognized, and then another face, a big brown smiling face; very lovely it looked now to him-almost as lovely as his wife's, which floated in from the other side.

"He's all right now," said the cheery tenor voice from the big bearded face.

"Oh, Mr. McTurg; do you think so?"

"Ye-e-s, sir. He's all right. The fever's left him. Brace up, old man. We need ye yit awhile." Then all was silent again.

The well mouth cleared away its mist again, and he saw more clearly. Part of the time he knew he was in bed staring at the ceiling. Part of the time the well mouth remained closed in with clouds.

Gaunt old women put spoons of delicious broth to his lips, and their toothless mouths had kindly lines about them. He heard their high voices sounding faintly.

"Now, Mis' Bloom, jest let Mis' Folsom an' me attend to things out here. We'll get supper for the boys, an' you jest go an' lay down. We'll take care of him. Don't worry. Bell's a good hand with sick."

Then the light came again, and he heard a robin singing, and a catbird squalled softly, pitifully. He could see the ceiling again. He lay on his back, with his hands on his breast. He felt as if he had been dead. He seemed to feel his body as if it were an alien thing.

"How are you, sir?" called the laughing, thrillingly hearty voice of William McTurg.

He tried to turn his head, but it wouldn't move. He tried to speak, but his dry throat made no noise.

The big man bent over him. "Want 'o change place a little?"

He closed his eyes in answer.

A giant arm ran deftly under his shoulders and turned him as if he were an infant, and a new part of the good old world burst on his sight. The sunshine streamed in the windows through a waving screen of lilac leaves and fell upon the carpet in a priceless flood of radiance.

There sat William McTurg smiling at him. He had no coat on and no hat, and his bushy thick hair rose up from his forehead like thick marsh grass. He looked to be the embodiment of sunshine and health. Sun and air were in his brown face, and the perfect health of a fine animal was in his huge limbs. He looked at Robert with a smile that brought a strange feeling into his throat. It made him try to speak; at last he whispered.

The great figure bent closer: "What is it?"

"Thank-you."

William laughed a low chuckle. "Don't bother about thanks. Would you like some water?"

A tall figure joined William, awkwardly.

"Hello, Evan!"

"How is he?"

"He's awake today."

"That's good. Anything I can do?"

"No, I guess not. All he needs is somethin' to eat."

"I jest brought a chicken up, an' some jell an' things the women sent. I'll stay with him till twelve, then Folsom will come in."

Thereafter he lay hearing the robins laugh and the orioles whistle, and then the frogs and katydids at night. These men with greasy vests and unkempt beards came in every day. They bathed him, and helped him to and from the bed. They helped to dress him and move him to the window, where he could look out on the blessed green of the grass.

O God, it was so beautiful! It was a lover's joy only to live, to look into these radiant vistas again. A catbird was singing in the currant hedge. A robin was hopping across the lawn. The voices of the children sounded soft and jocund across the road. And the sunshine-"Beloved Christ, Thy sunshine falling upon my feet!" His soul ached with the joy of it, and when his wife came in she found him sobbing like a child.

They seemed never to weary in his service. They lifted him about and talked to him in loud and hearty voices which roused him like fresh winds from free spaces.

He heard the women busy with things in the kitchen. He often saw them loaded with things to eat passing his window, and often his wife came in and knelt down at his bed.

"Oh, Robert, they're so good! They feed us like Gods ravens."

One day, as he sat at the window fully dressed for the fourth of fifth time, William McTurg came up the walk.

"Well, Robert, how are ye today?"

"First-rate, William," he smiled. "I believe I can walk out a little if you'll help me."

"All right, sir."

And he went forth leaning on William's arm, a piteous wraith of a man.

On every side the golden June sunshine fell, filling the valley from purple brim to purple brim. Down over the hill to the west the light poured, tangled and glowing in the plum and cherry trees, leaving the glistening grass spraying through the elms and flinging streamers of pink across the shaven green slopes where the cattle fed.

On every side he saw kindly faces and heard hearty voices: "Good day, Robert. Glad to see you out again." It thrilled him to hear them call him by his first name.

His heart swelled till he could hardly breathe. The passion of living came back upon him, shaking, uplifting him. His pallid lips moved. His face was turned to the sky.

"O God, let me live! It is so beautiful! O God, give me strength again! Keep me in the light of the sun! Let me see the green grass come and go!"

He turned to William with trembling lips, trying to speak:

"Oh, I understand you now. I know you all now."

But William did not understand him.

"There! there!" he said soothingly. "I guess you're gettin' tired." He led Robert back and put him to bed.

"I'd know but we was a little brash about goin' out," William said to him as Robert lay there smiling up at him.

"Oh, I'm all right now," the sick man said.

"Matie," the alien cried, when William had gone, "we knew our neighbors now, don't we? We never can hate or ridicule them again."

"Yes, Robert. They never will be caricatures again-to me."

11. A"GOOD FELLOW'S" WIFE

I

LIFE in the small towns of the older West moves slowly-almost as slowly as in the seaport villages or little towns of the East. Towns like Tyre and Bluff Siding have grown during the last twenty years, but very slowly, by almost imperceptible degrees. Lying too far away from the Mississippi to be affected by the lumber interest, they are merely trading points for the farmers, with no perceivable germs of boom in their quiet life.

A stranger coming into Belfast, Minnesota, excites much the same lanquid but persistent inquiry as in Belfast, New Hampshire. Juries of men, seated on salt barrels and nall kegs, discuss the stranger's appearance and his probable action, just as in Kittery, Maine, but with a lazier speech tune and with a shade less of apparent interest.

On such a rainy day as comes in May after the corn is planted-a cold, wet rainy day-the usual crowd was gathered in Wilson's grocery store at Bluff Siding, a small town in the "coulee country." They were farmers, for the most part, retired from active service. Their coats were of cheap diagonal or cassimere, much faded and burned by the sun; their hats, flapped about by winds and soaked with countless rains, were also of the same yellow-brown tints. One or two wore paper collars on their hickory shirts.

McIlvaine, farmer and wheat buyer, wore a paper collar and a butterfly necktie, as befitted a man of his station in life. He was a short, squarely made Scotchman, with sandy whiskers much grayed and with a keen, in-tensely blue eye.

"Say," called McPhail, ex-sheriff of the county, in the silence that followed some remark about the rain, "any o' you fellers had any talk with this feller Sanford?"

"I hain't," said Vance. "You, Bill?"

"No; but somebody was sayin' he thought o' startin' in trade here."

"Don't Sam know? He generally knows what's goin' on.',

"Knows he registered from Pittsfield, Mass., an' that's all. Say, that's a mighty smart-lookin' woman o' his."

"Vance always sees how the women look, Where'd you see her?"

"Came in here the other day to look up prices."

"Wha'd she say 'bout settlin'?"

"Hadn't decided yet."

"He's too slick to have much business in him. That waxed mustache gives 'im away."

The discussion having reached that point where his word would have most effect, Steve Gilbert said, while opening the hearth to rap out the ashes of his pipe, "Sam's wife heerd that he was kind o' thinkin' some of goin' into business here, if things suited 'im first-rate."

They all knew the old man was aching to tell something, but they didn't purpose to gratify him by any questions. The rain dripped from the awning in front and fell upon the roof of the storeroom at the back with a soft and steady roar.

"Good f'r the corn," McPhail said after a long pause.

"Purty cold, though."

Gilbert was tranquil-he had a shot in reserve. "Sam's wife said his wife said he was thinkin' some of goin' into a bank here-"

"A bank!"

"What in thunder-"

Vance turned, with a comical look on his long, placid face, one hand stroking his beard.

"Well, now, gents, I'll tell you what's the matter with this town. It needs a bank. Yes, sir! I need a bank."

"You?"

"Yes, me. I didn't know just what did ail me, but I do how. It's the need of a bank that keeps me down."

"Well, you fellers can talk an' laugh, but I tell yeb they's a boom goin' to strike this town. It's got to come.. W'y, just look at Lumberville!"

"Their boom is our bust," was McPhail's comment.

"I don't think so," said Sanford, who had entered in time to hear these last two speeches. They all looked at him with deep interest. He was a smallish man. He wore a derby hat and a neat suit. "I've looked things over pretty close-a man don't like to invest his capital" (here the rest looked at one another) "till he does; and I believe there's an opening for a bank."

As he dwelt upon the scheme from day to day, the citizens, warmed to him, and he became "Jim" Sanford. He hired a little cottage and went to housekeeping at once; but the entire summer went by before he made his decision to settle. In fact, it was in the last week of August that the little paper announced it in the usual style:

Mr. James G. Sanford, popularly known as "Jim," has decided to open an' exchange bank for the convenience of our citizens, who have hitherto been forced to transact business in Lumberville. The thanks of the town are due Mr. Sanford, who comes well recommended from Massachusetts and from Milwaukee, and, better still, with a bag of ducats. Mr. S. will be well patronized. Success, Jim!

The bank was open by the time the corn crop and the hogs were being marketed, and money was received on deposit while the carpenters were still at work on the building. Everybody knew now that he was as solid as oak.

He had taken into the bank, as bookkeeper, Lincoln Bingham, one of McPhail's multitudinous nephews; and this was a capital move. Everybody knew Link, and knew he was a McPhail, which meant that he "could be tied to in all kinds o' weather." Of course the McPhails, McIlvaines, and the rest of the Scotch contingency "banked on Link." As old Andrew McPhail put it:

"Link's there, an' he knows the bank an' books, an' just how things stand"; and so when he sold his hogs he put the whole sum—over fifteen hundred dollars—into the bank. The McIlvaines and the Binghams did the same, and the bank was at once firmly established among the farmers.

Only two people held out against Sanford, old Freeme Cole and Mrs. Bingham, Lincoln's mother; but they didn't count, for Freeme hadn't a cent, and Mrs. Bingham was too unreasoning in her opposition. She could only say:

"I don't like him, that's all. I knowed a man back in New York that curled his mustaches just that way, an' he wa'n't no earthiy good."

It might have been said by a cynic that Banker Sanford had all the virtues of a defaulting bank cashier. He had no bad habits beyond smoking. He was genial, companionable, and especially ready to help when sickness came. When old Freeme Cole got down with delirium tremens that winter, Sanford was one of the most heroic of nurses, and the service was so clearly disinterested and magnanimous that everyone spoke of it.

His wife and he were included in every dance or picnic; for Mrs. Sanford was as great a favorite as the banker himself, she was so sincere, and her gray eyes were so charmingly frank, and then she said "such funny things."

"I wish I had something to do besides housework. It's a kind of a putterin' job, best ye can do," she'd say merrily, just to see the others stare. "There's too much moppin' an' dustin'. Seems 's if a woman used up half her life on things that don't amount to anything, don't it?"

"I tell yeh that feller's a scallywag. I know it bull the way 'e walks 'long the sidewalk," Mrs. Bingham insisted to her son, who wished her to put her savings into the bank.

The youngest of a large family, Link had been accustomed all his life to Mrs. Bingham's many whimsicalities.

"I s'pose you can smell he's a thief, just as you can tell when it's goin' to rain, or the butter's comin', by the smell."

"Well, you needn't laugh, Lincoln. I can," maintained the old lady stoutly. "An' I ain't goin' to put a red cent o my money into his pocket-f'r there's where it 'ud go to."

She yielded at last, and received a little bankbook in return for her money. "Jest about all I'll ever get," she said privately; and thereafter out of her' brass-bowed spectacles with an eagle's gaze she watched the banker go by. But the banker, seeing the dear old soul at the window looking out at him, always smiled and bowed, unaware of her suspicion.

At the end of the year he bought the lot next to his rented house and began building one of his own, a modest little affair, shaped like a pork pie with a cupola, or a Tamo'-Shanter cap-a style of architecture which became fashionable at once.

He worked heroically to get the location of the plow factory at Bluff Siding, and all but succeeded; but Tyre, once their ally, turned against them, and refused to consider the fact of the Siding's position at the center of the county. However, for some reason or other, the town woke up to something of a boom during the next two years. Several large farmers decided to retire and live off the sweat of some other fellow's brow, and so built some houses of the pork-pie order and moved into town.

This inflow of moneyed men from the country resulted in the establishment of a "seminary of learning" on the hillside, where the Soldiers' Home was to be located. This called in more farmers from the country, and a new hotel was built, a sash-and-door factory followed, and Burt McPhail set up a feed mill.

And this improvement unquestionably dated, from the opening of the bank, and the most unreasoning partisans of the banker held him to be the chief cause of the resulting development of the town, though he himself modestly disclaimed any hand in the affair.

Had Bluff Siding been a city, the highest civic honors would have been open to Banker Sanford; indeed, his name was repeatedly mentioned in connection with the county offices.

"No, gentlemen," he explained firmly, but courteously, in Wilson's store one night; "I'm a banker, not a politician. I can't ride two horses."

In the second year of the bank's history he went up to the north part of the state on business, visiting West Superior, Duluth, Ashland, and other booming towns, and came back full of the wonders of what he saw.

"There's big money up there, Nell," he said to his wife.

But she had the woman's tendency to hold fast to what she had, and would not listen to any plans about moving.

"Build up your business here, Jim, and don't worry about what good chances there are somewhere else."

He said no more about it, but he took great interest in all the news the "boys" brought back from their annual deer hunts "up North." They were all enthusiastic over West Superior and Duluth, and their wonderful development was the never-ending theme of discussion in Wilson's store.

II

The first two years of the bank's history were solidly successful, and "Jim" and "Nellie" were the head and front of all good works and the provoking cause of most of the fun. No one seemed more carefree.

"We consider ourselves just as young as anybody," Mrs. Sanford would say, when joked about going out with the young people so much; but sometimes at home, after the children were asleep, she sighed a little.

"Jim, I wish you was in some kind of a business so I could help. I don't have enough to do. I s'pose I could mop an' dust, an' dust an' mop; but it seems sinful to Waste time that way. Can't I do anything, Jim?"

"Why, no. If you 'tend to the children and keep house, that's all anybody asks of you."

She was silent, but not convinced. She had a desire to do something outside the walls of her house-a desire transmitted to her from her father, for a woman inherits these things.

In the spring of the second year a number of the depositors drew out money to invest in Duluth and Superior lots, and the whole town was excited over the matter.

The summer passed, Link and Sanford spending their time in the bank-that is, when not out swimming or fishing with the boys. But July and August were terribly hot and dry, and oats and corn were only half-crop; and the farmers were grumbling. Some of them were forced to draw on the bank instead of depositing.

McPhail came in, one day in November, to draw a thousand dollars to pay for a house and lot he had recently bought.

Sanford was alone. He whistled. "Phew! You're comin' at me hard. Come in tomorrow. Link's gone down to the city to get some money."

"All right," said McPhail; "any time."

"Goin' t' snow?"

"Looks like it. I'll haf to load a lot o' ca'tridges ready fr biz."

About an hour later old lady Bingham burst upon the banker, wild and breathless. "I want my money," she announced.

"Good morning, Mrs. Bingham. Pleasant-"

"I want my money. Where's Lincoln?"

She had read that morning of two bank failure-one in Nova Scotia and one in Massachusetts-and they seemed providential warnings to her. Lincoln's absence confirmed them.

"He's gone to St. Paul-won't be back till the five-o'clock train. Do you need some money this morning? How much?"

"All of it, sir. Every cent."

Sanford saw something was out of gear. He tried to explain. "I've sent your son to St. Paul after some money-"

"Where's my money? What have you done with that?" In her excitement she thought of her money just as she hand handed it in-silver and little rolls and wads of bills.

"If you'll let me explain-"

"I don't want you to explain nawthin'. Jest hand me out my money."

Two or three loafers, seeing her gesticulate, stopped on the walk outside and looked in at the door. Sanford was annoyed, but he remained calm and persuasive. He saw that something had caused a panic in the good, simple old woman. He wished for Lincoln as one wishes for a policeman sometimes.

"Now, Mrs. Bingham, if you'll only wait till Lincoln-"

"I don't want 'o wait. I want my money, right now."

"Will fifty dollars do?"

"No, sir; I want it all-every cent of it-jest as it was."

"But I can't do that. Your money is gone-"

"Gone? Where is it gone? What have you done with it? You thief-"

"'Sh!" He tried to quiet her. "I mean I can't give you your money-"

"Why can't you?" she stormed, trotting nervously on her feet as she stood there.

"Because-if you'd let me explain-we don't keep the money just as it comes to us. We pay it out and take in other-"

Mrs. Bingham was getting more and more bewildered. She now had only one clear idea-she couldn't get her money. Her voice grew tearful like an angry child's.

"I want my money-I knew you'd steal it-that I worked for. Give me my money."

Sanford hastily handed her some money. "Here's fifty dollars. You can have the rest when-"

The old lady clutched the money, and literally ran out of the door, and went off up the sidewalk, talking incoherently. To everyone she met she told her story; but the men smiled and passed on. They had heard her predictions of calamity before.

But Mrs. McIlvaine was made a triffe uneasy by it "He wouldn't give you y'r money? Or did he say he couldn't?" she inquired in her moderate way.

"He couldn't, an' he wouldn't!" she said. "If you've got any money there, you'd better get it out quick. It ain't safe a minute. When Lincoln comes home I'm goin' to see if I can't-"

"Well, I was calc'latin' to go to Lumberville this week, anyway, to buy a carpet and a chamber set. I guess I might 's well get the money today."

When she came in and demanded the money, Sanford was scared. Were these two old women the beginning of the deluge? Would McPhail insist on being paid also? There was just one hundred dollars left in the bank, together with a little silver. With rare strategy he smiled.

"Certainly, Mrs. McIlvaine. How much will you need?" She had intended to demand the whole of her deposit-one hundred and seventeen dollars-but his readiness mollified her a little. "I did 'low I'd take the hull, but I guess seventy-five dollars 'll do."

He paid the money briskly out over the little glass shelf. "How is your children, Mrs. McIlvaine?"

"Purty well, thanky," replied Mrs. McIlvaine, laboriously counting the bills.

"Is it all right?"

"I guess so," she replied dubiously. "I'll count it after I get home."

She went up the street with the feeling that the bank was all right, and she stepped in and told Mrs. Bingham that she had no trouble in getting her money.

Alter she had gone Sanford sat down and wrote a telegram which he sent to St. Paul. This telegram, according to the duplicate at the station, read in this puzzling way:

E. O., Exchange Block, No. 96. All out of paper. Send five hundred noteheads and envelopes to match. Business brisk. Press of correspondence just now. Get them out quick. Wire.

12. SANFORD

Two or three others came in after a little money, but he put them off easily. "Just been cashing some paper, and took all the ready cash I can spare. Can't you wait till tomorrow? Link's gone down to St. Paul to collect on some paper. Be back on the five o'clock. Nine o'clock, sure."

An old Norwegian woman came in to deposit ten dollars, and he counted it in briskly, and put the amount down on her little book for her. Barney Mace came in to deposit a hundred dollars, the proceeds of a horse sale, and this helped him through the day. Those who wanted small sums he paid.

"Glad this ain't a big demand. Rather close on cash today," he said, smiling, as Lincoln's wife's sister came in.

She laughed, "I guess it won't bust yeh. If I thought it would, I'd leave it in."

"Busted!" he said, when Vance wanted him to cash a draft. "Can't do it. Sorry, Van. Do it in the morning all right. Can you wait?"

"Oh, I guess so. Haf to, won't I?"

"Curious," said Sanford, in a confidential way. "I don't know that I ever saw things get in just such shape. Paper enough-but exchange, ye know, and readjustment of accounts."

"I don't know much about banking, myself," said Vance, good naturedly; "but I s'pose it's a good 'eal same as with a man. Git short o' cash, first they know -ain't got a cent to spare."

"That's the idea exactly. Credit all right, plenty o' property, but-" and he smiled and went at his books. The smile died out of his eyes as Vance went out, and he pulled a little morocco book from his pocket and began studying the beautiful columns of figures with which it seemed to be filled. Those he compared with the books with great care, thrusting the book out of sight when anyone entered.

He closed the bank as usual at five. Lincoln had not come couldn't come now till the nine-o'clock accommodation. For an hour after the shades were drawn he sat there in the semidarkness, silently pondering on his situation. This attitude and deep quiet were unusual to him. He heard the feet of friends and neighbors passing the door as he sat there by the smoldering coal fire, in the growing darkness. There was something impressive in his attitude.

He started up at last and tried to see what the hour was by turning the face of his watch to the dull glow from the cannon stoye's open door.

"Suppertime," he said and threw the whole matter off, as if he had decided it or had put off the decision till another time.

As he went by the post office Vance said to McIlvaine in a smiling way, as if it were a good joke on Sanford:

"Little short o' cash down at the bank."

"He's a good fellow," McIlvaine said.

"So's his wife," added Vance with a chuckle.

III

That night, after supper, Sanford sat in his snug little room with a baby on each knee, looking as cheerful and happy as any man in the village. The children crowed and shouted as he "trotted them to Boston," or rode them on the toe of his boot. They made a noisy, merry group.

Mrs. Sanford "did her own work," and her swift feet could be heard moving to and fro out in the kitchen. It was pleasant there; the woodwork, the furniture, the stove, the curtains-all had that look of newness just growing into coziness. The coal stove was lighted and the curtains were drawn.

After the work in the kitchen was done, Mrs. Sanford came in and sat awhile by the fire with the children, looking very wifely in her dark dress and white apron, her round, smiling face glowing with love and pride-the gloating look of a mother seeing her children in the arms of her husband.

"How is Mrs. Peterson's baby, Jim?" she said suddenly, her face sobering.

"Pretty bad, I guess. La, la, la-deedle-dee! The doctor seemed to think it was a tight squeak if it lived. Guess it's done for-oop 'e goes!"

She made a little leap at the youngest child and clasped it convulsively to her bosom. Her swift maternal imagination had made another's loss very near and terrible.

"Oh, say, Nell," he broke out, on seeing her sober, "I had the confoundedest time today with old lady Bingham-"

"'Sh! Baby's gone to sleep."

After the children had been put to bed in the little alcove off the sitting room, Mrs. Sanford came back, to find Jim absorbed over a little book of accounts.

"What are you studying, Jim?"

Someone knocked on the door before he had time to reply.

"Come in!" he said.

'Sh! Don't yell so," his wife whispered.

"Telegram, Jim," said a voice in the obscurity.

"Oh! That you, Sam? Come in.

Sam, a lathy fellow with a quid in his cheek, stepped in. "How d' 'e do, Mis' Sanford?"

"Set down-se' down."

"Can't stop; 'most train time."

Sanford tore the envelope open, read the telegram rapidly, the smile fading out of his face. He read it again, word for word, then sat looking at it.

"Any answer?" asked Sam.

"All right. Good night."

"Good night."

After the door slammed, Sanford took the sheet from the envelope and reread it. At length he dropped into his chair. "That settles it," he said aloud.

"Settles what? What's the news?" His wife came up and looked over his shoulder.

"Settles I've got to go on that nine-thirty train."

"Be back on the morning train?"

"Yes; I guess so-I mean, of course-I'll have to be-to open the bank."

Mrs. Sanford looked at him for a few seconds in silence. There was something in his look, and especially in his tone, that troubled her.

"What do you mean? Jim, you don't intend to come back!" She took his arm. "What's the matter? Now tell me! What are you going away for?"

He knew he could not deceive his wife's ears and eyes just then, so he remained silent. "We've got to leave, Nell," he admitted at last.

"Why? What for?"

"Because I'm busted-broke-gone up the spout-and all the rest!" he said desperately, with an attempt at fun. "Mrs. Bingham and Mrs. McIlvaine have busted me-dead."

"Why-why-what has become of the money-all the money the people have put in there?"

"Gone up with the rest."

"What 've you done with it? I don't-"

"Well, I've invested it-and lost it."

"James Gordon Sanford!" she exclaimed, trying to realize it. "Was that right? Ain't that a case of-of-"

"Shouldn't wonder. A case of embezzlement such as you read of in the newspapers." His tone was easy, but he avoided the look in his wife's beautiful gray eyes.

"But it's-stealing-ain't it?" She stared at him, bewildered by his reckless lightness of mood.- "It is now, because I've lost. If I'd'a won it, it 'ud 'a' been financial shrewdness!"

She asked her next question after a pause, in a low voice, and through teeth almost set. "Did you go into this bank to-steal this money? Tell me that!"

"No; I didn't, Nell. I ain't quite up to that."

His answer softened her a little, and she sat looking at him steadily as he went on. The tears began to roll slowly down her cheeks. Her hands were clenched.

"The fact is, the idea came into my head last fall when I went up to Superior. My partner wanted me to go in with him on some land, and I did. We speculated on the growth of the town toward the south. We made a strike; then he wanted me to go in on a copper mine. Of course I expected-"

As he went on with the usual excuses her mind made all the allowances possible for him. He had always been boyish, impulsive, and lacking in judgment and strength of character. She was humiliated and frightened, but she loved and sympathized with him.

Her silence alarmed him, and he made excuses for himself. He was speculating for her sake more than for his own, and so on.

"Cho-coo!" whistled the far-off train through the still air.

He sprang up and reached for his coat.

She seized his arm again. "Where are you going?" she sternly asked.

"To take that train."

'When are you coming back?"

"I don't know." But his tone said, "Never."

She felt it. Her face grew bitter. "Going to leave me and-the babies?"

"I'll send for you soon. Come, goodbye!" He tried to put his arm about her. She stepped back.

"Jim, if you leave me tonight" ("Choo-choo!" whistled the engine) "you leave me forever." There was a terrible resolution in her tone.

"What do you mean?"

"I mean that I'm going to stay here. If you go-I'll never be your wife-again-never!" She glanced at the sleeping children, and her chin trembled.

"I can't face those fellows-they'll kill me," he said in a sullen tone.

"No, they won't. They'll respect you, if you stay and tell 'em exactly how-it-all-is. You've disgraced me and my children, that's what you've done! If you don't stay-"

The clear jangle of the engine bell sounded through the night as with the whiz of escaping steam and scrape and jar of gripping brakes and howl of wheels the train came to a stop at the station. Sanford dropped his coat and sat down again. + "I'll have to stay now." His tone was dry and lifeless. It had a reproach in it that cut the wife deep-deep as the fountain of tears; and she went across the room and knelt at the bedside, burying her face in the clothes on the feet of her children, and sobbed silently.

The man sat with bent head, looking into the glowing coal, whistling through his teeth, a look of sullen resignation and endurance on his face that had never been there before. His very attitude was alien and ominous.

Neither spoke for a long time. At last he rose and began taking off his coat and vest.

"Well, I suppose there's nothing to do but go to bed."

She did not stir-she might have been asleep so far as any sound or motion was concerned. He went off to the bed in the little parlor, and she still knelt there, her heart full of anger, bitterness, sorrow.

The sunny uneventfulness of her past life made this great storm the more terrifying. Her trust in her husband had been absolute. A farmer's daughter, the bank clerk had seemed to her the equal of any gentleman in the world-her world; and when she knew his delicacy, his unfailing kindness, and his abounding good nature, she had accepted him as the father of her children, and this was the first revelation to her of his inherent moral weakness.

Her mind went over the whole ground again and again, in a sort of blinding rush. She was convinced of his lack of honor more by his tone, his inflections, than by his words. His lack of deep regret, his readiness to leave her to bear the whole shock of the discovery—these were in his flippant tones; and everytime she thought of them the hot blood surged over her. At such moments she hated him, and her white teeth clenched.

To these moods succeeded others, when she remembered his smile, the dimple in his chin, his tender care for the sick, his buoyancy, his songs to the children-How could he sit there, with the children on his knees, and plan to run away, leaving them disgraced?

She went to bed at last with the babies, and with their soft, warm little bodies touching her side fell asleep, pondering, suffering as only a mother and wife can suffer when distrust and doubt of her husband supplant confidence and adoration.

IV

The children awakened her by their delighted cooing and kissing. It was a great event, this waking to find mamma in their bed. It was hardly light, of a dull gray morning; and with the children tumbling about over her, feeling the pressure of the warm little hands and soft lips, she went over the whole situation again, and at last settled upon her action.

She rose, shook down the coal in the stove in the sitting room, and started a fire in the kitchen; then she dressed the children by the coal burner. The elder of them, as soon as dressed, ran in to wake "Poppa" while the mother went about breakfast-getting.

Sanford came out of his bedroom unwontedly gloomy, greeting the children in a subdued manner. He shivered as he sat by the fire and stirred the stove as if he thought the room was cold. His face was pale and moist.

"Breakfast is ready, James," called Mrs. Sanford in a tone which she meant to be habitual, but which had a cadence of sadness in it.

Some way, he found it hard to look at her as he came out. She busied herself with placing the children at the table, in order to conceal her own emotion.

"I don't believe I'll eat any meat this morning, Nellie. I ain't very well."

She glanced at him quickly, keenly. "What's the matter?"

"I d'know. My stomach is kind of upset by this failure o' mine. I'm in great shape to go down to the bank this morning and face them fellows."

"It's got to be done."

"I know it; but that don't help me any." He tried to smile.

She mused, while the baby hammered on his tin plate. "You've got to go down. If you don't-I will," said she resolutely. "And you must say that that money will be paid back-every cent."

"But that's more'n I can do-"

"It must be done."

under the law-"

re's nothing can make this thing right except paying every cent we owe.

goin' to have it said that my children-that I'm livin' on somebody else. If you don't pay these debts, I will. I've thought it all out. If you don't stay and face it, and pay these men, I won't own you as my husband. I loved and trusted you, Jim-I thought you was honorable-it's been a terrible blow-but I've decided it all in my mind."

She conquered her little weakness and went on to the end firmly. Her face looked pale. There was a square look about the mouth and chin. The iron resolution and Puritanic strength of her father, old John Foreman, had come to the surface. Her look and tone mastered the man, for he loved her deeply.

She had set him a hard task, and when he rose and went down the street he walked with bent head, quite unlike his usual self.

There were not many men on the street. It seemed earlier than it was, for it was a raw, cold morning, promising snow. The sun was completely masked in a seamless dust-gray cloud. He met Vance with a brown parcel (beefsteak for breakfast) under his arm.

"Hello, Jim! How are ye, so early in the morning?"

"Blessed near used up."

"That so? What's the matter?"

"I d'know," said Jim, listlessly. "Bilious, I guess. Headache—stomach bad."

"Oh! Well, now, you try them pills I was tellin' you of." Arrived at the bank, he let himself in and locked the door behind him. He stood in the middle of the floor a few minutes, then went behind the railing and sat down. He didn't build a fire, though it was cold and damp, and he shivered as he sat leaning on the desk. At length he drew a large sheet of paper toward him and wrote something on it in a heavy hand.

He was writing on this when Lincoln entered at the back, whistling boyishly. "Hello, Jim! Ain't you up early? No fire, eh?" He rattled at the stove.

Sanford said nothing, but finished his writing. Then he said, quietly, "You needn't build a fire on my account, Link."

"Why not?"

"Well, I'm used up."

"What's the matter?"

"I'm sick, and the business has gone to the devil." He looked out of the window.

Link dropped the poker, and came around behind the counter, and stared at Sanford with fallen mouth.

"Wha'd you say?"

"I said the business had gone to the devil. We're broke busted-petered-gone up the spout." He took a sort of morbid pleasure in saying these things.

"What's busted us? Have-"

"I've been speciflatin' in copper. My partner's busted me."

Link came closer. His mouth stiffened and an ominous look came into his eyes. "You don't mean to say you've lost my money, and Mother's, and Uncle Andrew's, and all the rest?"

Sanford was getting irritated. "- it! What's the use? I tell you, yes! It's all gone-very cent of it."

Link caught him by the shoulder as he sat at the desk. Sanford's tone enraged him. "You thief! But you'll pay me back, or I'll-"

"Oh, go ahead! Pound a sick man, if it'll do you any good," said Sanford with a peculiar recklessness of lifeless misery. "Pay y'rsell out of the safe. Here's the combination."

Lincoln released him and began turning the knob of the door. At last it swung open, and he searched the money drawers. Less than forty dollars, all told. His voice was full of helpless rage as he turned at last and walked up close to Sanford's bowed head.

"I'd like to pound the life out o' you!"

"You're at liberty to do so, if it'll be any satisfaction." This desperate courage awed the younger man. He gazed at Sanford in amazement.

"If you'll cool down and wait a little, Link, I'll tell you all about it. I'm sick as a horse. I guess I'll go home. You can put this up in the window and go home, too, if you want to."

Lincoln saw that Sanford was sick. He was shivering, and drops of sweat were on his white forehead. Lincoln stood aside silently and let him go out.

"Better lock up, Link. You can't do anything by staying here."

Lincoln took refuge in a boyish phrase that would have made anyone but a sick man laugh: "Well, this is a —— of a note!"

He took up the paper. It read:

BANK CLOSED

TO MY CREDITORS AND DEPOSITORS

Through a combination of events I find myself obliged to temporarily suspend payment. I ask the depositors to be patient, and their claims will be met. I think I can pay twenty-five cents on the dollar, if given a little time. I shall not run away. I shall stay right here till all matters are honorably settled.

JAMES G. SANFORD

Lincoln hastily pinned this paper to the windows ash so that it could be seen from without, then pulled down the blinds and locked the door. His fun-loving nature rose superior to his rage for the moment. "There'll be the devil to pay in this burg before two hours."

He slipped out the back way, taking the keys with him. "I'll go and tell uncle, and then we'll see if Jim can't turn in the house on our account," he thought as he harnessed a team to drive out to McPhail's.

The first man to try the door was an old Norwegian in a spotted Mackinac jacket and a fur cap, with the inevitable little red tippet about his neck. He turned the knob, knocked, and at last saw the writing, which he could not read, and went away to tell Johnson that the bank was closed. Johnson thought nothing special of that; it was early, and they weren't very particular to open on time, anyway.

Then the barber across the street tried to get in to have a bill changed. Trying to peer in the window, he saw the notice, which he read with a grin.

"One o' Link's jobs," he explained to the fellows in the shop. "He's too darned lazy to open on time, so he puts up notice that the bank is busted."

"Let's go and see."

"Don't do it! He's watchin' to see us all rush across and look. Just keep quiet, and see the solid citizens rear around."

Old Orrin McIlvaine came out of the post office and tried the door next, then stood for a long time reading the notice, and at last walked thoughtfully away. Soon he returned, to the merriment of the fellows in the barbershop, with two or three solid citizens who had been smoking an after-breakfast cigar and planning a deer hunt. They stood before the window in a row and read the notice. McIlvaine gesticulated with his cigar.

"Gentlemen, there's a pig loose here."

"One o' Link's jokes, I reckon."

"But that's Sanford's writin'. An' here it is nine o'clock, and no one round. I don't like the looks of it, myself."

The crowd thickened; the fellows came out of the blacksmith shop, while the jokers in the barbershop smote their knees and yelled with merriment.

"What's up?" queried Vance, coming up and repeating the universal question.

McIlvaine pointed at the poster with his cigar.

Vance read the notice, while the crowd waited silently.

"What ye think of it?" asked someone impatiently. Vance smoked a moment. "Can't say. Where's Jim?"

"That's it! Where is he?"

"Best way to find out is to send a boy up to the house." He called a boy and sent him scurrying up the street.

The crowd now grew sober and discussed possibilities. "If that's true, it's the worst crack on the head I ever had," said McIlvaine. "Seventeen hundred dollars is my pile in there." He took a seat on the windowsill.

"Well, I'm tickled to death to think I got my little stake out before anything happened."

"When you think of it-what security did he ever give?" McIlvaine continued.

"Not a cent-not a red cent."

"No, sir; we simply banked on him. Now, he's a good fellow, an' this may be a joke o' Link's; but the fact is, it might 'a' happened. Well, sonny?" he said to the boy, who came running up.

"Link ain't to home, an' Mrs. Sanford she says Jim's sick an' can't come down."

There was a silence. "Anybody see him this morning?" asked Wilson.

"Yes; I saw him," said Vance. "Looked bad, too." The crowd changed; people came and went, some to get news, some to carry it away. In a short time the whole town knew the bank had "busted all to smash." Farmers drove along and stopped to find out what it all meant. The more they talked, the more excited they grew; and "scoundrel," and "I always had my doubts of that feller," were phrases growing more frequent.

The list of the victims grew until it was evident that nearly all of the savings of a dozen or more depositors were swallowed up, and the sum reached was nearly twenty thousand dollars.

"What did he do with it?" was the question. He never gambled or drank. He lived frugally. There was no apparent cause for this failure of a trusted institution.

It was beginning to snow in great, damp, driving flakes, which melted as they fell, giving to the street a strangeness and gloom that were impressive. The men left the sidewalk at last and gathered in the saloons and stores to continue the discussion.

The crowd at the railroad saloon was very decided in its belief. Sanford had pocketed the money and skipped. That yarn about his being at home sick was a blind. Some went so far as to say that it was almighty curious where Link was, hinting darkly that the bank ought to be broken into, and so on.

Upon this company burst Barney and Sam Mace from "Hogan's Corners." They were excited by the news and already inflamed with drink.

"Say!" yelled Barney, "any o' you fellers know any-thing about Jim Sanford?"

"No. Why? Got any money there?"

"Yes; and I'm goin' to git it out, if I haf to smash the door in."

"That's the talk!" shouted some of the loafers. They sprang up and surrounded Barney. There was something in his voice that aroused all their latent ferocity. "I'm goin' to get into that bank an' see how things look, an' then I'm goin' to find Sanford an' get my money, or pound - out of 'im, one o' the six."

"Go find him first. He's up home, sick-so's his wife."

"I'll see whether he's sick 'r not. I'll drag 'im out by the scruff o' the neck! Come on!" He ended with a sudden resolution, leading the way out into the street, where the falling snow was softening the dirt into a sticky mud.

A rabble of a dozen or two of men and boys followed Mace up the street. He led the way with great strides, shouting his threats. As they passed along, women thrust their heads out at the windows, asking, "What's the matter?" And someone answered each time in a voice of unconcealed delight:

"Sanford's stole all the money in the bank, and they're goin' up to lick 'im. Come on if ye want to see the fun."

In a few moments the street looked as if an alarm of fire had been sounded. Half the town seemed to be out, and the other half coming-women in shawls, like squaws; children capering and laughing; young men grinning at the girls who came out and stood at the gates.

Some of the citizens tried to stop it. Vance found the constable looking on and ordered him to do his duty and stop that crowd.

"I can't do anything," he said helplessly. "They ain't done nawthin' yet, an' I don't know-"

"Oh, git out! They're goin' up there to whale Jim, an' you know it. If you don't stop 'em, I'll telephone f'r the sheriff, and have you arrested with 'em."

Under this pressure, the constable ran along after the crowd, in an attempt to stop it. He reached them as they stood about the little porch of the house, packed closely around Barney and Sam, who said nothing, but followed Barney like his shadow. If the sun had been shining, it might not have happened as it did; but there was a semi-obscurity, a weird half-light shed by the thick sky and falling snow, which somehow encouraged the enraged ruffians, who pounded on the door just as the pleading voice of the constable was heard.

"Hold on, gentlemen! This is ag'inst the law

"Law to -!" said someone. "This is a case f'r something besides law."

"Open up there!" roared the raucous voice of Barney Mace as he pounded at the door fiercely.

The door opened, and the wife appeared, one child in her arms, the other at her side.

"What do you want?"

"Where's that banker? Tell the thief to come out here! We want to talk with him."

The woman did not quail, but her face seemed a ghastly yellow, seen through the falling snow.

"He can't come. He's sick."

"Sick! We'll sick 'im! Tell 'im t' come out, or we'll snake 'im out by the heels." The crowd laughed. The worst elements of the saloons surrounded the two half-savage men. It was amusing to them to see the woman face them all in that way.

"Where's McPhail?" Vance inquired anxiously. "Some-body find McPhail."

"Stand out o' the way!" snarled Barney as he pushed the struggling woman aside.

The wife raised her voice to that wild, animal-like pitch a woman uses when desperate.

"I shan't do it, I tell you! Help!"

"Keep out o' my way, or I'll wring y'r neck fr yeh." She struggled with him, but he pushed her aside and entered the room.

"What's goin' on here?" called the ringing voice of Andrew McPhail, who had just driven up with Link.

Several of the crowd looked over their shoulders at McPhail.

"Hello, Mac! Just in time. Oh, nawthin'. Barney's callin' on the banker, that's all."

Over the heads of the crowd, packed struggling about the door, came the woman's scream again. McPhail dashed around the crowd, running two or three of them down, and entered the back door. Vance, McIlvaine, and Lincoln followed him.

"Cowards!" the wife said as the ruffians approached the bed. They swept her aside, but paused an instant be-fore the glance of the sick man's eye. He lay there, desperately, deathly sick. The blood throbbed in his whirling brain, his eyes were bloodshot and blinded, his strength was gone. He could hardly speak. He partly rose and stretched out his hand, and then fell back.

"Kill me-if you want to-but let her-alone. She's-"

The children were crying. The wind whistled drearily across the room, carrying the evanescent flakes of soft snow over the heads of the pausing, listening crowd in the doorway. Quick steps were heard.

"Hold on there!" cried McPhail as he burst into the room. He seemed an angel of God to the wife and mother.

He spread his great arms in a gesture which suggested irresistible strength and resolution. "Clear out! Out with ye!"

No man had ever seen him look like that before. He awed them with the look in his eyes. His long service as sheriff gave him authority. He hustled them, cuffed them out of the door like schoolboys. Barney backed out, cursing. He knew McPhall too well to refuse to obey.

McPhail pushed Barney out, shut the door behind him, and stood on the steps, looking at the crowd.

"Well, you're a great lot! You fellers, would ye jump on a sick man? What ye think ye're all doin', anyhow?"

The crowd laughed. "Hey, Mac; give us a speech!"

"You ought to be booted, the whole lot o' yeh!" he replied.

"That houn' in there's run the bank into the ground, with every cent o' money we'd put in," said Barney. "I s'pose ye know that."

"Well, s'pose he has-what's the use o' jumpin' on

"Git it out of his hide."

"I've heerd that talk before. How much you got in?"

"Two hundred dollars."

"Well, I've got two thousand." The crowd saw the point.

"I guess if anybody was goin' t' take it out of his hide, I'd be the man; but I want the feller to live and have a chance to pay it back. Killin' 'im is a dead loss."

"That's so!" shouted somebody. "Mac ain't no fool, if he does chaw hay," said another, and the crowd laughed. They were losing that frenzy, largely imitative and involuntary, which actuates a mob. There was something counteracting in the ex-sheriff's cool, humorous tone.

"Give us the rest of it, Mac!"

"The rest of it is clear out o' here, 'r I'll boot every mother's son of yeh!"

"Can't do it!"

"Come down an' try it!"

McIlvaine opened the door and looked out. "Mac, Mrs. Sanford wants to say something-if it's safe."

"Safe as eatin' dinner."

Mrs. Sanford came out, looking pale and almost like a child as she stood beside her defender's towering bulk. But her face was resolute.

"That money will be paid back," she said, "dollar for dollar, if you'll just give us a chance. As soon as Jim gets well enough every cent will be paid, If I live."

The crowd received this little speech in silence. One or two said, in low voices: "That's business. She'll do it, too, if anyone can."

Barney pushed his way through the crowd with contemptuous. curses. "The — she will!" he said.

"We'll see 't you have a chance," McPhail and McIlvaine assured Mrs. Sanford.

She went in and closed the door.

"Now git!" said Andrew, coming down the steps. The crowd scattered with laughing taunts. He turned and entered the house. The rest drifted off down the street through the soft flurries of snow, and in a few moments the street assumed its usual appearance.

The failure of the bank and the raid on the banker had passed into history.

V

In the light of the days of calm afterthought which followed, this attempt upon the peace of the Sanford home grew more monstrous and helped largely to mitigate the feeling against the banker. Besides, he had not run away; that was a strong point in his favor.

"Don't that show," argued Vance to the post office- "don't that show he didn't intend to steal? An' don't it show he's goin' to try to make things square?"

"I guess we might as well think that as anything."

"I claim the boys has a right t' take sumpthin' out o' his hide," Bent Wilson stubbornly insisted.

"Ain't enough t' go 'round," laughed McPhail. "Besides, I can't have it. Link an' I own the biggest share in 'im, an' we can't have him hurt."

McIlvaine and Vance grinned. "That's a fact, Mac. We four fellers are the main losers. He's ours, an' we can't have him foundered 'r crippled 'r cut up in any way. Ain't that woman of his gritty?"

"Gritty ain't no name for her. She's goin' into business."

"So I hear. They say Jim was crawling around a little yesterday. I didn't see.

"I did. He looks pretty streak-id-now you bet."

"Wha'd he say for himself?"

"Oh, said give 'im time-he'd fix it all up."

"How much time?"

"Time enough. Hain't been able to look at a book since. Say, ain't it a little curious he was so sick just then-sick as a p'isened dog?"

The two men looked at each other in a manner most comically significant. The thought of poison was in the mind of each.

It was under these trying circumstances that Sanford began to crawl about, a week or ten days after his sickness. It was really the most terrible punishment for him. Before, everybody used to sing out, "Hello, Jim!"- or "Mornin', banker," or some other jovial, heartwarming salutation. Now, as he went down the street, the groups of men smoking on the sunny side of the stores ignored him, or looked at him with scornfull eyes.

Nobody said, "Hello, Jim!"-not even McPhail or Vance. They nodded merely, and went on with their smoking. The children followed him and stared at him without compassion. They had heard him called a scoundrel and a thief too often at home to feel any pity for his pale face.

After his first trip down the street, bright with the December sunshine, he came home in a bitter, weak mood, smarting, aching with a poignant self-pity over the treatment he had received from his old cronies.

"It's all your fault," he burst out to his wife. "If you'd only let me go away and look up another place, I wouldn't have to put up with all these sneers and insults."

"What sneers and insults?" she asked, coming over to him.

"Why, nobody 'll speak to me."

"Won't Mr. McPhail and Mr. McIlvaine?"

"Yes; but not as they used to."

"You can't blame 'em, Jim. You must go to work and win back their confidence."

"I can't do that. Let's go away, Nell, and try again." Her mouth closed firmly. A hard look came into her eyes. "You can go if you want to, Jim, I'm goin' to stay right here till we can leave honorably. We can't run away from this. It would follow us anywhere we went; and it would get worse the farther we went"

He knew the unyielding quality of his wife's resolution, and from that moment he submitted to his fate. He loved his wife and children with a passionate love that made life with them, among the citizens he had robbed, better than life anywhere else on earth; he had no power to leave them.

As soon as possible he went over his books and found out that he owed, above all notes coming in, about eleven thousand dollars. This was a large sum to look forward to paying by anything he could do in the Siding, now that his credit was gone. Nobody would take him as a clerk, and there was nothing else to be done except manual labor, and he was not strong enough for that.

His wife, however, had a plan. She sent East to friends for a little money at once, and with a few hundred dollars opened a little store in time for the holiday trade-wallpaper, notions, light dry goods, toys, and millinery. She did her own housework and attended to her shop in a grim, uncomplaining fashion that made Sanford feel like a criminal in her presence. He couldn't propose to help her in the store, for he knew the people would refuse to trade with him, so he attended to the children and did little things about the house for the first few months of the winter.

His life for a time was abjectly pitiful. He didn't know what to do. He had lost his footing, and, worst of all, he felt that his wife no longer respected him. She loved and pitied him, but she no longer looked up to him. She went about her work and down to her store with a silent, resolute, uncommunicative air, utterly unlike her former sunny, domestic self, so that even she seemed alien like the rest. If he had been ill, Vance and McPhail would have attended him; as it was, they could not help him.

She already had the sympathy of the entire town, and McIlvaine had said: "If you need more money, you can have it, Mrs. Sanford. Call on us at any time."

"Thank you. I don't think I'll need it. All I ask is your trade," she replied. "I don't ask anybody to pay more'n a thing's worth, either. I'm goin' to sell goods on business principles, and I expect folks to buy of me because I'm selling reliable goods as cheap as anybody else."

Her business was successful from the start, but she did not allow herself to get too confident.

"This is a kind of charity trade. It won't last on that basis. Folks ain't goin' to buy of me because I'm poor-not very long," she said to Vance, who went in to congratulate her on her booming trade during Christmas and New Year.

Vance called so often, advising or congratulating her, that the boys joked him. "Say, looky here! You're gom' to get into a peck o' trouble with your wife yet. You spend about hall y'r time in the new store."

Vance looked serene as he replied, "I'd stay longer and go oftener If I could."

"Well, if you ain't cheekier 'n ol' cheek! I should think you'd be ashamed to say it."

"'Shamed of it? I'm proud of it! As I tell my wife, if I'd 'a' met Mis' Sanford when we was both young, they wouldn't 'a' be'n no such present arrangement."

The new life made its changes in Mrs. Sanford. She grew thinner and graver, but as she went on, and trade steadily increased, a feeling of pride, a sort of exultation, came into her soul and shone from her steady eyes. It was glorious to feel that she was holding her own with men in the world, winning their respect, which is better than their flattery. She arose each day at five o'clock with a distinct pleasure, for her physical health was excellent, never better.

She began to dream. She could pay off five hundred dollars a year of the interest-perhaps she could pay some of the principal, if all went well. Perhaps in a year or two she could take a larger store, and, if Jim got something to do, in ten years they could pay it all off-every cent! She talked with businessmen, and read and studied, and felt each day a firmer hold on affairs.

Sanford got the agency of an insurance company or two and earned a few dollars during the spring. In June things brightened up a little. The money for a note of a thousand dollars fell due-a note he had considered virtually worthless, but the debtor, having had a "streak o' luck," sent seven hundred and fifty dollars. Sanford at once called a meeting of his creditors, and paid them, pro rata, a thousand dollars. The meeting took place in his wife's store, and in making the speech Sanford said:

"I tell you, gentlemen, if you'll only give us a chance, we'll clear this thing all up-that is, the principal. We can't-"

"Yes, we can, James. We can pay it all, principal and interest. We owe the interest just as much as the rest." It was evident that there was to be no letting down while she lived.

The effect of this payment was marked. The general feeling was much more kindly than before. Most of the fellows dropped back into the habit of calling him Jim; but, after all, it was not like the greeting of old, when he was "banker." Still the gain in confidence found a reflex in him. His shoulders, which had begun to droop a little, lifted, and his eyes brightened.

"We'll win yet," he began to say.

"She's a-holdin' of 'im right to time," Mrs. Bingham said.

It was shortly after this that he got the agency for a new cash-delivery system, and went on the road with it, traveling in northern Wisconsin and Minnesota. He came back after a three weeks' trip, quite jubilant. "I've made a hundred dollars, Nell. I'm all right if this holds out, and I guess it will."

In the following November, just a year after the failure, they celebrated the day, at her suggestion, by paying interest on the unpaid sums they owed.

"I could pay a little more on the principal," she explained, "but I guess it'll be better to use it for my stock. I can pay better dividends next year."

"Take y'r time, Mrs. Sanford," Vance said.

Of course she could not escape criticism. There were the usual number of women who noticed that she kept her 'young uns" in the latest style, when as a matter of fact she sat up nights to make their little things. They also noticed that she retained her house and her furniture.

"If I was in her place, seems to me, I'd turn in some o' my fine furniture toward my debts," Mrs. Sam Gilbert said spitefully.

She did not even escape calumny. Mrs. Sam Gilbert darkly hinted at certain "goin's on durin' his bein' away. Lit up till after midnight some nights. I c'n see her winder from mine."

Rose McPhail, one of Mrs. Sanford's most devoted friends, asked quietly, "Do you sit up all night t' see?"

"S'posin' I do!" she snapped. "I can't sleep with such things goin' on."

"If it'll do you any good, Jane, I'll say that she's settin' up there sewin' for the children. If you'd keep your nose out o' other folks' affairs, and attend better to your own, your house wouldn't look' like a pigpen, all' your children like A-rabs."

But in spite of a few annoyances of this character Mrs. Sanford found her new life wholesomer and broader than her old life, and the pain of her loss grew less poignant.

VI

One day in spring, in the lazy, odorous hush of the afternoon, the usual number of loafers were standing on the platform, waiting for the train. The sun was going down the slope toward the hills, through a warm April haze.

"Hello!" exclaimed the man who always sees things first. "Here comes Mrs. Sanford and the ducklings."

Everybody looked.

"Ain't goin' off, is she?"

"Nope; guess not. Meet somebody, prob'ly Sanford."

"Well, somethin's up. She don't often get out o' that store."

"Le's see; he's been gone most o' the winter, hain't he?"

"Yes; went away about New Year's."

Mrs. Sanford came past, leading a child by each hand, nodding and smiling to friends-for all seemed friends. She looked very resolute and businesslike in her plain, dark dress, with a dull flame of color at the throat, while the broad hat she wore gave her face a touch of piquancy very charming. Evidently she was in excellent spirits, and laughed and chatted in quite a carefree way.

She was now an institution at the Siding. Her store had grown in proportions yearly, until it was as large and commodious as any in the town. The drummers for dry goods all called there, and the fact that she did not sell any groceries at all did not deter the drummers for grocery houses from calling to see each time if she hadn't decided to put in a stock of groceries.

These keen-eyed young fellows had spread her fame all up and down the road. She had captured them, not by beauty, but by her pluck, candor, honesty, and by a certain fearless but reserved camaraderie. She was not afraid of them, or of anybody else, now.

The train whistled, and everybody turned to watch it as it came pushing around the bluff like a huge hound on a trail, its nose close to the ground. Among the first to alight was Sanford, in a shining new silk hat and a new suit of clothes.

He was smiling gaily as he fought his way through the crowd to his wife's side. "Hello!" he shouted. "I thought I'd see you all here."

"W'y, Jim, ain't you cuttin' a swell?"

"A swell! Well, who's got a better right? A man wants to look as well as he can when he comes home to such a family."

"Hello, Jim!. That plug 'll never do."

"Hello, Vance! Yes; but it's got to do. Say, you tell all the fellers that's got anything ag'inst me to come around tomorrow night to the store. I want to make some kind of a settlement."

"All right, Jim. Goin' to pay a new dividend?"

"That's what I am," he beamed as he walked off with his wife, who was studying him sharply.

"Jim, what ails you?"

"Nothin'; I'm all right."

"But this new suit? And the hat? And the necktie?" He laughed merrily-so merrily, in fact, that his wife looked at him the more anxiously. He appeared to be in a queer state of intoxication-a state that made him happy without impairing his faculties, however. He turned suddenly and put his lips down toward her ear. "Well, Nell, I can't hold in any longer. We've struck it!"

"Struck what?"

"Well, you see that derned fool partner o' mine got me to go into a lot o' land in the copper country. That's where all the trouble came. He got awfully let down. Well, he's had some surveyors to go up there lately and look it over, and the next thing we knew the Superior Mining Company came along an' wanted to buy it. Of course we didn't want to sell just then."

They had reached the store door, and he paused.

"We'll go right home to supper," she said. "The girls will look out for things till I get back."

They walked on together, the children laughing and playing ahead.

"Well, upshot of it is, I sold out my share to Osgood for twenty thousand dollars."

She stopped and stared at him. "Jim-Gordon Sanford!"

"Fact! I can prove it." He patted his breast pocket mysteriously. "Ten thousand right there."

"Gracious sakes alive! How dare you' carry so much money?"

"I'm mighty glad o' the chance." He grinned.

They walked on almost in silence, with only a word now and then. She seemed to be thinking deeply, and he didn't want to disturb her. It was a delicious spring hour. The snow was all gone, even under the hedges. The roads were warm and brown. The red sun was flooding the valley with a misty, rich-colored light, and against the orange and gold of the sky the hills stood in Tyrian purple. Wagons were rattling along the road. Men on the farms in the edge of the village could be heard whistling at their work. A discordant jangle of a neighboring farmer's supper bell announced that it was time "to turn out."

Sanford was almost as gay as a lover. He seemed to be on the point of regaining his old place in his wife's respect. Somehow the possession of the package of money in his pocket seemed to make him more worthy of her, to put him more on an equality with her.

As they reached the little one-story square cottage he sat down on the porch, where the red light fell warmly, and romped with the children, while his wife went in and took off her things. She "kept a girl" now, so that the work of getting supper did not devolve entirely upon her. She came out soon to call them all to the supper table in the little kitchen back of the sitting room.

The children were wild with delight to have "Poppa" back, and the meal was the merriest they had had for a long time. The doors and windows were open, and the spring evening air came in' laden with the sweet, suggestive smell of bare ground. The alert chuckle of an occasional robin could be heard.

Mrs. Sanford looked up from her tea. "There's one thing I don't like, Jim, and that's the way that money comes. You didn't-you didn't really earn it."

"Oh' don't worry yourself about that. That's the way things go. It's just luck."

"Well, I can't see it just that way. It seems to me just-like gambling. You win' but-but somebody else must lose."

"Oh well, look a-here; if you go to lookin' too sharp into things like that, you'll find a good 'eal of any business like gamblin'."

She said no more, but her face remained clouded. On the way down to the store they met Lincoln.

"Come down to the store, Link, and bring Joe. I want to talk with yeh."

Lincoln stared, but said, "All right." Then added, as the others walked away, "Well, that feller ain't got no cheek t' talk to me like that-more cheek 'n a gov'ment mule!"

Jim took a seat near the door and watched his wife as she went about the store. She employed two clerks now, while she attended to the books and the cash. He thought how different she was, and he liked (and, in a way, feared) her cool, businesslike manner, her self-possession, and her smileless conversation with a drummer who came in. Jim was puzzled. He didn't quite -understand the peculiar effect his wife's manner had upon him.

Outside, word had passed around that Jim had got back and that something was in the wind, and the fellows began to drop in. When McPhail came in and said, "Hello!" in his hearty way, Sanford went over to his wile and said:

"Say, Nell, I can't stand this. I'm goin' to get rid o' this money right off, now!"

"Very well; just as you please."

"Gents," he began, turning his back to the. counter and smiling blandly on them, one thumb in his vest pocket, "any o' you fellers got anything against the Lumber County Bank-any certificates of deposit, or notes?"

Two or three nodded, and McPhail said humorously, slapping his pocket, "I always go loaded."

"Produce your paper, gents," continued Sanford, with a dramatic whang of a leathern wallet down into his palm. "I'm buying up all paper on the bank."

It was a superb stroke. The fellows whistled and stared and swore at one another. This was coming down on them. Link was dumb with amazement as he received sixteen hundred and fifty dollars in crisp, new bills.

"Andrew, it's your turn next." Sanford's tone was actually patronizing as he faced McPhail.

"I was jokin'. I ain't got my certificate here."

"Don't .matter-don't matter. Here's fifteen hundred dollars. Just give us a receipt, and bring the certif. any time. I want to get rid o' this stuff right now."

"Say, Jim, we'd like to know jest-jest where this windfall comes from," said Vance as he took his share.

"Comes from the copper country," was all he ever said about it.

"I don't see where he invested," Link said. "Wasn't a scratch of a pen to show that he invested anything while he was in the bank. Guess that's where our money went."

"Well, I ain't squealin'," said Vance. "I'm glad to get out of it without asking any questions. I'll tell yeh one thing, though," he added as they stood outside the door; "we'd 'a' never smelt of our money again if it hadn't 'a' been f'r that woman in there. She'd 'a' paid it alone if Jim hadn't 'a' made this strike, whereas he never'd 'a'-Well, all right. We're out of it."

It was one of the greatest moments of Sanford's life. He expanded in it. He was as pleasantly aware of the glances of his wife as he used to be when, as a clerk, he saw her pass and look in at the window where he sat dreaming over his ledger.

As for her, she was going over the whole situation from this new standpoint. He had been weak, he had fallen in her estimation, and yet, as he stood there, so boyish in his exultation, the father of her children, she loved him with a touch of maternal tenderness and hope, and her heart throbbed in an unconscious, swift determination to do him good. She no longer deceived herself. She was his equal-in some ways his superior. Her love had friendship in it, but less of sex, and no adoration.

As she blew out the lights, stepped out on the walk, and turned the key in the lock, he said, "Well, Nellie, you won't have to do that any more."

"No; I won't have to, but I guess I'll keep on just the same, Jim."

"Keep on? What for?"

"Well, I rather like it."

"But you don't need to——"

"I like being my own boss," she said. "I've done a lot o' figuring, Jim, these last three years, and it's kind o' broadened me, I hope. I can't go back where I was. I'm a better woman than I was before, and I hope and believe that I'm better able to be a real mother to my children." Jim looked up at the moon filling the warm, moist air with a transfiguring light that fell in a luminous mist on the distant hills. "I know one thing, Nellie; I'm a better man than I was before, and it's all owin' to you."

His voice trembled a little, and the sympathetic tears came into her eyes. She didn't speak at once—she couldn't At last she stopped him by a touch on the arm.

"Jim, I want a partner in my store. Let us begin again, right here. I can't say that I'll ever feel just as I did once I don't know as it's right to. I looked up to you too much. I expected too much of you, too. Let's' begin again, as equal partners." She held out her hand, as one man to another. He took it wonderingly.

"All right, Nell; I'll do it."

Then, as he put his arm around her, she held up her lips to be kissed. "And we'll be happy again-happy as we deserve, I s'pose," she said with a smile and a sigh.

"It's almost like getting married again, Nell-for me." As they walked off up the sidewalk in the soft moon-light, their arms were interlocked.

They loitered like a couple of lovers.

THE END

Made in the USA
Las Vegas, NV
17 November 2021

34700217R00105